AUTOMATIC SAFE DOG

Jet McDonald

Automatic Safe Dog
by Jet McDonald

Publication Date: February 2011

Copyright 2011, Jet McDonald.

Cover art and design by Jasmin Topalusic and David Rix -
copyright 2011.

Author Photo by blueskies Photography

Paperback
ISBN: 978-1-908125-01-9

www.eibonvalepress.co.uk

Jet McDonald is a writer, musician and storyteller. His fiction has been published in *Subtle Edens - An Anthology of Slipstream Fiction* from Elastic Press, *Catastrophia* from PS Publications and *Blind Swimmer* from Eibonvale Press. His work has been included in *The Idler* and *Paraphilia Magazine*. He is a member of spoken word collective *Heads and Tales* and in 2008 won the Missouri Review Audio Fiction Award for his contemporary spoken fiction. He has performed his stories and music at festivals across the UK including Glastonbury Festival and the Hay on Wye Literary Festival. His freaky folk band *Jetfly* have been aired on BBC 6 radio and toured nationally with four albums. In May 2010 Jet began an overland cycle tour to India.

Contents

A Foreword by Allen Ashley

JET'S PET SOUNDS

What is this book about? Dogs, certainly. Humans, too. The future of furniture? Partly. Also: modern life; consumer culture; ethics and morality and the lack thereof; inventions, be they useful or otherwise. But mostly I believe that this story is about identity. Narrated by a hero who takes an assumed name partway into the tale – the ludicrously zeitgeist moniker of Terribly "Telby" Velour. Who is he really? Initially quite low on the conventional employment ladder – a dog comber on the shop floor, later a road sweeper – he incredibly reinvents himself in the way that is only possible in the modern world of vacuous hyperbole and becomes a creative consultant to Pet Furnishings. He has many of the other characters fooled by his imposture. Telby is our narrator, our viewpoint, our moral compass in this warped very near future world. He is Everyman, the little guy against the big corporation, the working class hero. Or just a chancer riding his luck while it lasts.

Questions about identity bring me to a consideration of this book's author. You see, I first knew Jet McDonald as Josh McDonald. Indeed, I even published him as such in my anthology *Subtle Edens* (Elastic Press, 2008). Entitled, *Luxury Flats*, it was one of his first published stories. The tale had undergone a couple of rewrites – part of the learning curve – but was now nestled amongst pieces by Joel Lane, Mike O'Driscoll and Nina Allan. I invited him to the book launch, expecting him to turn up perma-tanned, in a pinstripe suit with a portfolio of properties under his arm – largely due, I now realise, to the story title! Of course Josh / Jet was much more modern and easygoing and animated than my ridiculous expectation. He read from his story and won the art competition, too.

I moved on to another editing project – *Catastrophia* (PS Publishing) – and Mr. McDonald placed another story with me. He had now settled on "Jet", marrying up a literary presence with the musical identity of his band Jetfly. This new offering suggested he had made strides even in the two years or so since I'd taken the first story.

And now we have *Automatic Safe Dog*. Have you ever wondered what really goes on in those several floors of Canary Wharf (or Priscilla Towers as it's styled in the novel)? Have you ever pondered exactly what "creative types" get up to all day? No, I don't mean writers and musicians like us, I mean those hot air merchants in "Ideas" or "Development", the clowns who create new products that nobody needs and then somehow make us feel we can no longer live without them. Jet takes us to the heart of this question and the answers are strange, very strange. There are not enough novels focused so closely on the world of work, even if Jet's satirical dissection of consumerism adds more than a touch of the surreal to proceedings. Think *Bartleby* crossed with *Smallcreep's Day* and you're partly there. The author sprinkles in a pinch of J. G. Ballard and a measure of William Burroughs to the concoction. *Automatic Safe Dog* is a somewhat picaresque piece – if the pace ever looks like flagging, there's sure to be an intriguing new madcap character along at any moment and a bizarre scenario in which they encounter the young lovelorn Telby. One of my favourites amongst the comedic array is Ibore Davidson – a voracious, copper-skinned lovely who lives in a penthouse apartment on the top floor of a multi-storey car park. Really. Best of all, however, is Telby's (male) secretary Abel.

This latter is straight out of the "too posh for this job" school and does nothing all day – not even adequately taking messages – because he is actually a writer engaged on a one syllable a day quest to write either the perfect poem or the great novel. Pompous and self-absorbed doesn't cover it. When Abel finally gets his first paragraph finished and you finally see what this immortal line becomes . . . you know that Jet McDonald is right on the button with his satire and you are in the hands of a wonderfully witty writer.

This is a funny, pleasingly ridiculous and yet commendably plausible book. Like all the best stories, it will change the way you look at certain things. Jet's skewed vision makes us think anew about the assumptions our culture is based upon. And that's got to be a good thing. The lunatics may not have entirely taken over the asylum but the hollow men are certainly running the multi-nationals, holed up somewhere in the bowels of the office blocks and the twelfth floors of skyscrapers.

Read on. Enjoy. Are you sitting comfortably? Pet Furnishings will see that you are… for a while at least.

- Allen Ashley, London 2010

AUTOMATIC SAFE DOG ↓

JET McDONALD

"At the risk of sounding like the poet William Blake, the cause of some phobias manifested by dogs is baffling. The majority of gun dog training books go to some lengths discussing gun shyness or the fear of the loud and sudden noises and offer some advice on how to deal with the disorder."

Brian. D. Plummer, *The Development of the Dog*

"Those who restrain desire, do so because theirs is weak enough to be restrained; and the restrainer or reason usurps its place and governs the unwilling. And being restrained it by degrees becomes passive till it is only the shadow of desire..."

William Blake, *The Marriage of Heaven and Hell*

Prologue

A funny thing happened on the way to my head but I can't remember what it was...

Anyway there was this dog, right, and they sawed its legs off so they had to pull it round on the stumps. Eventually the stumps wore down to a polished sheen but there was this friction problem. So they put castors on the stumps, you know, the kind they have on the bottom of sofas and armchairs, and pulled it round on that. This caught on in a big way and someone had the great idea of combining Crufts with the Ideal Home Exhibition. The combination of soft furnishings and pets levered open a whole new retail niche. There were hundreds of Pet Furnishing warehouses across the country and I worked for one of them. Some of my friends worked in the leg sawing department but I couldn't stand that. It wasn't the sawing so much as having to tranquilise the dogs and I was a real needle phobic. So I worked on the shop floor. I was a dog-comber, like in car showrooms you need to polish up the cars to a telling gloss, I combed the mutts to a fine satiny layering, for shop floor walkabouts. And that was where I met Ravenski Helena Goldbird, the most beautiful woman I had ever seen.

chapter 1
AUTOMATIC SAFE DOG

I remember the tips of her fingers flashing as she fiddled with her name badge. And when she opened her mouth, resonant transatlantic tones poured through her voice like sovereigns down an iron drainpipe. I'd heard rumours of course, whispers in the canteen, sniffs over the cashtills. Ravenski was from a higher plane, she had descended from the peaks of power, she had flown in from the great blue yonder to detail our every move. And here, today, she was with me, combing dogs.

"So where are you from?" I asked tentatively, my thumb pressed against the teeth of my comb.

"I was bought from a Romanian orphanage." She stared at me with dark brown eyes. "My parents got me in an adoption deal. They're American, real rich. They came over to England to be even richer but live in castles." She drew a circle with the point of her trainers on the tiled floor. "But I didn't want to be cooped up. I wanted to work with the real people…"

Ravenski Helena Goldbird. I turned the name over and over in my mind. I imagined it written under the lid of a grand piano, the trademark of a quality design. I imagined my fingers running up and down the keys and then tracing the gold signature, the back of my hand against the hard lip of the lid.

"…they wanted me to go to board meetings," she went on, "but I wasn't having none of it. I demanded to be on the shop floor with the real people and my father's best buddies with the chairman of Pet Furnishings, and so…"

I took her hand in mine and guided it through the thick white hair of a Highland terrier. Ravenski's skin was so pale it melted into the fur and at first I thought we'd lost the comb but she pulled it through and the mutt didn't feel a thing, just rolled on its castors backwards and forwards, wagging the remnants of its clipped tail, wag bone, butt cartilage.

"You've got the makings of a real dog comber," I told her and she showed me her fingernails, each one embedded with a small diamond.

"I have to have them replaced every time the nails grow out."

"I'd be well expensive," I said, "I bite mine."

"That's why my parents made me have it done because the "nail-stop" varnish wasn't working and I was a real nibbler."

And it was then that we felt bonded, super glued by accident, skin to skin. Well, that's how I felt we felt; I didn't ask her and she picked at the diamonds with the teeth of her comb. I wanted to cup my hands and catch a jewel, if one popped out, but I didn't, you know, want to appear uncivilised. So I watched and the diamonds didn't come away just made fleeting prisms as she played them into the light.

And then we sought out a Dalmatian and sat on it. All the dogs at Pet Furnishings have reinforced backs made from runners of Teak. They're carefully inserted, just above the dog's spine, to give reinforcement for placing the derriere; 'Placing the derriere', that's what we had to tell the customers (appendix 4 of the P.F. handbook: 'Making the Customer Feel At Home'). Most of the time further padding wasn't needed, and the dogs enjoyed being sat upon, a bit of extra attention before they were wheeled away; well that's what it said in the handbook. Anyhow, there were Ravenski and I sitting on the Dalmatian and she says:

"How fast do these babies go?"

"They're pulled along by traction, that's the beauty of Pet Furnishings, everything's under YOUR control." I made the holding the leash sign with thumb and forefinger like they did in the adverts.

"Don't give me that crap. I bet you can build up some speed if you push them hard enough." She put her legs astride the Dalmatian and made me do the same. "I reckon you can ride 'em like a hobby horse." She stretched out her legs in front of us. The dog yapped a little.

"I'm not sure they're serviced for this."

"Don't be such a kill joy." She tugged the Dalmatian's ears, and pushed it forward on its castors, using her legs to give her traction. "Pick up your tootsies boy or we're not going to roll."

I did as I was told; she was Ravenski Helena Goldbird after all and we had, well we had a 'bond'. She had thick-soled trainers and full muscular calves so she could really build up some speed. Anyway, there we were castoring across the tiled floor on the back of the yapping Dalmatian, when I saw Mr Hollenbrook, the shop floor manager.

"Go left," I shouted at Ravenski.

"Why?"

"It's Mr Hollenbrook."

"Hokenbock?"

"The shop floor manager."

"Who cares?" She extended her stride and we accelerated towards a rack of dog bowls.

"I'm due for an extra pay star."

"You've got to ride the wave honey."

"Go left," I hollered. Ravenski leant towards the checkouts and we cornered on the dogs two left castors, the right side rising up as we tilted. We continued behind the tall shelves of dog cushions and were at the apex of our ellipse when there was a snap, an anxious yelp, and we collapsed together on top of the broken Dalmatian. Ravenski lay close to me. I could feel her chest pressing against mine; the button of a nipple.

"What happened?" she said, dismounting the wreckage.

"You, err we, snapped it."

"What?"

"We broke the Dalmatian, right across the middle by the looks of it."

"Ugh."

"Don't worry. Mr Hollenbrook can't see us from here."

"Ugh."

I followed Ravenski's gaze. The dog had indeed snapped, so evidently that the back now made a 'V' with its head and front legs levered to one point, its hind paws and tail crooked to the other. It lay on one side, a wounded pedigree, its body an arrow pointing to the fire exit.

Ravenski put her hands to her flushed cheeks and squealed:

"The tail's still moving."

And yes, the dog's stumpy cartilage continued to wag; its hind stumps jittering on the plastic floor.

"Spinal reflex, quite impressive isn't it?"

"It's terrible." Ravenski began to bite her nails, one by one, including their diamond highlights. Of course I wanted to comfort her but was unable to detach myself from the idea of those swallowed diamonds. I imagined myself surreptitious in a toilet cubicle panning for the expensive gems.

"Is it still alive?"

"What?"

"The dog, is it still alive?"

I knelt beside the Dalmatian and searched for its small heart. I found the point of the snapped Teak runner prodding through the ribs and felt a momentary and confusing tingle of excitement. I moved my hand further across and found a limp beat.

"It's alive, not for long though."

"Oh the poor dog," howled Ravenski. She fell to her knees and stroked between its eyes. "What's its name?"

"The Velvet Derriere. Type D23."

"Oh poor dog, poor twenty three."

I couldn't help but follow Ravenski's robbed and ragged fingernails as she tugged at the Dalmatian's coat. Suddenly the mutt turned its head and snapped at Ravenski. She flinched, but too slowly and the dog bit into her fingers and they snaked with blood. I pulled the dog's jaw back and removed her hand. It was then that I heard footsteps and saw the familiar leather shoes of Mr Hollenbrook approaching by the dog cushion stand.

"Listen," I said to Ravenski, "you've got to pull yourself together. I'll lose my job if Mr Hollenbrook finds this." She put her fingers in her mouth and sucked and tried to nod. "We've got to straighten the mutt," I said. I made her take the back end while I took the muzzle end and we pulled tight as if rejoining a crumpled Christmas cracker. The dog straightened, giving one last bleat, and I felt the tension drift from its jaw. Just then Mr Hollenbrook came around the corner. We continued to hold onto the mutt.

"Ah hallo Ravenski. Are you being looked after?" She bit her lip and nodded. He turned to me. "What are you showing the young lady?"

"I'm just demonstrating how smooth and straight we make the dog's spine, for the derriere."

"Oh yes, very good. Our teak runners come all the way from Fiji. We use the finest woods."

Ravenski smiled thinly, I noticed a trickle of blood running down the dog's leg. I tightened my grip around the muzzle.

"Well I won't keep you." Mr Hollenbrook gave a slight bow to Ravenski and moved on, hands palm in palm behind his back.

Ravenski allowed herself to cry, tears splashing onto the Dalmatian's spotted back.

"Please don't be sad," I said. Ravenski released the dog and it fell into itself.

"Dead," she said and sobbed.

"Yes pretty well." I let go.

"I killed it."

"Well we both killed it; I think it was our combined weight. They have a limited floor span anyway. We recommend a replacement every three years."

She began to gasp.

"Shhh," I hushed, "Mr Hollenbrook might hear you. Look, all we've got to do is take it to the disposal centre. I know the spade man there, he's a good friend."

"I can't bear it any more."

"All we've got to do is carry the dog, straight, just like before. No one will know."

"I want to go home."

"Come on, pick up the mutt." She stood there, motionless, clutching her bleeding fingers. "Look," I said, "you wanted a taste of real life, real people, well this is it, here, now, and we're in *it* together." I took her hands. "We have a bond you and me, you may not think so but we do, I can tell." I looked into her brown eyes; tinsel brimmed by the strip lights. "Will you do this? For me, for the common people?" She squeaked and nodded and flushed. And I knew then that there was a passion between us. My heart beat like a lunatic and I thought I might have one of my fits or a full on B.P.E.

But I breathed carefully and I calmed myself and we each took one end of the dog, and hauled it across the shop floor. Music piped through the in-store Tannoy, 'Unchained Melody', one of my favourites.

I wasn't aware at first but I had started to move us both in time to the music and we turned in a waltz, round and round, using the dog as the pivot of our promenade.

The song heightened its refrain. *Oh my darling…*

Ravenski looked uncertain, shaky and I tried to reassure her. "This melody is so enchanting, don't you find?" We continued in a circle, pulling the strut of the dog ever tighter.

I need your love… Ravenski's knuckles were white and bright as our waltz advanced towards the leash selection.

And time goes by…

"You know Ravenski, if I can call you that, I feel so close to you. I feel like we have a special bond, a real SOMETHING." The shop floor spun around us; the cash tills, the tied up dog furniture, the grooming accessories, the racks of tasselled edgings, the haberdashery…all blurring into the strip light flood. I looked at Ravenski, her tiny square teeth biting her rose lip, her pale face the one definite thing in the blur.

… can dooo so much.

"You know the only the only thing that separates us," I said, "is a broken dog."

I neeeed your love.

It was then that the dog gave way. Its spotted hide, weakened by the initial puncture of the teak runner, ripped at the rib cage and its innards slopped out, mostly over Ravenski's shoes.

I lost my job of course. Ravenski's father made sure of that. I was forced to sweep up leaves on the roads by the industrial estate. Through every season I swept, the green, the yellow, the orange, the brown and sometimes, as I shovelled, I thought of Ravenski.

I was told she went to a detox clinic. I'm not sure what she was detoxed from. Dog innards I suppose. She returned to Pet Furnishings and took a post on the executive board. It was she who was responsible for the Automatic Safe Dog. They developed a microchip that you could puncture through the dog's skull; 'With the chip of a mallet, the dog has habit.' The chip was studded into the dog's motor cortex and pet sofas and divans were made automatic and safe so they didn't howl, bite, shit or piss until programmed at preset intervals. This made for not just safer but cleaner furnishings. Our customers forever complained of the times that their mutt would whine to be let out, just when they needed to pet it, or love it or sit down for a cup of tea, and then they'd have to deal with the inevitable mud in the castors or dew in the tassels. But Ravenski changed all that with her bold new ideas and leapt up the career ladder, far away from the 'real' people.

One day, while I was sweeping, I found a copy of 'Fortune' magazine in the gutter. I saw her photo; she was power dressed in a trouser suit with arching shoulder pads. I could see that she still bit her nails though; both hands down to the quick, and her eyes no longer had that sparkle, a sparkle I thought I remembered in the folding of leaves.

Chapter 2
Hairy Teeth

I'd always wanted to meet Ravenski again but now we were even further apart on the ladder; her bitten fingers round the highest rung, mine reaching for the lowest. Our initial rendezvous was particularly unsuccessful. She was visiting the local Pet Furnishings, the one where we first met, to open its new service centre; 'Automatic Dog Fast Through'. There was a high level of security and ever since the Dalmatian incident I hadn't been welcome, so I had to go undercover. I was certain that when Ravenski saw my face I would be pressed into her hybrid bosom with open arms. So I hid in a pile of leaves. I accumulated the mound just off the entrance to the warehouse and burrowed into its mulching heart. I waited there, sweating, until the press unleashed their firefight of camera shutters and then I starjumped into her path. A few of the drier leaves fluttered away as I ran across the red carpet.

"Ravenski, remember me, your hope, your common chalice?" But I didn't even get to meet her. She was swamped by her bodyguards and the police marched me off to a charge of public disorder, with leaves.

I had to rethink my advances with a more intelligent inclination. I decided if she wasn't going to come to me then I would go to her; to the big city, to the land of the fat, to London. More specifically Lydon, that region of London that marks the edge of the docklands, an area some people say they can't locate. An urban inroad at the frontiers of development so carefully built into unrealised real estate that some say it has been squeezed into a portion of the city that doesn't exist. How they could say this when the area declares itself in bold concrete plazas and towering waterside escarpments with windows like the reflecting scales of huge circuit boards is beyond my ken. How they could announce it hard to find when it is so obviously there, more familiar to me than Old London itself, with its grubby Palace and Parliament, I don't know.

So I rented a flat at the fringes of this district and became a lift attendant at Priscilla wharf, the soaring harbourside development where Ravenski worked. When I say, "I became a lift attendant", I don't mean I transformed into one straight away. It was more of a gradual moulding, an incremental design. I started off as a cleaner at the wharf, slopping out corridors, emptying the ashtrays, rifling the drawers for telling executive memos that enlarged my corporate vocabulary. And then I progressed to the post room, unwrapping parcels and steaming envelopes, absorbing further markers of executive genealogy until I applied for and was accepted as lift attendant. I still rifled and unwrapped and steamed but this time it was through the open files of gnawing mouths; the office insects, their incisors forever sticky with knowing gossip on 'Pet Furnishings Ltd'. They didn't really need an attendant but as the personal officer explained, "it gives a human touch". I shouted out the floor with each ring of the bell; "Floor number eleven, legs eleven" and the legs would centipede out to their paper tunnels, gabbling industrial secrets into the air conditioned air. It was by this means that I learned that the executive board were recruiting for a new research strategist; 'a big bull in the creative china store' was 'vital to give impetus to flagging markets.' This, I decided, was how I would work my way into the heart of the company and win Ravenski's hand.

I continued to listen and plan my application as I rode the lifts, mimicking the nuances and facial tics of the corporate body. The only blip in my transformation was an unfortunate B.P.E. whilst riding the lifts. I've experienced B.P.E.s from adolescence and, despite intensive investigation from scans to E.E.G. tracings (where wires were attached to my head like a clump of seaweed), no one has been any the wiser. My child psychiatrist told me I was unique and this has always given me an element of pride.

I was about three weeks into my job and travelling between the eleventh and twelfth floor when our movement came to an abrupt halt. It was then that I had a Brief Period of Evangelism or B.P.E. I was reaching for the maintenance phone and was convulsed, made upright and experienced an overwhelming desire to save the world in the Lord's name. I laid my hand on the nearest head, a man with goggle thick glasses who was holding a wedge of printed spreadsheets, and bade him: "Kneel to the floor young man". He was bald and I was sweaty so there was a certain amount of slippage but he did as he was told and buckled to the floor, apparently assuming this was part of the emergency procedure. "Witness me," I proclaimed. The power-dressed clerks looked on blankly as I began the sermon.

"This man has sinned as all men have sinned and only with his piety and your love can he, and you, now be redeemed. Do you hear me? I say DO YOU HEAR ME?" A mousey woman with a bob who was holding a jiffy bag said "yes". The others shuffled awkwardly and discovered out the shine of their shoes. "This planet is a gravity of sin and only the Lord can rise us up!"

"Excuse me," said the bald one beneath my blessing, "can I stand up? I have sciatica and…"

"Stay, you heart-torn sinner." I reached out my free hand to the mousey woman with the bob. "Spit in my hand."

"Sorry?"

"Spit in my hand. For the unbaptised shall be prisoners of the dungeon of hell." She looked at me meekly, as the meek are want, and the lift juddered down a few centimetres in its rails.

She dribbled a pocket of phlegm into my cupped hand and I smeared it on the bald one's head.

"Rise, for you have been born again and your new name shall be LOVE." The bald one got up and shuffled his spreadsheets into alignment. The spittle began to roll across his forehead like the mucous of a cracked egg.

"HALLELUJAH," I shouted as a nondescript businessman in the corner began to hyperventilate. There was a muttering as the occupants sensed the contagion of the mad.   "Hallelujah," said the mousey woman, quietly, and the lift began to move again.

"The miracle of the poor made rich," I said and collapsed on the floor.

This was later shown to me on the CCTV. I couldn't remember much myself. If I saw the mousey woman I would get sudden shudders of rejoicing, somewhat like a flashback, but other than that it was a complete blank.

"A close call," the personnel officer said. "If it hadn't have been for this medical condition you'd have been sacked. You'll have to go to occupational health of course. One more episode and its sick leave or suspension."

Needless to say this speeded up my plans to advance for the post of research strategist. One more evangelical chorus between the eleventh and twelfth floor and it would have been swept leaves and eternal damnation.

I felt by this point I had the necessary executive knowledge but lacked the wardrobe and more importantly the face. I needed some new design to smuggle my seductions to Ravenski. Unable to afford the clothes or the plastic surgery, I resorted to a more ragged means of procurement.

I had only read of charitable muggings in the papers but the idea appealed and was relatively simple. I jumped on an accounts clerk in the lift when he had his back turned and pulled his jacket off. He stared at me aghast and demanded it back. I pointed out the little gold sticker I'd pressed onto his shirt 'Save the tiny ill babies from slow death (I gave and saved)' and explained that his jacket would be recycled into research funds and by the fourteenth floor he had relented. I told him the tiny ill baby he had saved was called Jasmine and he would be sent a milk tooth in due course. I later sent him a sheep's molar in a matchbox.

Getting hold of the trousers was much harder and, bearing in mind my previous B.P.E., I thought another charitable mugging unwise. So I just plain mugged someone. No real damage done of course. I left the victim with his wallet and a jockstrap on the night bus to Ealing. I placed a sheep's molar in a matchbox on his lap. I thought this had a poetic reiteration to it; as if there could be some aesthetic redemption to my crimes, a rhyming calling card to the scan of my forensic verse. I imagined the hapless shift worker examining the tooth between thumb and forefinger, turning it around, discovering its tobacco crevices, as the bus carried him off, half naked, into the halogen night. I stood by the bus stop and measured his trousers to my waist.

Next of course I had to steal a face and leave a tooth. An eye for an eye…but no, not the Stanley knife for me. It's not the cutting so much as the having to anaesthetise the skin and I'm a real needle phobic. So I left the lift job and carefully set about constructing my identity through other means. I grew a beard and then groomed and pruned it to a goatee and sideburns. Changing the voice was simple; cotton wool in the cheeks altered the structure and tonality of my syllables and I left a sheep's molar in a matchbox under my pillow to nibble at my mind. I dreamt of cancers with hairy teeth and sleeptalked with cotton wool in my mouth, eventually being woken by my own howling, chomping on some imaginary growth.

I practiced my interview technique with ascetic devotion. Every morning I was up at seven, sat in front of the mirror, cotton wool in my cheeks, fuffing out my list of engineered qualifications and bogus research breakthroughs. This would be followed with an hour for lunch, then out with the old cotton wool and in with the new as I spent the afternoon dispatching a fictional career into C.V. form, muttering my exotic hobbies out loud and brushing my chin against the computer screen as if the one might bristle with the other. I had a short supper break with yesterday's refried beans, some new cotton wool, and then back to the mirror.

"I have always been research driven. I was always more interested in the sweet wrappers than the sweets…I like rock climbing and canoeing. Yes I'm a member of the rock canoeing club, up granite face and then down stream…Every Sunday and then off to the pub… of course relaxation is very important. For every work ethic there must be a work leisure…Well I see my role as being a bull in the china store, breaking a few plates for the sake of a dinner set…" On and on I would continue with this, into the early hours, until I found myself muttering false promises into the mirror's surface, where I'd fallen asleep.

So magnificently was the transformation progressing that I took it out into the streets and blathered to the grocer about the size of his tomatoes and had he thought of throwing them at passing white vans as a way of splashing his currency around town. The grocer laughed. He was a tobacco chewer and spat cud onto my face. I took a piece of cotton wool out of my mouth and wiped the phlegm away with that. The grocer took hold of my loose cheek and wagged it between thumb and finger. "You've got lovely Polish cheeks," he said. I never went back to the grocers after that. Vegetable and fruit are for peasants who can't afford their meat. That's what my cousin used to say, bless his cholesterol soggy ashes, and I agree up to a point, well as far as mangoes. I mean who can resist mangoes; frivolous, fibrous, juice melting eggs of Eden, the only fruit that dissolves into honey and leaves you with floss between your teeth. But, for now, mangoes were out, cotton wool was in; twenty four hours a day, with dried food and sips of water all my mouth could accommodate.

And on the sixteenth day the mirror winked at me, coal eyed and bunker bruised but sparkling green in the irises. I was a made man; 'Terribly Velour' or 'Telby' or 'T' for short. Shot from the canon of the neon valley, I was tip top ready for executive stardom. "Telby Velour," the bearded lips whispered back at me, "T for short but gin for the long, long lunches." I could feel my cotton wool sodden with saliva. Ravenski's magazine photo, cut out and placed on my bedside, smiled in recognition. I hooked out the cotton wool from my cheeks, dropped it onto her picture and turned off the light, not dreaming, not sleep talking or no one there to hear.

chapter 3

Brush Your Teeth

On the morning of the interview, skyscraper shadows pointed towards the wharf like unopened ledgers. I chased the gulls across them, singing 'Yankee Doodle Dandy'. The little litter that there was made cabarets with the wind; a hamburger carton gaped and lolled its tomato tongue. A crisp packet gusted up in a wire bin and then drifted down, a weary kite in a cage. I jumped them all in my pin stripe suit, a paper file under my arm, a currency of false C.V.s and forged affidavits. Oh yes, goatee Velour was rock hopping to the top of the mountain. I skipped out of the last long shadow and through the stalls of the many-gated entrance and into the elevator.

The new lift assistant had been in the job long enough not to feel obliged to give the prefix 'floor', only the number. So we elevated in a count up: "one, two, three, four, five..." His voice raising a pitch with each integral development. It may sound overly bold but I was rushing with confidence that day. The previous night I had mangoed out in front of the window watching the city lights flicker on and off like a distant stadium scorecard. I had scraped and sucked the mango in one last indulgence. And as I flossed with its fibres in the early morning, I felt a gift fall into my hands; a chip of the mango stone that had lodged between cheek and tooth. And in the patterns of this chip there was plainly a silhouette of Ravenski's profile; a sign I was certain. So I put the chip in my wallet, in the plastic photo slip, and returned it to a trouser pocket. It was this wallet that I could feel against my thigh as I jumped over the litter and gulls, the small Braille of Ravenski's seed hard against the trammels that led to my pelvis and the bladder stone.

The bladder stone has been growing inside me for years. It irritates, yes, and sometimes I feel it rolling and plopping in its cavity but the doctor said not to bother unless it gave me colic which it hadn't so far, so far. I think the bladder stone is probably not a stone but a seed and is pre germinal, awaiting some kind of light, shone across and down the belly, and then it will break and crumble and grow its rich calcium through my blood. The poet in me tries to break it down like this but I suppose the operation will one day have to come. On the day of the interview, all I could feel was the nub of the mango chip, the float and splash of the bladder stone was nothing, the thought of a fountain nib on my contract the most purposeful flourish.

Up the elevator; "six, seven, eight, nine, ten…" My feet made little jigs on the thin carpet and I had to syncopate it to the piped country music as a few faces looked my way. Gosh I was high. I felt a wave of tingles run through me, leaving behind a sweaty kelp of body hair; "eleven, twelve, thirteen, fourteen…" The lift attendant reached falsetto. I desperately needed a pee.

"I need a pee," I said to him. I said this not because I thought he could help but because it might relieve some of the tension.

"The nearest toilets are on floor twelve," he said, descending half an octave.

I looked enviously at the cleaner's mop bucket. Onward and upwards we continued and as we reached the twentieth floor, and his voice reached a Disney squeak, I knew I needed the toilet more than anything else.

"Does floor twenty have a toilet?" I asked.

"No sir. The nearest toilet is floor twelve." His voiced dropped a relative canyon. I knew of course that the nearest toilet was on the twelfth floor, a peculiarity of Priscilla's plumbing no one had been able to explain and I had to leave on the twentieth floor and then run down the stairs to search out the urinals and pee against the ceramic, only to discover that the flow was red.

"Oh no not now," I thought and indeed then, the excruciating pain of a splinter of calcium in one of my kidney tubes began to stab through the curtain of adrenaline. "Almighty." I ran back up the stairs taking them two and then three at a time.

I waited in the reception room, writhing in discomfort, hands enveloped around my fictitious file. The pain came in waves. I chewed at the cotton wool in my cheeks and tasted mango but morphine was what I needed.

"Mr. Velour, would you like to come through." I was shown by the personnel officer into a board room which was divided by a long mahogany table, with the interview panel on the other side; two high ranking executives and, yes Ravenski, the third, leafing through a copy of my C.V. She was power dressed and magnificent in her dark eyed beauty. The very sight of her made me quiver and my pain eased as I took the central chair facing them.

"Good Morning Mr. Velour." The chairman of the panel got up to welcome me. He was a bony man, with half rim glasses and he held out a spindly arm. "Mr Strachen, Head of Product Enquiry, and this is Ibore Davidson, Fleet Market Division." He indicated a woman in a velvet rust coloured dress with a squashed silver insect broach. I took her hand and noticed she had a firm, almost metallic, touch. "And Ravenski Goldbird," he nodded to his left, "Head of Corporate Research and Development." I held her bitten fingers once more in mine and found her touch at once familiar and energizing. I sat and the wave of kidney colic returned. "Ahhh," I screamed inside.

Strachen began the questioning "So err Mr..."

"AHHHH," I screamed once more to myself.

"Velour," offered Ravenski.

"Yes, Mr. Velour. What do you think you have to offer this company?"

"A...A...A consistently original approach to research and development. In an era, a, a..."

"Yes?" Ravenski looked up from my C.V. and all I wanted to do was scream, pee blood and kiss her dark red lips.

"In an era of maximum competition I can offf..," the pain increased to a peak and then subsided, "...fer maximum gains for minimum outlay. As I think you'll see from my C.V. I have a long and varied career in research and, from cabbage leaf pesticides to cigarette robotics, every input has offered substantial profit gains to the organizations concerned."

"So why Pet Furnishings?" Ibore Davidson caught me with a flinty eye.

"Pet Furnishings is a company that has always impressed me with its bold initiatives and simple but effective insights into consumer needs. I think everyone around this table would agree that the simplest ideas are the most effective and the remarkable combination of the dog with contemporary furnishings is one such revolutionary but altogether obvious insight, an insight so obvious," the pain returned, "that it requires genius, pure genius." I squeaked and tried to make it look like a swell of corporate emotion.

"Yes," said Ravenski, "I can see that you feel very strongly about this Mr. Velour. Do you have any insights that you think might widen P.F.s portfolio?"

"InsIGHTs?" I wrapped my legs into a squirming knot and held the underside of the chair like an ejector seat and then shouted: "WELL I THINK THE DOG IS MULTIFACETED."

The interview panel rocked back, as if swept by the ferocity of my intuition.

"Can you explain that further?" asked Strachen tentatively.

"YES, yes." The pain eased. "Yes." I exhaled. "I can." Ibore nodded encouragement. "A dog is not only a man's favourite furnishing, as P.F. has demonstrated, but also a leisure and sports fixture and a means of home security. If we can tap into and exploit these other key canine features, then we can yank a whole pack of new markets from the canine kennel." I made the 'Holding the Leash' sign and untangled my legs.

Ibore wrote something on my C.V. and turned to Ravenski, who continued.

"I see you are a rock canoeist. That must require a lot of stamina?"

"Oh yes," I said, "freestyle climbing without the rope but with a canoe on your back is a top-heavy experience but…," the stone shifted in its kidney tube, "…ALTOGETHER INVIGORATING." The stone eased back again. "Canoeing down the rapids is so refreshing. Yes," I relaxed and smiled, "refreshing."

Ravenski raised her eyebrows. "Have we met somewhere before?"

"No I don't believe we have." I wondered if the calcium fragment had crumbled.

"I'm sure I know you from somewhere."

I chewed on my cotton wool. The taste of mango had gone, my mouth was dry. "If only we could have met before, it would have been a REAL PLEASURE."

Ravenski shuffled her notes. "Let's move on to your referees. I see they all are Middle Eastern corporations and we haven't, as yet, received any replies. Surely British firms could vouch for you?"

"The problem has been my creative virility. I was, if you like, poached by the Middle Eastern firms because of my unusual talents and the British companies became bitter. I was a bull in the creative china shop and they just couldn't cope. I really believe that you need to BREAK A FEW PLATES if you want to make a brand new dinner set."

"I couldn't agree more," said Strachen.

"Ahum," interrupted Ravenski, "as an employee of Pet Furnishings do you think you might defect from us. Steal our wares, defeat us with your duplicity." She tapped her bitten nails on the mahogany table top.

"That depends," I fixed her with my most certain gaze, "if you can COPE WITH A BULL in the creative china store."

"I can see," she replied, "that you put your opinions very forcefully."

I rubbed my hand over my bladder. "A bull has to have HORNS."

"Can you give us an example," she said, "of how you have been a 'bull in the creative china store'?"

"I once threw a bunch of pub darts up in the air and they pinned down a whole set of branding ideas, as well as a few minor executives."

"Mmm," said Ravenski. She appeared irritated and removed her hands from the table top.

"Do we have any further questions?" Strachen turned to the women either side. Ravenski stared through a window, concealing her hands under the desk. Ibore Davidson sucked the end of her biro and gazed at my tie knot. "Well then, thank you Mr Velour." Strachen rose from his seat and shook my hand. "We'll let you know as soon as we can, within the next couple of days." Ravenski continued to look away.

I left the interview borne down by the double weight of an anchor in my heart and a stone in my bladder. Whatever the outcome, I felt I had failed; failed in Ravenski's eyes that fell on me with contempt and then flickered away in dismissal. The elevator seemed to bear down with added speed in my sullen gravity. I watched the grains of grit wash along the ceramic of the twelfth floor urinals, as the pain dissolved. I had the bitter taste of a broken seed, a taste I tried to swallow as I went home on the bus. I pulled out the balls of cotton wool from my mouth and showed them to the old woman sitting beside me:

"My mouth is so bitter."

She looked from the cotton wool to my face and then reached into her own mouth and removed her upper dentures from her blackened gums. "These taste of porridge."

The old lady taught me an important lesson then and I grasped the balls tight.

"Thank you," I said to her.

"Anytime," she said, dribbling.

That night, in my room, I poured the wax from my scented candles over those cotton wool balls. I poured more and more until they became waxed tombs of cotton. I took a knife and cut her message into each one. "Brush your teeth." I rubbed ink into the cut grooves and balanced the prophetic tablets on the windowsill overlooking the city. I brushed my teeth for the fifth time that evening and eventually there was no bitter taste as I sank to bed. I took out the chip of the mango stone from my wallet and turned it in my palm, savouring Ravenski's profile. I searched out the mango stone from the bin where I had thrown it and pushed both the chip and the stone deep into the earth in the bedside pot plant.

"Moss," I thought as I fell asleep, "moss is a good fertilizer or is it tea leaves?"

The next day I decided to go to the doctors: I was tired of this bladder stone colic. The local G.P. surgery was built from a series of Portakabins painted in health service pea. My doctor was admiring the view out of his plastic shed;

"Two years they've been building." I joined him by the window and we surveyed the quarried hole together. "Foundations of the new practice," he explained. He pointed out the rusting girders and the oil curdled puddles.

"Money run out?" I said sympathetically.

"There was always enough money," he said. "It was me. I made them stop."

"You?"

"Isn't it picturesque? The way the cast iron cables worm into the air like severed nerves?"

"Um…"

"There's nothing like the bitten maw of a building site. I had to fight for it of course." He put on a whining voice; "'We need new services', they said, 'It's not good for the patients', they said, 'Where will we put the physiotherapy block?' On and on. 'yada, yada, yada.' Can they not appreciate art? Can they not understand the built environment in all its…"

"About my problem," I said

"Your problem?" He turned to me.

"My indescribable pain."

"Oh yes, *your* pain." He returned reluctantly to his desk and I explained to him about my colic.

"An operation," he concluded, not without a little relish, as if this was to be his only pleasure in the disinfected room.

"But I don't have time."

"Well you'll have to make some time then." He seemed impatient and tried to smile as if to indicate the end of the consultation.

I noticed his poor dentition. "How often do you brush your teeth?" I asked him.

"What?"

"Do you brush your teeth everyday or just, occasionally?"

"Well I have to say I'm a bit of a tooth libertarian…," he started to warm to the subject. "Once every three days is my maximum. There's enough on my consulting plate without brooding on enamel plaques. A bit of dental neglect gives me quite a hedonistic thrill. Teeth, you see, are the dentist's preserve."

"But if you don't brush your teeth you could end up with gum disease, decay, and, even, dentures."

He smiled with what were clearly brown, sticky teeth. "Isn't it decadent? Halitosis is a bit of a problem though." He leaned forward. I leaned away.

"About my bladder stone?"

"Yes, the stone." He closed his tarry smile and fell into his swivel chair.

"Isn't there some kind of truss?" I asked

"I'm afraid not. All I can offer you is pain killers, or the operation."

"Painkillers?"

"We used to use suppositories but they banned those for obscure reasons."

"What kind of painkiller?"

"Pethidine mainly…as an injection."

"An injection?"

"You know, sharp, pointy, thing."

"I can't give myself injections."

"Well surprisingly you can. A Commons Committee decided that suppositories were 'a bit French' and 'rather queer' and that injections were far more suitable. It was during the Conservative resurgence a few years back. There's a very interesting debate in one of the Sunday magazines, you should read it.

"It's not the Pethidine so much, it's just I'm…needle phobic."

The G.P. picked up a drawing pin, loose on his desk, and pushed it between thumb and forefinger. "We can cure that," he said, "by repeated exposure." He dropped the drawing pin and picked it up again. I watched his fingers with horror. "Ritual enforcement of painful pressure," he explained, "our psychologist has been on a course."

"No, thank you."

"She still has a few places left."

"No really, I'm fine."

"Well, all I can offer you are the injections."

"It doesn't seem like I have much of a choice."

"You could choose not to have them."

"And then choose pain?"

"It's still a choice, Mr," he checked his notes, "Velour."

"Very well."

"O..," the doctor filled out a prescription with his gold fountain pen. "K. There you go." He handed me the script with a flourish.

"Thank you."

"My pleasure." He smiled with his brown teeth.

*

I waited at home to hear the outcome of the interview. I felt my chances were slim, given Ravenski's palpable disdain, but I still brushed the soil of the pot plant expectantly. Meanwhile I was occupied with the problem of the colic and the Pethidine injections. I would have to attend to the pain but I couldn't really imagine pulling up a tug of skin to inject. My flat was self-contained and I couldn't ask my unknown neighbours for help. It seemed presumptuous to ask them for a jar of coffee let alone a morphine hit.

As so often, accident provided the answer. Skewering a lamb kebab I slipped and pricked myself in the thumb. I was spared all of the anticipatory anxiety and immediately began setting up a Pethidine Accidental Injection System or PRAXIS as I dubbed it. I ate the lamb bloody and undercooked in celebration.

For a test run, I put the PRAXIS next to the telephone. The theory being that, in my involuntary reach for the handset, I would nick myself with the needle, avoiding any preparatory fear, and then push the plunger down to give the required dose. I set up the syringe by the hall phone using some strong black masking tape and was able to test the system the next morning when, staggering from bed in the unholy stupor of the newly woken, the phone rang. I reached out and was jabbed in the forearm. I pushed the barrel home and administered its dose. I felt myself becoming pleasantly high.

"Helllloooo."

"Mr Velour, this is Frances Blencoe from Personnel at Pet Furnishings."

"Ahhhh Helllooooooo," I slurred with pleasure.

"Have I caught you at a bad time?"

"No not at alllll. Simply purrrfect."

"You don't sound so well."

"No, no I'm fiiiiine and yourshelf?"

"I'm…well."

"You soond adorable, delishshus even."

"Umm yes. Bad news I'm afraid you didn't get the post."

"Oh well, that's reeelly no problem. Mmmmm, no problem."

"I would be happy to see you this morning to let you know what other vacancies we have available."

"That's mighttee kind of yoossh. I'll be right along."

"I know this is upsetting but we could have other line vacancies."

"Mmmm yes that's good. You sound well, you sound so good, do you feeeel good? You have a lovely voish."

"Well thank you, thank you very much." I imagined her blushing and my loins flickered with excitement. "I'll see you later this morning then?"

"You shure will. You shhooz will. Mmmm."

"Bye then Mr Velour." I thought I heard her giggle.

"Byee Franshish."

I replaced the receiver and slumped across the wall with a fixed smile. Black spots floated across my eyes like poppy seeds and then disappeared.

When I arrived at Priscilla, I was at the tail end of my Pethidine comedown and I stumbled off the bus platform. Nevertheless I was smartly dressed and had decided to accept defeat with grace. I would take a lowly post at the organisation and rework my strategies towards Ravenski. I walked through the milling reception and was about to press the call button for the elevator, when two large security men emerged from the crowd and forced me into a wheelchair. I struggled until I saw the smiling face of Frances Blencoe, the personnel officer I had met at the interview. She put a finger to her lips and whispered; "Don't worry, this is all part of the plan." The guards wheeled me into an elevator behind the reception desk, marked 'transport lift', and we rattled into the bowels of Priscilla. I was pushed from the elevator along a narrow corridor to a heavy wooden door. Frances opened it and I was guided through.

"Welcome to the executive board," she said with a flourish.

I was in a large oak panelled room with a board table in the middle. Sitting alongside the table were the executives of Pet Furnishings and at the far end the company's chairman, Howard Mantle. He was enthroned in a leather chair, a portly sack of a man, trussed in braces. He wore a sharp Italian suit whose pin stripes had crumpled into contours around his belly. He elbowed his weight forward to address me. "Ah Velour, welcome."

"Stand up," whispered Frances. She rubbed, perhaps caressed, the side of my neck.

I tried to get up but slipped and fell back into the chair which then toppled so its underside faced the table and the soles of my shoes paddled at the executives. I hoped I hadn't trodden in any dog turd on the way. A security guard helped me to my feet and I warily went over to the chairman and shook his fat palm.

"Welcome, welcome," Mantle said, appearing to suppress a burp, "I understand you are to be our Research Supervisor."

I gaped and put my fingers into my mouth to remove the boiled sweet I'd been sucking. "But Frances said…" I turned back to the personnel manager.

"Don't worry," said Frances, "it's all part of the 'camouflage'."

"Oh yes 'camouflage'," Mantle released my hand, "take a seat and I'll explain." He gestured to an empty place midway along the board table. It was right next to Ravenski. My heart beat like a foundry. Ravenski, meanwhile, stared at the ceiling. I noticed the brass mount that described my position; 'Terribly Velour, Research Project Supervisor.' Ravenski made a tutting noise as I tried to sneak my sweet under a blotter.

"Well then Mr Velour," continued Mantle. I tried to adjust into the uncomfortable shape of someone else's buttock crease. "Camouflaging is our method of corporate confidentiality. We conduct all our meetings down here while a number of stand-ins conduct similar meetings on the top floor, as cover. Industrial espionage continues to be a problem." I nodded dumbly. "We found whole dossiers of corporate ideas were being haemorrhaged through elevator gossip." He again suppressed a burp. "So we made the elevator ride shorter and in the opposite direction. And you being our newest weapon," he mimed a gun with his hand and cocked his thumb, "we felt we needed to keep you hidden, so we kept the appointment a secret, even to yourself. Indeed as far as Personnel," he nodded towards Frances, "and the rest of the company are concerned you will be a cleaning manager, a mop head." He paused and took a sip of water and the other executives raised their tumblers in reflection. I noticed the tip of his thumb was blackened, by ink or a bruise I couldn't tell. "I don't have time to introduce the rest of the board," he went on, "but I'm sure that will happen. You will be mainly working with Ms. Goldbird," he nodded at Ravenski who was to my left "and Ibore Davidson". He turned to Ibore Davidson who was at my right. She tapped a gold pen against her white teeth. "You will also meet with Denis McCloy, our marketing man," he blinked at a youthful executive with blonde hair beside Ibore, "and next to him Morgan Wenlock, accounts". I craned forward to see a bald man with a pencil thin moustache. He nodded stiffly like a Luftwaffe pilot.

"Morgan *L* Wenlock," the man said quietly. "It's Morgan *L* Wenlock."

"What we need," interrupted Mantle, crashing his hand on the table, "is a bull in the creative china store and I understand you have those qualities." The water jugs lapped their undrunk contents onto the pale blotters.

"Yes sir," I said, "I do."

"I want your proposal by next week and remember Velour, no barking, just talking."

"No barking, just talking," echoed the board and Mantle prised himself from his seat and left by a door at the far end. When he had gone, the executives slunk in their seats and the businesslike atmosphere dissipated into chatter.

I noticed a scattering of fingernail clippings on the blotter in front of me. I looked either way to see if anyone else had noticed.

"I suppose we'll have to have a meeting," snarled Ravenski, "I'm not happy about this appointment, not happy at all. But we'll have to be *businesslike* won't we. I hope you have some business sense." She leant forward and sniffed at my suit as if trying to quantify its quality and then leant back. "My secretary will make an appointment with your secretary, unless," she showed her incisors, "you want your secretary to make an appointment with mine."

"No, no, your secretary's fine."

"Good." She flung a silk scarf over her shoulder and left.

Ibore Davidson tapped me on the wrist.

"You can see me anytime," she said and puckered her orange lipsticked lips.

The young executive with the blonde hair, took me by the arm.

"Sorry Ibore, Telby and I need to talk."

He dragged me through a side door, halfway along the board room. It was the executive toilets. I marvelled at its ceramic splendour. An attendant sat by the door and handed me a towel.

"Listen Telby." The executive ushered me across to the washbasins and looked about him cautiously.

"You are again?"

"Denis McCloy, advertising." He made the peace sign with his right hand. I noticed he had smart but floppy blonde hair. He was dressed in a pin stripe suit and had a kipper tie with a cartoon picture of a fighter plane coming into attack. He had blue eyes and short, quick teeth.

"Now listen, you need to tell me what your plans are so I can start doing the design work."

"What, now?"

"I have to make Mugs, T shirts, Toothbrush holders with your creative bull of a project. I have to bribe T.V. execs, pay for D.J.'s coke, and get Editors drunk on Claret. I've got to sell them something and I need to know now."

"Can't it wait till next week?"

"Nothing waits till next week in this game boy."

"But I've only just arrived."

"Life is a catapult, Velour, and you're in the sling."

"Do I have to tell you right now, here, in the toilets? Can't my secretary contact your secretary?"

"That's for the girls, boy. All the real dirt gets wiped here. Hey do you?" he sniffed, "you know?" He sniffed again.

"I'm not sure."

"It's the only way to move." He produced a wrap of paper and hissed at the toilet attendant who turned his back. "If my juices aren't running I put fruit in the squeezer."

"I don't quite..."

"Look," he went over to a toilet cubicle and knelt in front of the seat, unfolding the paper on the rim, "at least give me a feeling, a vibe, you know?" His hair flopped about his youthful, startled face.

"Well, its, umm..."

He sniffed at the toilet seat. "Sorry I used your line up but I forgot to have breakfast." The seat cover fell and hit him on the head. He rubbed it briefly with his hand and flicked his hair back. "So what's the vibe?"

"Well…"

"Come on, come on. Budda, budda, budda." He made machine gun impressions with his fists until he pounded into my chest. "So what's the demon, Mr Dream man?"

"Dogs," I said.

"What?"

"Dogs."

"Dogs, schmogs, this is Pet Furnishings for godsake, what's new about dogs?" He yanked at my tie like a chain pull.

"The multifaceted dog."

"Tell me more baby."

"Well the dog has many attributes and I intend to exploit them all."

"I like it, like a cube right, and every side has a different meaning, roll the dice and rock baby for the dog is hot and casino, right?"

"Right."

He let go of my tie and sniffed. "I'll get creatives to send you a mock up by this afternoon. Take it easy." He made the peace sign again, buttoned up his suit and left the toilet, giving the attendant a note.

I rubbed at my goatee. I felt things were moving too fast. I looked in the mirror and could see that the cotton wool balls had shifted and my cheeks had become malignant with the lump. I squeezed the protrusions back into place and rubbed at my goatee some more. "Ideas," I said out loud.

"Give me some cash and I'll give you an idea," said the toilet attendant.

"What kind of idea?" I turned to him. He was wearing a long janitors coat that reached down to his ankles and was buttoned up to his chest. His black polyester tie shone in the artificial light.

"The first idea's free," he said, "but after that there's an incremental payscale."

It was my turn to look cautiously from side to side. "O.K.," I said

He picked up a paper napkin, drew a repeating curl on it with a biro, and pressed it into my hand.

"That's not an idea," I said, "that's you trying to get the biro to work."

"I'll charge you for the next one."

"There's nothing to charge for."

"It's an idea," he reiterated.

"It's a curl," I said and stuffed it in my pocket and walked out.

"Remember," he called after me, "I'm charging for the next one."

Ibore Davidson blocked my way into the boardroom.

"I'm so sorry, I'm sooo accident prone. But I was thinking we ought to do lunch. You know, chew the cud, share some sushi."

"I just need to sort myself out."

"I'll see you at your office then, at one. It's on me." She raised her plucked eyebrows. "We're going to get on perfectly I can see. By the way, check your flies."

I looked down at my groin; the zipper had a small shiny bauble attached, like a Christmas decoration.

"Sleight of hand," she said over her shoulder, "I learnt it from an old magician." She winked.

I slumped in my chair in the empty boardroom as a cleaner went from place to place collecting biros and throwing them into a bin bag like discarded wands. I fiddled with my zipper, trying to remove the bauble but my nails were too bitten. I could see my face reflected in it, the cotton wool grimace distorted into an insane smile.

Chapter 4

DANCE FUNK
EAT SHOP

DANCE FUNK
EAT SHOP

Frances Blencoe took me to my office by the stairs, as the lift was broken. I noticed how the seams in her tights made an alluring detour into the hollow behind her knees before tracking up her thighs and behind her skirt.

"Hey ho Francis. Do you think you could slow down a little. It's just…"

"No time, Mr Velour, no time at all…"

We were somewhere around the sixth floor when I ran out of steam and Frances disappeared ahead of me. There was a cupboard on this landing and poking out of the partly closed door was a foot, a foot with a polished black shoe and a white sock. Hesitantly I opened the door and discovered a man in a sharp suit slumped on the floor. His head was propped up by the shelves behind and his chin pressed against his chest. A thin frogspawn of saliva burbled on his lips and he coughed flecks of blood into the phlegm. His chest rose and fell in sudden starts as if it could not carry the full burden of his breathing. By one hand was a plastic bottle, and by the other, a dog leash.

"Telby, where have you been!" Frances Blencoe's voice echoed down the stairwell and she arrived, flushed and breathless giving off a curious odour of sweat, Chanel No 5 and hairspray.

"I found him in the cleaning cupboard," I said. "He doesn't look very well. I wonder if we should…"

"There's nothing to worry about," said Francis. "He's just," she took a deep breath, "a drunk."

"A drunk?"

"He's a dog walker. They're all drunkards. I believe Mr Timpson does a screen at interview but a lot of them end up," she nodded at the man in the cupboard, "boozers."

"He doesn't look very well to me."

"He's been boozing."

I watched him froth pinkly at the lips. "Perhaps he needs some assistance."

"I'll get someone to clean up later."

"I didn't know our dogs could walk up stairs."

"It's probably one of those new models. I'm sure you're working on that kind of thing yourself."

"Yes, yes of course."

A black puddle oozed around a mop next to the man's body. There was a whiff of cordite in the air, cordite and piss.

"Not very hygienic," I thought, closed the door on the man's foot, and hurried on up the stairs.

Frances took me to my office and promptly left, the seams of her tights flickering behind her.

"Abel," said my secretary offering his hand, "I'm profound."

"You're what?"

"I'm profound."

"In what way?"

"I'm a writer, I'm only doing this to pay the bills. In fact, I'm an undiscovered great." Abel seemed to have an impossibly long body, not thin, but long, as if all his mass had been extruded without losing the breadth. He had enormous nostrils like the vents of jet engines from which a few hairs fluttered beneath the roar of his breathy pronouncements. His teeth clacked between thin lips like a series of mahjong tablets from which the offending spots had been wiped. His puppety arms were continually restless in florid piques of outrage and condescension.

"Also I don't do shorthand, it cramps my style."

"Do you think you could contact Ms. Goldbird's secretary to arrange a meeting?"

"Oh, but she's such a floozy."

"Who?"

"Ms. Goldbird's secretary."

"Does that affect meetings?"

"No but it makes for very dull conversations."

"Could you show me to my office?"

"That way," he pointed with a firm 'Every Man Must Do His Duty' finger. "Past the water cooler."

I noticed something moving in the plastic tub. I bent down and found a fish in it.

"Abel?"

"Yes?" He turned his head like a nut on a bolt.

"Why is there a fish swimming in the water cooler?"

"It's a Pampas fish; it gobbles up the detritus and keeps the water clean. They harvest them from whales."

"Doesn't it, you know, contaminate the water?"

"It makes a very nutritious effluent. It charges the water with vitamins, electrifies it with micronutrients. I add them to my bath at home."

"Your bath?"

"They nibble my body perfectly clean. And it is only when I am perfectly clean that I write my best work. I get out before they micronutrient."

There was no name on my door, just a faded plywood rectangle where the last occupant's sign had been removed. Splinters of wood emerged from the four screw holes where the plate had been levered away.

"Please don't slam the door when you go in," Abel shouted, "I have to think."

My office was of a box standard business design. There was a thin beige carpet, a painted black hardwood desk, polystyrene tile walls and, on two of the walls, framed colour prints. The view however was extraordinary. Three full-length windows formed the fourth side of the room and I had a magnificent vista across the docks. I watched the boats move across the waters, the seagulls swoop across the sky and an ambulance creep along the forecourt towards a collapsed man.

"BANG." There was a sudden noise from the walls like a car backfiring. I looked about me but the room had the same innocuous formality.

"Pipes," said Abel who had snuck up unnoticed, "they make bangs and puffs like one of those steam engines. Plays havoc with my ideas." I ushered him out and there were no more bangs but I could still hear distant tapping sounds like lanyards knocking against flagpoles.

I'd always found Priscilla's plumbing strange; pipes going overhead in the canteen, hoses under the tables in the typing pools, radiators that hung between the striplights in the stairwells and now it was banging and clunking and making a repetitive "tap, tap, tip, tip, tap, tap." I traced the noise to behind the office walls and found it to be most amplified just below the framed print of a Turner sunset. "Tap, tip, tap, tip." The tapping faded and then returned through the wall opposite the Turner painting, at its loudest just below a framed Warhol print of Marilyn Monroe. "Tip, tap, tap, tip."

I sat back at the desk and listened to the rally of noises from one side to the other. It seemed as if the Tippity Taps of the Turner painting would continue and pause and then the Tippity Taps of the Marilyn would fill this space until the Turner would begin again. It was as if a pipe rattling conversation was being conducted over my head. On and on it went like some infernal ping pong game. I shielded my ears with a couple of paperweights, until suddenly it disappeared and I was left alone with the background mutterings of Priscilla; the opening and closing of doors, the coughing of photocopiers and the trill of telephones from the floor below. I noticed that the carpet by my feet had black splashes like coffee stains.

I peered defensively over the desk. There was a broken executive toy, one of those 'Newton's Balls', made of stainless steel marbles that swing, one upon the other, on threads of nylon. The threads had broken and the balls lay around like broken tackle on the varnished wood. I was fiddling with the bauble on my flies when the phone rang.

"Miss Davidson is here for lunch," said Abel.

I got up from the chair and yanked at the bauble.

Ibore Davidson burst into the room. As she did so I unzipped my fly and the bauble tore from its clasp and rolled across the carpet towards her. She crushed it underfoot, rezipped my trousers and looked me straight in the eye.

"Let's do Lunch."

"Couldn't we have a sandwich?"

"Sandwiches are for the boys." She turned and regarded me over her shoulder, "and, I, am a woman."

"Of course."

Ibore paced out and I followed. I could feel fragments of bauble crunching under my sole.

Ibore leant over Abel's desk on her elbows. "Cancel all Mr Velour's appointments."

Abel winked at me as I edged around the door. "You move quick for a mop head."

"If Ms. Goldbird rings then..."

"I'll write you a poem," Abel glanced at Ibore beckoning across the room, "or maybe a crude limerick."

I left him sharpening his pencils.

The lifts were out of order and we took the stairs. "What's up with the lifts?" I said.

"There's a dog stuck in the winders."

"A dog?"

"A dog darling, you know dogs, canines, woofers."

"How did it get there?"

"I'm not a clairvoyant darling, maybe somebody let it off its leash." She tightened my tie and pushed me against a wall.

"Where are we going for food?"

"Lunch," said Ibore and showed her perfect white teeth.

"Food," I repeated.

"The Dance Funk Eat Shop."

"I'm sorry?"

"The Dance Funk Eat Shop. They play contemporary funk and serve the most exotic dishes."

"I thought they might be exotic."

"Oh you're so perceptive."

"Extrasensory." I made little antennae with my fingers and wriggled them from my forehead.

"And so very funny."

We tumbled down past the sixth floor and I paused outside the cupboard with its once protruding foot.

"Hurry up darling, I'm sooooo hungry."

I opened the door and found the body had gone. The mop, however, remained, slumped in its black puddle. I could still smell cordite and piss and unwashed dog hair.

Ibore breathed against my neck. "Hurry up darling, please hurry."

*

We took a cab from the wharf out of Lydon and arrived in Soho. We were walking or rather parading past the shops when I had to stop suddenly. There in a pizza parlour, at the window seat, I saw a shockingly familiar couple.

"What's the matter darling?"

I pointed. "It's us." And there, feeding each other pepperoni slices, were almost identical figures of Ibore and I. The Ibore woman was wearing the same clothes as Ibore and had the same tall body and startling white teeth and my double was, well, my double, right down to the goatee beard and paunchy cheeks. Though not quite as handsome I thought.

"Not quite as pretty," said Ibore.

"Who are they?"

"Oh they're just actors, members of the reciprocal executive board, the ones that meet on the top floor. It's all part of the camouflage. If we go to lunch, then they go to lunch, if we go to a sauna, then they go to a sauna, if we undress in the hot afternoon heat they…"

"They're feeding each other pizza."

"I know," said Ibore and pouted. "We, on the other hand, have enormous expense accounts."

In the window, past the couple, I saw a man kneeling on the floor, he had his head in his hands and the backs of his hands were spattered black. I couldn't tell whether he was in the restaurant or if it was a reflection in the glass. I went to look behind but Ibore had her hand on my back. "Darling, we'll miss our hors d'oeuvres."

"Did you see…?"

"This way."

"BANG." I tried to turn but Ibore had already taken hold of my shirt and was dragging me along the pavement.

"What was that?"

"What?"

She nipped down a sidestreet and I was led to a flashing neon sign; 'Dance Funk Eat Shop'. The words flashed one after the other below a luminescent man and woman doing a cancan on the back of a whale. The whale spouted as the figures reached the water hole and they were blown upwards in disarray.

"That noise."

"You really ought to calm down, my darling. Relax."

She cajoled me through the door. A waitress walked, well not so much walked as funk-danced, to meet us. She made a strange jigging movement with her hips and took us over to a high table.

"Where are the seats?" I said.

"This isn't a sit down meal Telby; you dance."

The opening bass line of a 70's disco hit came over the speakers and she began to move her shoulders in motion. She had long blonde hair that fell around her face in two glossy waves. The waves gained their own momentum as she danced, as if she were screen-testing for a shampoo commercial. She had tanned bronzed skin and startling blue eyes like flashes of Atlantic surf. Her teeth were long and strong and sharp.

"Won't we get cramp, with all this eating and dancing?" I shouted.

"Not with bone marrow darling; it just slips down." She began to make a figure of eight with her body. The thick pillar through the centre of the table was translucent and gulped inky bubbles like a lava lamp.

"Bone marrow?"

"It's the new thing."

"You mean cans of marrow?"

"Oh no darling, it's completely fresh, just made to those timeless canned recipes."

"I have to use the w.c.," I shouted above the music.

"Dance baby dance," she called.

I tried to move my hips to the music and felt the bladder stone splashing in its cavity. A waitress funked past. She was wearing a one piece leotard, ankle warmers and trainer pumps.

"Toilet?" I asked her. The waitress star jumped and landed, leaning over her right knee, hands clasped together into a gun shape, pointing to a door with a dancing neon man on the front. "Thank you."

In the washrooms I found the toilet cleaner leaping and sliding across the floor to a hot disco classic. I nodded to him, "funky toilet music." He fell onto his knees and glided up to offer me a towel. I waived him aside and went over the washbasins to replace my cotton wool. I slicked my hand through my hair and flicked a coin to the cleaner. He spun, caught it and flipped it into a jar. I danced back to the table in what I hoped was a funky way.

"Ah just in time," said Ibore. A waitress placed a silver box in front of each of us and then joined a high kicking conga. Ibore had toned down her funk dancing and was now just cameling her head either side of the pillar. Finally she stopped and allowed only her eyes to switch from side to side.

"Eat and enjoy," she said and opened her box.

I flicked open the lid and found a ballerina in a jewellery case. The ballerina had bent knees, in a plié, and was spinning around to a clinking version of 'Unchained Melody'. It had a piece of salmon in its outstretched arms.

Ibore tore the ballerina from behind her lid and sucked out the fillet. She winked and gave a burp. All I could think about as the ballerina span was of my first meeting with Ravenski.

"What's the matter, don't you like it?" Ibore began to camel her head backwards and forwards to a new funk track. But the only tune that mattered was the dying metallic clunk of my wound down ballerina. "Memories," I said.

"You have to live for the moment honey." She leant over, snapped the figurine from my box and sucked out the flesh.

Before I could remonstrate, a waiter and a waitress arrived with plates of gelatinous marrow. They danced and waved the chunks about in time to the music.

Ibore jutted out to snatch a cube of marrow with her mouth and then another and another. The lights went into strobe and she became a many headed hydra in their spectral flash.

"Dance Funk Eat Shop," she shouted at me

"Couldn't we just eat," I shouted back.

"Nobody 'just eats'" she said. "It's a taste dance sensation."

The waitress launched herself into a high kicking jump and landed by the table. She waved the plates of marrow around my body, in synchrony to the beat.

I managed to pick off a piece by holding her arm and found the curd was sweet, dimpled with salt. I picked off another and then another until my mouth was bulging with the food. I swallowed, in gulps, in time to the music. The waitress broke free and offered the next morsel by my mouth. I bit out. The marrow was wizened and fatty; it lingered and then lodged at the back of my throat. I waved my hands about in panic. The waitress mimicked my movements as if to follow a lead. Ibore shouldered her to one side. I began to asphyxiate and clawed at my Adam's apple. Ibore scratched her own throat and swivelled her body in time. "It tastes so goood, doesn't it?" She fluttered her eyelashes.

I gave a sudden expulsive cough and catapulted the soggy piece of marrow into Ibore's face. It slid down and slopped into her cupped hands. She looked at it and then me, wordless. The waiter and waitress continued to funk dance. Ibore picked up the piece of marrow between thumb and forefinger and guided it towards her lips.

I ran from the restaurant and hailed a cab all the way home, the sound of distorted guitar still warbling in my ears like a drowning castrato.

I sneaked into Priscilla early the next morning. There were five people outside the office, in a queue, they were all carrying mops of white string spattered with black. They were dignified and held their cleaning utensils by their sides in a military fashion.

"He's here already," said one.

"He's shorter than I thought," said another.

"Can I help you?"

"We're a delegation," said the first. He was a middle aged man with straw hair and plastic spectacles. His teeth were stumpy. "We've come to see you about our mops, we went to our supervisor but he wouldn't listen…"

"Hang on." I sighed. The corporate world seemed too frantic even for my aspirations. I retreated to my office. Through the windows, I could see that the collapsed man on the concourse had gone, though somehow I expected him to be still there, the ambulance to have passed him by, wailing in the distance. I picked up a couple of the Newton's balls and tried to juggle them.

"BANG," the plumbing shuddered behind the walls and I dropped them. They fell on the floor and I kicked them around the dirty carpet. They made a sound like French boules on clay. The door rattled.

"Come in."

The delegation trooped through carrying their mops and stood in line. The straw haired one stepped out of rank, mop by his side.

"I'm sorry to bother you so early Mr Velour but we wanted a moment of your time. You are the new cleaning services manager?"

"Yes." I tightened my mouth around my cotton wool balls.

"We have a request."

"Yes?"

"Well you know how some companies have tractors and industrial machines they move to music?"

"Err..."

"We have learnt to move our mops to popular classics. If you'll permit me." He took a tape recorder from one of his colleagues and placed it on the floor in front of him.

I uncurled my fingers to the line of mops. "Mop dancing?"

"No, we are the first mop martial arts dance troupe."

Tchaikovsky's 1812 bleated out in a synthesized score from the tape recorder. I tried to shout above the music but the group had already formed a circle and they were crisscrossing in front of me, turning somersaults, using their mops as props. Two separated from the group and began to spar using the handles as sticks to jab and parry while the others thumped theirs in time to the music.

"This is wrong," I shouted, "dance should be pure, should be couple dancing, should be waltzing." I croaked to be heard and the 'z' in waltzing becoming a hissing candlewick. The troupe raised their poles and waved the mops in the air like uprooted wigs. My nostrils burned with the acrid odour of disinfectant. "Stop," I screamed, "stop."

But then the music segued into the Moonlight Sonata and the troupe filed into line in front of me, wafting their spattered mop heads like anemones in a rock pool tide. The movement had a certain beauty and I sank into my chair. They raised the mops towards the ceiling, rocked them at the light fittings and then glided, one between each other, until the music petered away and they curled into themselves, evening creatures, sliding the mops to their chests.

The tape ran its length and the recorder switched off with a snap. I gave a cupped clap into the silence and the mop martial arts troupe stood and bowed.

"There wasn't much martial art in the last bit. I liked the last bit," I said.

"It was a meditative form: Tai Chi Mop."

"Oh."

"We'd like the company to sponsor us."

"In what way?"

"Well for a start the mops." He shoved a mop into my face. "Feel that." I tentatively touched the tasselled threads and the crusts of the black spots. "Industrial grade string recombinants," he went on, "we'd like a cotton weave, for exhibition use only."

"Well I..."

"And," he waved the mop up and down, "see that?" I shook my head. "No flexion, we propose to have metal ratchets on the end of the pole, to allow four degrees of motion, up, down, left and right." He demonstrated with the mop and I followed it, transfixed. He returned the mop to his side. "So what's your opinion?"

"I'll see what I can do."

"You won't regret it."

"No I'm sure I won't."

"Thank you for your time." He picked up his tape recorder and the group left one by one.

I lay my cheek on the desk and dozed and when I sat up I found some old post-it notes stuck to me. 'Keep to the shadows', said one, 'Walk in single file,' said another.

My neck ached, so I lay on the thin beige carpet, star shaped among the Newton's balls and coffee stains and closed my eyes.

I woke to see Morgan L Wenlock standing over me, one foot either side. He was wearing a perfectly fitted grey pinstripe suit and a small, knotted tie. When he spoke, his moustache inched on his upper lip like a worm. His teeth had a sharp, filed, edge.

"Oh it's Morgan isn't it," I said, "Morgan..."

"Morgan *L* Wenlock."

"Accounts isn't it?" I attempted to prop myself up by my elbows.

"You're a hell of man," he said.

"Thank you".

"We should have brunch. I have a whole other side to my personality."

"I'm quite busy at the moment."

"The L stands for *Lola* by the way," he let his tongue rest on the 'L' and flicked his bald head back as if once a mane of flowing hair. "Morgan *L*ola Wenlock."

"That's a lovely name."

"We can discuss the seasonal audit figures over a sorbet and...," he lingered over the syllables, "a blackberry flan."

Before I could reply he had sprinted away, barging past Ravenksi.

"That was Morgan," I said tentatively, "the L stands for..."

"I know what the L stands for." Ravenksi peered down at me, amidst the silver balls and black spots. "Did you know my secretary has been trying to contact your secretary all morning?" She twisted a leopard print silk scarf around her neck and lifted up her chin so I could see a tiny freckle.

"Err my secretary isn't here. He's...thinking." From my position on the floor I admired the smooth muscles of her calves. They had a pleasant arc, like the runners of a rocking chair.

"This is a company Velour. A company." She adjusted her scarf as if to allow her bosom extra freedom. "I don't have time to play games."

"No." I sat up and tried to push away some of the Newton's balls.

"My office, three o clock."

"Can I..?"

"Three o clock."

She turned and the hem of her skirt floated up an inch as if playing on an updraft.

*

The lift remained out of order and I was forced to take the stairs again. I wondered if one day Ravenski would admire my newly toned calves.

I was approaching the stairwell on the fourteenth floor when Denis McCloy jumped onto the landing, his brightly coloured tie swept over one shoulder. He pointed something at my head.

"BANG," he shouted.

Once I had lowered a protective forearm I found myself staring at McCloy's clasped hands, more precisely the index and middle digits of his left hand pressed against the index and middle of his right, a gun barrel, his thumbs cocked back like a trigger, his finger pointing straight between my eyes.

"Got ya," he said and blew at his fingertips, whistling away pretend gunsmoke. "Don't be a pixel Mr Schnitzel, its just a bit of fu, fu, fun…," he put his arm about my shoulders and put his mouth close to my ear, "till Daddy takes the gu, gu, gun away. You never heard of 'Fingerkilling'? It's a game me and the lads play, up and down the corridors. Gets yer eye in for when we go dog hunting, in the country."

He clenched his fingers and tracked an imaginary hound in an arc in front of us. There was a 'schlopping' sound and McCloy's pin stripe shirt billowed beneath his arm. He dropped his gun, folded his arms over the strange growth, and flushed red.

I took a step towards him. "Are you O.K.?"

But he shuffled sideways into a cleaning cupboard, closing the door behind him.

I went up and listened tentatively through the panel. "Shit, shit, shit," he whispered.

I eased the door ajar and looked through.

McCloy had taken off his shirt and tie and was naked from the waist up. From his armpit dangled a smooth plastic object, cupped at one end to fit into the sweaty hollow from where it hung by several wires. A little LED light flashed and it whirred and chirruped as he held it in his hand. He looked up and saw me and snuck the device back into his armpit where it seemed to fit snugly. He pressed his arm to his side, presumably to hold it in, and bit off lengths of gaffer tape from a roll he had in his other hand with which he used to fix the thing more tightly under his armpit. When he had finished dressing and reapplied his tie, he looked up.

"Don't tell anyone…"

"What is it?"

"I'll only tell you if you promise not to tell anyone else, ever."

"O.K."

"It's my Interpit."

"What?"

"A composite of phone, internet and video transmission plugged into the brachial nerve plexus and thence into my brain. I am connected twenty four hours a day, seven days a week into the worldwide telecommunications network. But you mustn't tell anyone, no one, you hear. No one must know the secret of my networking success, no one."

"So you're plugged into the worldwide web by your armpit?"

He lowered his voice and I crouched close so I could listen. "I have instant communication with anyone, anywhere in the world with a twitch of my forebrain. But you mustn't tell one person, you hear, no one."

"Doesn't it get a bit sweaty?"

"What?"

"Having the world in your armpit?"

"I wipe it with a J-cloth at lunchtimes."

"Ah."

"No one must know, remember, no one."

I nodded. The tap behind him dripped hesitantly into a bucket.

"A word of advice," he said, "the walls have ears. So be careful what you say and don't step on anybody's toes." He looked down at his own highly polished black shoes and slipped out of the room, waving a one handed finger gun over his shoulder. "See you in the country for some finger killing."

The pipe above the tap rattled and shuddered, jerking its tarry water into the pail. I closed the faucet and the dripping stopped but the pipe continued to shake as if trying to jerk out its fluids, uselessly, against the valve.

I continued up the stairs and on the sixteenth floor sensed someone behind me and spun round with a fingergun. But it was only a cleaner with his mop over one shoulder. He stared at my fingers blankly and then went on his way, dripping black spots on the steps as he went.

Ravenski's office was higher, wider and plusher than mine. Her view showed a mauve pollution band that diffused into the horizon. She had no Newton's balls, just a computer, a telephone and a wire ring notepad; blank on her desk. The walls of the office were decorated with abstract and thickly brushed oil paintings. She had a bowl of Bombay mix on her desk. I eyed it eagerly. Ravenski sat in a high steel chair behind her desk and I sat to one side in a smaller straight backed seat. She was wearing a brown spotted neckerchief. I put my hand next to the bowl of Bombay mix.

"So what have you got for me Velour? I haven't got all day."

"Well, as I said in my interview, I believe there is room for expansion into the multifaceted…"

"Yes, yes, I've heard all that before. I want to see some real ideas, some blueprints, not this chittle chattle. The development meeting is next week…" She paused to answer her phone. "Put him on hold, divert the other two… Well?"

I was mesmerized. She had a neat black bob that reached just below the nape of her neck like a parenthesis. She had a peaked nose and wide chestnut eyes that seemed, despite her ferocious energy, to signal some kind of autumn sadness. Her incisors were tiny, square and symmetrical, with pleasing gaps, like a mosaic. Her canines, I noticed, were long and precise and angular.

"Well?" She repeated. I watched her calves rub one upon the other in their russet tights. "WELL?"

I fumbled in my pocket, removed the paper napkin I had been given by the toilet attendant, and smoothed it out on her desk.

"There it is."

"And what is it, exactly?"

"A curling…"

"It looks like someone trying to get his biro to work."

"No really, it's an idea."

"What kind of idea?"

"A kind of…abstract…one."

"I don't have the time for this Velour."

I crept my fingers into the Bombay Mix and excavated a handful as I pushed the napkin further towards her with my other hand "It's a, err, spiral thing."

"BANG," the walls erupted with an exclamation.

I peered around but Ravenski continued, undaunted.

"You make the presentation yourself. I'm having nothing to do with it. I always felt your application for the post was so much hot air, a snort in a snowstorm."

"No, wait I can explain…"

"Not with that Mr Velour." She pushed the napkin across the desk. "Goodbye."

I picked up the drawing and left. But once outside the door my disappointment was overwhelmed by hunger and I used the napkin as a wrapper for the stolen Bombay mix. Ravenski's morsels tasted so much better than Ibore's - so much more refined.

It was only back home that I was forced to confront my failure. I had fallen yet again in the eyes of Ravenski and she had discarded her respect for me. I stared at the blighted napkin of my honour and the beginnings of the bladder stone colic returned, shooting strands of pain to my groin with a punishing inevitability. I set up the Pethidine Accidental Injection System with a heavy heart, pinned it just below the shower head and brushed my teeth fiercely. My enamel ached as I felt over the soil where the mango stone was interred, as if it might offer some growth and then slept intermittently, tortured by spasms of colic and uncurling roots of ideas. A car backfired in the streets or perhaps in my dreams.

I awoke with a pain in my belly. I put my hand there and found a black fluid where I had spilt my coffee from the night before. I rolled out of bed and wobbled across the floor to the kitchen, picking up the crumpled napkin from the table and making for the bathroom, turning the mark round as if different angles might offer a solution. I reached through the shower curtain for the tap and was pricked in the arm by the

Pethidine injection. I pushed the plunger home, slumped to the shower base and squatted there, dozing, as the pain subsided.

I woke an hour later with cramps in my legs. The shower had been dripping on my head. In my hands was the crumpled napkin; the water had smeared the sketch into a blotch of odd familiarity.

"That's it," I shouted as I jumped to my feet, "that's it." The needle stabbed me in the neck. I couldn't dress quickly enough as I hurried to Priscilla to develop my new strategy, my hand to the wound.

"You're late," said Abel.

"Any messages?"

"One."

"And?"

"I can't remember. I've been working on my iambics."

"Who?"

"The Greek canon mainly, I hope to translate Homer's Third Odyssey."

"Who was the message from?"

"Young woman or man. Flighty sounding."

I closed the door to my office and then opened it again.

"Third odyssey? I thought he only did one?"

"I'm extrapolating with an iambic slide rule."

I ignored him. "Get me the head of bioscience."

"My iambics will suffer."

"Goddam your iambics, get me the head of bioscience."

"No more poems for you."

"I don't want any."

"Man cannot live on bread and water alone."

"Get me the head of ..."

"I know, I know, bring me the head on a platter." He threw his slide rule on the desk and marched over to the water cooler.

*

The Head of Bioscience, Mr Ballistrade, arrived two hours later. He was wearing a white coat and I noticed a phleb of greenish slime on its tails.

"I came as soon as your secretary told me."

"Which was?"

"Ten minutes ago, in the canteen. I must say I'm looking forward to working with you Mr Velour. How can we help?" He seemed genuinely keen, despite his air of bedraggled science and his eyes moved with an oily glint.

I unfolded my curl on the crumpled napkin and proceeded to elaborate. He left some hours later saying he would begin work immediately.

I felt I deserved a siesta and was dozing on my blotter when Ibore marched in with a compass point stride. She lifted one of her orange heels onto the desk so I could see the seam of her tights and then held me with a fierce metallic gaze.

"I love it when a man spits dog food in my face. How about dinner, tonight?"

"Um."

She plucked a steel fountain pen from the breast pocket of her trouser suit and dashed her address on my blotter. "8.00pm sharp. We can discuss business and its pleasures. Home cooking. No funk." She whipped around and her jacket flared up to reveal a narrow belted waist. She left the door open.

Her address diffused into the blotter. And, like a Rorschach test, I imagined I could see in it desires that reflected my own carnality; twisted limbs on a couch, a frantic confusion of lines: "Studio Seven, Top Floor, 109 Battersea Park, Battersea. Ring bell slowly." The last full stop spread its ink like an encroaching planet in the flecks of the blotter universe.

"The Big Bang," said Abel as he put his head through the door.

"What is?"

"The last great mystery, I'm leaving to write a poem about it."

It occurred to me that women were like the laws of relativity, in that they only seemed to be interested in my universe when I ignored them. I put a thumb on the blotting punctuation and it spread beyond, encroaching on the black splashes and spots.

*

Ibore lived in what appeared to be a car park. It was of the multi-storey variety in a concrete and steel design. I went up to the barrier and an attendant from a booth ambled out to greet me.

"Can I help?"

"I'm here to see Miss Davidson, Ibore Davidson."

"Top floor, keep following the arrows."

"And where do I get out of the car park?"

"That's where she lives; top level."

"So this isn't a car park?"

"No it's a car park studio development."

"Oh."

I followed the arrows. Each floor was separated into parking spaces except for one corner which had been partitioned off and developed into a self contained flat with polished marble effect walls. The stairwell smelt of urine and stale vegetables and there was a liberal sprinkling of rubbish, apart from the area around the flats where a neat red carpet lead up to a formal door. A few cars were parked next to each studio, amongst the hundreds of empty spaces. As I continued up the ramps, I was sure I could see creeping growths on the concrete but on closer inspection they turned out to be streaks of oil and skid marks. At times I was certain I could see bruised blotches, floating across my sight like the blebs of lava lamps. I blinked and they would disappear but it made me wonder at my eyesight. I rubbed my eyes and experienced the yellow streaks that come when sight is pressed inwards, when the funnel to the brain is disturbed. And at this I relaxed, it was a reminder that my hands and my mind could meet in a physical loop, that I was the one in control, and I waved at the shadows, the unknown darkness and saw no further blebs and continued up the car park, keeping to the glare of the artificial lights.

Slumped against a pillar on level five I came across a man in a dirty overcoat with a bottle in his hand. Warily, I stepped into the shadows to take a closer look. He had a matted beard, interposed with flakes of food, and reeked of alcohol and piss. As far I could tell he was asleep.

I kicked him gently. He coughed and groaned but didn't wake. I kicked him again and this time he belched and began to snore. I kicked him a third time, hard in his stomach and then again and again, until shocked by my own viciousness, I held back, my foot lame in revulsion. The drunk opened his eyes, leant to one side and vomited, flecks of blood streaking his convulsion. Then he staggered to his feet and off into the car park, leaving a shadow behind him on the concrete. I returned to the striplights and continued up the stairwell.

Ibore had the penthouse suite on the top floor. I took a sniff of the flowers in the oriental vases on either side of her door, and pressed the bell. It rang with a slowly dissolving chime. The ink from my thumb made a smeared print on the ivory nipple of her button and I was trying to wipe it away when she opened the door, one arm holding up a sweep of fiery and translucent evening gown.

"Telby, you found me."

"Lovely setting," I said. "Looks a bit like a car park."

"Urban chic; don't you just love it? There's a burnt out car on level three."

"I must have missed it."

"We have a beggar, you know, who wanders all over the site on Friday evenings." She widened her eyes. "A *real* homeless person."

I politely raised my eyebrows as she took my coat and hooked it onto a carved antique stand with plated fittings on the horns.

The flat had a golden glow. Standard lamps stood in corners of the hall to echo the radiance and multimedia paintings hung in the aureoles of light, squares of metal nailed into their cubist geometries. I followed her backless gown into the lounge at the end of the hall.

"Sit down. I'll fix a G and T."

I took a seat on a Great Dane sofa. The Great Dane was Automatic Safe; its castors had been locked and its eyes closed. I could just make out the moist flare of its muzzle as it breathed. I brushed the dog's soft skin, a short fawn hide. It was, I noticed, a D37, the old Autumn collection. The sofa faced a frameless window whose glass went from floor to ceiling forming the fourth wall of the room. It created an engulfing view of the city landscape; a circuiting of tower blocks and dual carriageways and transmitter pylons. To my left there was a widescreen television, to my right a huge ceramic cockerel and in front a coffee table inlaid with bright copper coins. They had been polished to a shine and the profile of each altered so the monarch now had her head tilted back, her mouth open, laughing. I sat on the back of the Great Dane and was admiring the view through the full length windows when I became aware of a squeaking sound. I looked up and saw a brass lamp swinging from a pendulum attached to the light fitting. It swept the room, wending and wefting its glow, back and forth.

"Ambience," said Ibore as she walked in with two glasses.

"A bit squeaky," I said.

"Oh yes." She removed an oil can from the coffee table in front of the sofa and then, standing on tiptoes, held the lamp so she was pulled from side to side like a fake fire flame, her tanned body transparent through the thin material. She squirted a bit of lubrication into the hinge and released the pendulum which returned to its silent arc above us. She nestled next to me on the bench and gave me a drink. It tasted of wormwood.

"G and T," she said, arching her blond eyebrows, "with a hint of absinthe. So, tell me…."

"Yes?"

"Just tell me."

"Anything in particular?"

"Anything?"

"Lovely view," I nodded at the windows.

"Beautiful isn't it?"

"Mmm," I tipped the glass to my lips, encouraged by the neutrality of the conversation, "you can see so much."

She bent over, low, in front of me and stretched along the bench so her belly rested on my lap and then picked up a remote control before returning to her original position, so her body and breasts rippled over my legs.

"It's not actually the view of the city; it's the view of the city behind the wall reproduced on a panorama screen. That whole wall, my steel, is a projection. This," she pointed at the cityscape, "is life size but this," she waved the remote towards the window, "is even bigger." The view focused on a single tower block which enlarged to fill the electronic frame. "And again." The lens pulled to a single office at which a man was bent over a computer. "And again." The wall was filled with the head and shoulders of the man and the image of a dancer on his screen; a ballerina spinning round and round throwing pixels into the air. "Enough," said Ibore and thumbed the remote so the wall resolved to the real sized cityscape, "Let's talk about the business of pleasure."

"Can business be pleasure?"

"Every transaction," she said and parted her lips, "is an exchange of gifts."

I picked out the ice cube from my glass and absent-mindedly popped it in my mouth.

"Raph, raph, raph," I said through the ice.

She pointed at my neck. "You've got a love bite."

"Oh no," I readjusted the ice cube so I could speak, "that's a, um, mosquito bite."

"You naughty devil, you've got a secret lover haven't you?"

"Not at all," I said, picturing Ravenski, the romance of my dreaming.

"So you're a free man," she said, "a wild rancher lost to the outback of his desires?"

"Well …"

She leant across, took my head in her hands and then kissed and bit at my neck, over the hypodermic bruise. Reflexively I chomped on the ice cube and it cracked. She moved to my mouth, pulled out the ice cube with her teeth and spat it onto the floor.

"I always knew you wanted me," she said and spread her lips across mine. I hesitated but then responded to the easy dissolution of the chill, her tongue warming the cavities in my teeth. We grappled in a fearsome tangle, clawing at each others clothes until her copper coloured bra straps hung listless over her tanned shoulders and her lacy knickers crept below the rim of her hip bones. She whipped the belt from my trousers so they fell and put her thumb over the edge of my boxers and we both stood facing one another against the city widescreen, each with the other's fingers on the fringes of our carnal imaginations.

"Now my love, my steel," she said.

"My steel?"

"My prop," she said and ripped my boxers down to reveal a healthy erection which she guided to the sofa. I clawed off her underwear and we had sex in as many positions as I could muster for her, until the dog fell over. She shouted "Don't come, don't come," and pulled herself away before leading me to the next coupling.

"Shouldn't we be using protection?" I shouted.

"I'm safe, are you?" She pushed her hands against my face, smearing my cheeks, pressing the cotton wool balls against my teeth.

"Of course."

We ended up doing it on the coffee table. Ibore on all fours, me taking her from behind, my hands cupped under her breasts. As our rhythm escalated I noticed the cityscape in front of us magnifying in jumps. Ibore had the heel of one hand on the remote control and with each pump forward was accidentally pressing a button. She had her head down, deep in the processes of her orgasm, but I couldn't help but notice the magnifications of the screen that we made with each thrust. The view expanded to the rooftops of the tower blocks, then focused on a passing plane with a red flashing light, enlarged again so the plane filled the whole wall and then a single cabin window, until finally, as Ibore howled, it became the face of a fat businessman eating his airline meal. Noodles dribbled from his mouth. He turned to look at us with a Soya sauced string hanging from his lips.

"Madness," I shouted.

"Taoist," shouted Ibore.

The screen focused on the passenger's eye; fat, fleshy, jaundiced, his pupil an eclipse in a blue iris. He blinked and Ibore collapsed under me, taking us down to the edge of the sofa. We lay there panting as the screen ratcheted back to the cityscape.

"My steel," she said, "a bit rusty but then stainless is so tomorrow and tomorrow," she yawned, "is so yesterday." Behind us the dog paddled its castors in the air.

Later, as she made coffee, Ibore outlined the manifesto of our relationship.

"You need to change your image," she said. "Luckily I know all the right people." She handed me my drink and smiled.

I slept badly in Ibore's bed, guilty in the caresses that I half imagined were Ravenski's. But by the morning I had decided to pursue the relationship, if only for its carnal and career rewards. Ibore caressed my beard as I woke. "Isn't business such pleasure?" I put on my suit while she watched from under the duvet. "Don't forget, after work, your image."

I left silently for Priscilla. I wondered, as I held my tie knot between thumb and forefinger, what Ibore's image might entail. I pulled up the knot to my neck so it pushed against the Adams apple, a stifle to its bob. The car park attendant raised the barrier as I left. He winked at me.

"Pleasant evening Sir?"

I tried to respond but was unable to loosen the tie.

"You'll want a Windsor knot sir, that'll be one of those grannies."

I tugged at the tie on the bus to work, as if pulling on my own lead and it loosened in the slowest of measures as we choked forward in the commuter judder. When it finally came loose, I fell asleep and missed my stop by miles. When I awoke it was to find myself whistling, as if adrift from the dream of a song.

"You're late," said Abel. He had his legs up on the desk and was cutting a quill with a penknife.

"Important business."

"Important business shagging Rusty Busts."

"Now listen here Abel…"

"I'm all ears Mr Velour."

"Don't use that language."

"I speak no other apart from Homeric Greek, which is somewhat redundant in day to day transactions." He pointed the quill at me.

"Get on with your translation then."

"Oh I'm bored of my translation, I'm back to the great novel."

"Well…do something."

"Oh I shall," he yawned, "I'm writing a syllable a day. My first one is Arrb…"

I went into my office and had barely sat down when he started knocking on the door. I flung it back, determined to assert my new power and virility.

"Look here, Abel I..."

Denis McCloy swept into the room carrying a large polystyrene cube that he held between both arms so it obscured his face. I just could see the bottom of his tie that depicted a Challenger tank rolling over bits of broken masonry.

"I've been trying to get hold of you for days Velour." He dropped the cube on my desk and it tilted lopsided from the phone.

"A mock up," he patted it on one corner, "of the multifaceted dog, Dicematic."

I looked at the thing more closely. It was the size of a small washing machine with six white sides on which the dark dots of a dice were marked. The dots were freshly painted and dripped here and there like wounds. From one side of the cube a plastic dogs head emerged and from other a plastic tail, arched up in static glee. Four doorstops made rubber feet at the bottom.

"It's part of the merchandising process," said McCloy, "go on, have a go."

"How?" I asked

"The holes Velour, just put a finger in." I did so and pulled out a boiled sweet. "I haven't finalised the expenses for all the free gifts," said McCloy, "but try the number one dot."

I went to the side with the plastic dog's head and pulled out a wrap of tracing paper.

"What's this?"

"A little bit of sniff for the broadcasting execs, top whack, no nose dribble." I handed it back to him. "No go on keep it," he said, "it's on me; well on accounts anyway."

"Thanks."

"Now watch this." McCloy hit the cube on one corner with his fist. It began to shake and judder and a variety of 'gifts'; a gold fountain pen, a lump of brown hash, a tea bag and some tickets to a film premiere, shuffled out, emerging from their holes like wormlife.

"Brilliant eh?" said McCloy

"Very um…"

"Enticing - that's the word you're looking for."

"Yes I suppose it is," I said, "now all we need is the thing itself." The cube stopped rattling, as if a clockwork spring inside had wound down.

"What?" said McCloy

"The new product."

"Don't worry about that Velour. It's the selling that's important not the making."

"But you've got to have something to sell."

"This is what we sell," McCloy hit the cube again, "the image." It started to rattle out its maggoty contents. "To the executives anyway," he shouted above the noise. "And let's face it who else counts? Don't worry about it Velour, relax. You know you should come out with me and the lads, do a bit of dog hunting." He made a finger gun and put it to his own head. "Work off a bit of steam." Then he laughed, picked up the cube and walked away, the taut skin on his young face quivering with the transmitted vibrations. I bent down to get the gifts and ran after him.

"You forgot your novelties," I shouted as he went through the reception.

"Keep them," he shouted back as I tried to push the things back into the holes but they immediately fell out, along with other, more brightly coloured, gratuities. I slipped up on a packet of wine gums and he was gone.

Abel peered over me as I sat on my backside in the litter.

"Who tore a hole in your Santa sack?"

"They're not mine."

"Freebees," announced Abel and picked up the gold fountain pen. "I collect fountain pens; perfect for draining the poison from snake fangs." He took off the cap and looked at the nib. "Just a hobby, of course. Freebees!" he shouted and a gaggle of P.A's appeared who, after a brief pause and appraisal of the goods, jumped in. They left me dazed and freebie picked, a locusted scarecrow in the plains of polyester carpet. A domestic twirled away with a brown lump. "I got the hash, I got the hash," she sang in a high diminishing refrain.

Abel squeezed the cartridge on his pen so the nib dribbled spots onto the carpet. "I feel another syllable coming on. Must dash." He ran off to the lifts holding his pen like a dirk, assassinating the air.

I got up, dusted myself off, and sought some peace in the office. But there again was that tapping sound from the walls, volleying from one side to the other, in some porous communication between the Marilyn Monroe print and the Turner sunset. I tapped my biro on my blotter, in time to the beats, and saw that the previous occupant had marked rows of dashes and blots, like a hangman conundrum. "Of course," I said out loud, "Morse code". Someone or something was trying to communicate through the pipes and the previous occupant had picked up their transmissions. All at once the tapping disappeared leaving only the hum of air conditioning and distant office machinations.

I gazed through the window at some street performers on the wharf forecourt below. They were gymnasts and flip flopped and tumbled from each others shoulders and made human pyramids and webs; an alphabet of limbs.

From afar they appeared to be contorting Lowry figures in a barren painting, breaking and reconstituting their bodies. I wondered why they continued doing this when their audience, a few office workers, passed so far away. I took out a fiver, folded it into a paper plane and threw it from a window. It disappeared from my sight but I imagined it gliding down and landing by the performer's feet, an easy tip. I searched my trouser pockets and found a box of matches from the 'Dance Funk Eat Shop'. I began to snap and bend them into a wooden frame, using glue from Abel's drawer until the matchstick model expanded into an intricate branching and seemed to me to become the blood supply of an irregular brain, weaving tendrils, an acrobatic intellect exemplified. I balanced the work on the desk and the setting sun's rays leant it the bloody aura of life. The acrobats had now long gone but I felt I had trapped them here, frozen in their geometric intimacies, their gestured thoughts. Somewhere here, somewhere within this mind, I was sure I would find the answer to the tapping walls.

Ibore burst into the room. "Come on boy, you need a makeover" She offered her lips for a kiss. I pressed them hard as she looked sideways at my matchstick brain.

"What's that, a skeleton?" she said, and stepped back to take a proper view.

"It's something I imagined," I said. "Ibore do you ever hear knocking from the…?"

Ibore leant over, snapped a matchstick from the construction, struck it on the sole of her high heeled shoe and put it to the sculpture.

"No," I shouted but the flame had already engulfed the lattice and it crumpled in a gulp of carbon. The smoke alarms sounded and I turned to Ibore, equally distressed.

She rubbed her fingers in the matchstick charcoal and then marked my eye sockets with a grey smudge.

"That shadow is so you, my steel. Let the makeover begin."

She dragged me from the room in the discordant blare of the fire alarms and we dodged the security guards that were running in the opposite direction. I was dragged down the stairs by Ibore, until both of us were left, panting, outside the forecourt reception. The tall glass doors reflected my face and stole it in a revolving carousel. Above us, Priscilla Tower reflected the sun in a thousand molten squares. Ibore held my head and kissed me, leaving lipstick traces around my mouth.

"I've hired a car," she said and on cue a black limousine rolled up from the underground garages next to Priscilla. I climbed in and, once behind the tinted windows, demanded an explanation from Ibore.

"Why did you burn my work?" I said

"What work?"

I tried to wipe the oily lipstick from around my mouth and could see in the glass reflection that it had smeared across my cheeks like rouge. "You burnt my matchstick model," I said.

"That was just a bit of fun." She handed me some paper towels from a cabinet in the door and I smeared the lipstick further round my face. "Aren't you having fun? Isn't life such a ride?" She kissed me again and bit at my lips and I pulled at her hair as the car accelerated and guttered through the traffic.

Our first stop was the basque makers: "Body Bod, For the Body in You"

"It's your chest, my steel. You need, well, you need more muscle." She draped a finger across my pectorals.

The basque makers looked like an old tailors from the outside but had various basques and bodices fitted onto mannequins in the shop window. 'Body Bod' was written in gold curling letters on the signboard. A bell rang as we went in and a short man appeared from the gloom. He had a thin moustache that wrapped slowly around his face like an ink line and blotched into fat sideburns. His shop had the pale conformity of a well worn trade; shirt drawers were racked to the ceiling behind wooden counters and there were tailors dummies, headless and limbless, trailing a measuring tape over one shoulder or around a waist like forgotten straps of underwear. The man gently stroked a brass rule, laid into the counter, and spoke with an Eastern European accent.

"Ah Miss Davidson. What can we do for you?" He turned to size me up with a keen tailor's eye. "A fitting for another gentleman?"

"*Another* gentleman?" I said.

"I've an extended family," said Ibore. "So many nieces and... nephews." She turned to the moustachioed man. "I want a tuck and widen, Mr Blanoff."

Mr Blanoff produced a metal tape measure, almost by sleight of hand, from his trouser sides and wrapped it about my chest. "Mmm yes, very tiny pectorvals. We shall soon sort out this matter." He whipped the band away and it zinged against my nipple.

"Ow."

"Get your shirt off," said Ibore.

I removed it reluctantly and put my hands over my nipples. "I'm shy."

"Geratin, it's a goot size." Mr Blanoff returned with a yellow basque with metal clasps down the side. He opened it like a suit of armour. "This should do the job. Lift up your arms." Ibore issued a commanding gaze and I raised my arms as Mr Blanoff pressed the corsetry around my waist and chest and flicked the metal clasps shut one by one. The bone underpinnings pushed below my pectorals and squeezed them high and wide.

Ibore dragged a fingernail across the new ridges. "So firm, you'll look great in a T shirt, my steel."

"It's bit uncomfortable," I said. I tensed my jaw so a cotton wool ball popped out and I had to reposition it with the point of my tongue.

"But the pain suits you. Show him the mirror Mr Blanoff."

He showed me and I saw a snared canary, frowning.

"Your steely glare," said Ibore, "it's so movie star."

"I feel so heroic," I said and pulled the corset up at the waist where it was digging into my hips.

"Schein," said Mr Blanoff, "beautiful."

"We'll take it." Ibore handed over a credit card and I put my shirt on over the basque. "Don't you feel better already?"

"Uhuh."

Ibore paid her respects to Mr Blanoff and he bowed. We climbed into the limousine with some difficulty, me having to bend straight at the waist. Ibore shoved me in and twined a wisp of hair around her finger.

"Now," she said, "for the locks."

"The locks?"

"Curlies. Don't worry; your image is entirely under my control. It's a matter of purpose and direction." The car careered around a corner and I rolled against the window, my nose pressed against the glass.

"But I don't feel under control."

"Take heart," said Ibore and put her hand down my back and began tightening the straps of the basque, "you're transitional."

The limousine braked abruptly and I bolted forwards and back and then quivered with the engine, like a vibrating thong. She removed her hand from the basque and patted me on the head. "There you go."

I tottered out onto the pavement, in front of; 'Chip Chop (Smart Sculpting for the Smart generation)'. A plastic comb on a set of wheels ran a switchback around the lettering on a little metal track.

"This is the smartest hairdressers in town."

"Do they let you have a cup of tea?"

"Vodka and lime," she said, "on the rocks."

As we went through the tinted double doors, Ibore advised me on protocol. "You normally have to book weeks in advance but I told them you were a somebody. So you have to be a somebody."

"A whobody?"

"A somebody."

"So who am I?"

"Make it up, steel. You've got a clever little brain." She tapped me on the forehead with an orange painted fingernail. "But make sure you're somebody interesting, somebody important, otherwise I'll never get a booking here again."

We sat on a bench and waited for my appointment while Ibore read a glossy magazine. A woman appeared with long black hair tied into a series of peacock feathers that trailed on the floor. She was carrying a piece of card the shape of a small satellite dish.

"Chin up," she said and applied the instrument around my neck and then tucked a gown into my shirt. "Nice pectorals," she added and nodded at Ibore.

"What's this?" I pointed at the thing.

"Hair and tears catcher," said Ibore

"Tears?"

"You have to pay for beauty, my steel."

"Come with me," commanded Peacock Hair and I followed, with a last nervous laugh towards Ibore.

"I'll see you in an hour," she said and set about applying some lipstick.

"Kneel," said Peacock hair and we approached a washbasin. I knelt behind the ceramic pew. "Put your hands behind your back." A ribbon was tied about my wrists to hold them firm. "My name is Tamsin, pleased to meet you." Tamsin filled the basin with cold water and proceeded to plunge my head into it, repeatedly.

"This-is-so-re-fresh-ing," I spat between the plunges.

"Yes," said Tamsin, "it loosens your root structures."

"Ah."

I noticed that the dish around my neck was full of soapy water. I pointed it out to Tamsin.

"Hang on, hang on." She sighed, bent down for a bucket under the mirror and then drained the water from a plug. She looked at her nails as it trickled into the pail, the water spotting black. But before I could protest, she had left, taking the bucket with her. "Stay there."

I dripped into my satellite dish. Tamsin hadn't replaced the plug and the water continued to trickle down my front.

"Hallo my name's Nigel." A young man in a kaftan appeared. He had long hair but this time in a pony tail which stretched down and wrapped around his waist like a belt. "I've come to revitalise your scalp."

"Are you the hairdresser?"

"No," he said with a flourish, "I am the apprentice."

Nigel pressed a little button underneath the ceramic and an oratorio started playing from hidden speakers. Nigel moved to its ebbs and peaks as he mouthed the words, diving in on my scalp with staccato pecks of his hands.

"That's a bit painful," I suggested.

"It's revitalising," he advised and increased the intensity of his pecking as the song reached its climax. "Hallelujah," Nigel boomed as the tears welled in my eyes and then abruptly the music stopped.

Nigel put his face close to mine. "Would you like a shot of vodka?"

"Yes please," I said, faintly sobbing.

"Ice and lime?"

"Please."

He returned with the tumbler and then wiped the tears from my cheeks with a napkin. "Nuala will be along shortly."

I went to take a frantic swig of the vodka but my hands were still bound behind my back and I tipped forward uselessly, like a plastic woodpecker on a pivot. Twenty minutes later Nuala arrived and poured my vodka down the sink. Nuala was short, her head was completely shaven and she had an Innuit face, round and ravishing. Her teeth were oddly triangular. She sat on my lap, her legs astride mine and gazed into my eyes.

"How do you feel?" she said.

"A bit tearful," I said.

"No, how do you *really* feel?"

"Um, happy?"

"That's right, and revitalised."

"Oh yes," I said, "revitalised."

"Good. Now its hair extensions, isn't it?"

"I think so."

"Long, double long, or super."

"Err…"

"Double long's good."

Nuala helped me into a chair with castors and wheeled me across to a mirror in another part of the salon. Then she set to work twisting my locks into hundreds of porcupine spikes, which she glued and set with a tube from the counter. She firmed the spikes with a hairdryer until they were pointy sharp and tested them with a fingertip. "Ouch. So what attachments would you like?"

"Um…"

"You can have 'Vogue', 'Elle', 'The Times', 'The Financial Times', 'The Guardian'…most periodicals really."

"What would you recommend?"

"You look like more of a Times man to me," said Nuala

"Fine, I'll have 'The Times'."

She disappeared and came back with a bucket full of sopping newspaper in a glue paste and then proceeded to roll the sheets into twists and attach them to the spikes of hair.

"Nice weather," she said as she fixed a stripping of the international news section.

"Nice," I said.

"So what do you do then?"

I searched my mind for a more or less interesting persona. "I'm an Islamic extremist," I said.

"That's lovely; we had an astronaut in from the NASA space programme last week…"

"Oh."

"Nice chap he was. Lovely chest."

We continued in this vein until she had finished attaching all the glued twirls of Times broadsheet.

"….so I said to him it must get awfully cold up there…."

I looked at my reflection in the mirror. I was a white rasta, newspaper dreadlocked in a kindergarten pasting frenzy.

"If only my head were a balloon," I said wistfully.

"Why?"

"You could papier-mâché the balloon and puncture the bit underneath to make a shell."

"Oh you are a funny one. What did you say you did?"

"I'm an extremist."

"Aren't we all honey? Would you like to see the back?"

As she held up the mirror I could make out the headline of an editorial curling round; "Arms trading for grain," it said.

"O.K?" She plucked at the strings of paper as if fluffing them out.

"Fine," I said and she blow-dried the glue until the hair piece was set.

Nuala undid the ribbons and unclasped the satellite dish. She tilted it to one side so a few tears could be collected from the tap underneath. She put them in a small bottle and handed it over. "It's a memento, no extra charge."

Ibore ran up and took my hands as I emerged from the salon. "Oh my Steel, you're transformed. Spin round for me."

I did as I was told.

"I don't believe it," she said, "you've gone for 'The Times'. The embarrassment." She looked away.

"What's wrong?"

"Nobody goes for 'The Times'. That's old style financial. You should have gone for 'Elle' or 'Chic Encounters' or something. Perhaps we can change it next week. I want you to tell everyone it's 'The Guardian'." She tutted and pulled at the paper strands "I hope they won't tell from the typeface."

She led me outside and into the streets. The rain was lashing down and I had to use an umbrella to keep my headpiece dry. As Ibore rushed me along, I was sure I saw black bleeding into the lamplight, slurring into the puddles and then I blinked and rubbed my eyes and it was gone.

We were driven to a private viewing at a Soho gallery. There I met Ernie and Charlene and Pettico and Tabs and lots of people with backless dresses and voices like new woodsaws.

"I simply love your hair," said Pettico, "Is it Chip Chop?"

"Yes," I said, drooping slightly with the alcohol and pain from the basque.

"Which paper?"

"The Guardian."

"Oh old style liberal. Paddy, that's my beau, he's got the New Left Review, in plats."

"Lovely," I said.

"BANG. BANG. BANG" There was the sound of gunfire from behind us, followed by a scream.

Pettico dropped her champagne glass and it shattered. I clenched my fingers into a gun shape and pointed over her shoulder at the noise.

Pettico followed the line of my arm to the bitten fingernails. She looked at me blankly.

"It's a finger gun," I said

She opened her mouth as if to say something but I had already started striding towards the gunfire. There were people running in the opposite direction, evening dresses hitched up above the knees, men with blotches of red wine spilt down their shirts. And against the tide I ran with my imaginary gun. I turned a corner to find Morgan Wenlock spreadeagled against the wall of the gallery, riveted through his palms so he hung by them. He was not in his business suit but in an ill-fitting red dress, so tight that his bones stuck out through the material. He was wearing an orange wig that had splayed up around his face like a rusty Brillo. Above the neckline of his dress was a pearl necklace and above this an open chest wound, the final rivet.

"Apparently the L stands for Lola," said the man next to me.

A crowd had gathered, craning over each other. "He worked for Pet Furnishings," the man continued. "Garrick," said another, "Garrick, Garrick."

There was an oil painting above Morgan. It was a portrait of two women in 19th century dress, drinking tea from tiny china cups. 'Tea for Two' read the title.

"Garrick, Garrick," whispered the man.

"Garrick?" I said.

"He's an Animal Liberation Liberationist, campaigns for the release of Animal Liberationists. Attacks people in Pet Furnishings." He nodded at Wenlock. "Apparently, the L stands for…"

"Yes," I said, "I know."

"I hope we can keep him there," said a tall man with a name badge. "We could call it 'Cococablamma for Lola'" He spread his hands out as if to illustrate. There was a slow chorus of approval. "We'd have to ask the police first of course."

Sirens stirred in the distance and the crowd reluctantly retreated, feet crunching on broken glass.

*

I gave my apologies to Ibore and, after getting steadily drunk on someone else's champagne, went home. I managed to unlock myself from the basque and fell onto the bed with a paper snap. My whole body ached and I set up a PRAXIS injection next to the bedside alarm. I felt I deserved a bit of pain relief. Tomorrow was the day of the board meeting; the moment when I would reveal my grand idea, my creative bull of a project. I turned over and the papier-mâché hair crackled about me.

I dreamt I was having a quiet meal with Ravenski in a perfectly White Room. We ate small mango chunks one by one from transparent saucers. The saucers had holes and the juice dripped out making black spots on the floor.

Chapter 5

~~Libiration~~
Liberation

The alarm roared into action and I put a hand out and received my PRAXIS injection in the arm. I pushed the plunger and welcomed the drug's easy caress. I spat out the cotton wool balls, sodden from the night before, gargled with mouthwash, and staggered into the shower. The water ran over my head and I put my hands up to the warmth and then rubbed my sore chest. It was then that I began to notice lines of black running along the hollows between my ribs.

I felt the damp newsprint of hair and realised it was ink. I pulled the shower curtain back, tripped onto the bathmat and started squeezing out the water. But the headpiece had already turned into a soggy pulp. I leant against the tiles and rocked back and forth against them, making reflected headlines, stilling myself to sleep. I eventually woke from dreams of 'Eastern conflict' in 'Village Ponds Sadness' too late for the beginning of my meeting.

Still, I insinuated myself into the basque, accepted the discomfort as a penance for my stupidity, and put on a tie behind the pulped haircut. I looked at the new styling with a hand mirror. Its paper strands had meshed together so the headlines now lapped into a hieroglyphic of symbols. The whole thing had become an Egyptian headdress wedge and I felt more like a Ramesean priest than an executive as I stepped out of the flat and walked to Priscilla wharf.

In my journey, I noticed a broken snooker cue sticking out of a skip. It was just the tip that had been snapped off and I yanked the thing out and used it as a prop, a staff. The other pedestrians gave me a wide birth and I saw their distance as respect for the wandering prophet rather than as fear of my eccentricity. The bus journey was especially successful. The old conductor took my arm and guided me to the disabled seat and I enjoyed the ride in splendid isolation. The staff at Priscilla were quite complimentary. "Oh very stylish, Mr Velour." The receptionist waved her glossed fingernails at me.

I told the guard I needed to get to the executive meeting immediately and he guided me to the lift behind the reception and thence the underground board room, brushing aside lesser clerks and accountants. I strode along the narrowing corridor and then waited as he pulled the door back and I made my entrance.

The executives turned towards me in a domino of astonishments. Mantle looked up from the far end of the table. He pointed. "You Velour, we have been waiting. Where is your research?"

"It's ready. In fact," I said, "I have a prototype." There was a gasp. "If you'll permit me." I lifted my cue above their heads and used it to press the intercom button in the middle of the mahogany table. "Get me Ballistrade, Head of Bioscience."

"Right away sir," the speaker replied and I waited, standing beside my seat, staff in hand, noble and papier-mâché wedge haired. A ripple of executive murmurs travelled far and wide.

As I stood there proudly with my staff I noticed the empty space Morgan Wenlock once occupied and in a blink I saw him spread-eagled against the wall of the gallery, his wig disparate, his moustache poised thin above his astonished mouth, his pearl necklace spattered with blood.

Ravenski seemed unsettled. I saw her draw a question mark on her blotter like a crook. Ibore, to my right, applied lipstick intently with a gold baton. The others tapped their biros ferociously against their blotters and shuffled their chairs a degree to one side so they didn't have to glance at the space Wenlock once occupied. Everyone else was ignoring him, and so, I decided, would I.

"What do you mean by coming at this hour?" said Mantle.

"I was developing my theories," I said, "if you want to be a real bull in the china shop, you have to polish your horns." Ballistrade bustled in with a cardboard box.

He put down the container, removed from it a second box, this time made of pine, and retreated.

"Ladies and Gentleman of the board," I manoeuvred my cue and put the tip under the pine lid. "I give you the dog in the box." I flicked it open and a dog's head popped out on a spring. It bobbed up and down for a while and then the jaw swung open and closed and the eyes rolled in their sockets. It was a Collie dog's head. "Arf," it said and then, "arf, arf."

There was a silence into which I unleashed my proposition.

"This," I pointed at the thing, "is not a real dogs head but in three months time we hope to be able to produce the genuine article, a dogs head on a spring, isn't that right Ballistrade?"

"We are developing the technology that will allow us to create a bioengineered dogs head," he continued, "we did toy with using actual dog tissue…"

"But," I tapped my stick on the table, "there are issues to do with public relations which despite our best efforts," I nodded respectfully at Denis McCloy, "may clog up the merchandising process."

"Nice Hairdo," whispered McCloy

I went on; "I want the Dog in the Box to be a portable delight for the lonely traveller, a comfort pet for those without the space to spare, convenience intimacy for the young professional. The Dog in the Box will be all of these and more. The first in a range of products that will explore and develop all that our canine friends have to offer." There was a mustering of applause from one end of the table until I silenced it with my staff. "In the meantime, as a taster for the mass markets, we hope to release," I nodded at Ballistrade and he produced a smaller container, "The Snail in the Box". I flipped its lid and a snail bounced out on the end of a spring. It flopped out of its shell, squelched and played its salivary antennae into the air.

"Note the interesting dynamic," I pointed with my snooker stick, "between the innate tardiness of the snail and the spring's rapid movement, creating a psychological release that makes this the ideal executive toy."

Mantle seemed to nod his head in appreciation and Mr Strachen stood up and began to clap in hearty swipes which his frame couldn't quite manage, until his half rim spectacles inched down his nose. And then the other executives joined him until the whole table shuddered in corporate approval. I removed my cue from the table and pushed my back straight with it, becoming once again the prophet, the research guru.

Mantle brought his fist down on the table and the room went silent. "Where," he roared, "is the furniture?"

"It's a new direction," I murmured, "the multifaceted dog."

"I like the furniture, I like the dog benches."

"Oh this is purely complementary," I said, "In the ideal home there would be a dog sofa and a dog in the box, we're just expanding the market."

He felt around his enormous stomach and burped. "Good. Bring me my tea and then on with the agenda."

I returned to my seat. I could feel the newsprint of my headpiece damp against my neck. Ibore winked. Ravenski expanded the doodle of her question mark. Mantle was brought his tea and the next item was announced: "The reciprocal committee's research findings."

I turned to Ravenski. "Reciprocal?"

"Oh the camouflage committee. They meet on the top floor and…" I smiled encouragement, delighted by her new, softer tones, "… we always check to see what they're up to. They're just a bunch of actors but we like to keep a tab on their pretend developments."

The reciprocal executives arrived, mainly the core research committee, who were more or less flamboyantly dressed versions of myself and Ravenski and Ibore. My reciprocal had not yet evolved a hieroglyphic hairdo and pulled discontentedly at his short locks as if affronted by my rapid styling.

"So," said Mantle, as he accepted another tray of tea, "what have you come up with?"

My alter ego stepped forward and erected a flip chart. He had a thin reedy voice and I pushed my pectorals out as he spoke. "We," he said and rolled over the front page, "have created 'Smile Clips'. On the sheet of paper beside him he had drawn a picture of a dog's face and at the corners of its mouth had sellotaped paper clips.

"Smile clips," said the weedy one, "will be placed at the corners of the dog's mouth to make it look perkier and the owner more pleased with his pet." He pointed at one of the clips and it fell off the chart. I tried to suppress my laughter. He flipped the chart. There was another dog's face, this time with a downturned mouth with paper clips at the corners. "And for those more melancholy moments," he said, "the sad dog or hang dog."

The executive board laughed politely and the reciprocal committee filed out. I adjusted my tie. The executives returned to earnestly tapping their biros against their blotters, interrupted by a crack every now and then as one bit into a nail. Mantle continued to roll out the agenda smothering any discomfort in his rotund momentum.

"Let's try and wrap up this meeting," said Mantle, "I've got a massage at midday." The agenda reeled onwards and, as the personnel department began their presentation, I imagined playing 'Pin the Tail on The Dog', with the melancholic canine sketched on the flipboard. The black spot of its cartoon eye drifted off the paper and over the top of the executives, it lingered somewhere about the ceiling, before suddenly returning to the dog's flat gaze. I blinked but the spot remained where it was, at the centre of its hieroglyphic eye, and I wondered instead at the vagaries of my own vision.

The meeting finished abruptly when Mantle had to relieve himself and I stood from the table to receive the congratulation of my peers.

"Brilliant presentation," said Strachen. He twirled his spectacles between thumb and forefinger. "I'm looking forward to more of your work." The glasses flew out of his grasp and he went off to find them.

"Nice moves," said Denis Mcloy. "Top dog."

Ibore gave me a bronzed kiss. "My steel, I always knew you were the real thing. I'll give you a bell later, must rush; one of my nephews is unwell."

One by one, they left the board room and I leant upon the oak panelled walls radiant with the glow from their praise. The dog on a spring and its snail companion nodded where they had been brushed by the passing executives. They seemed to be genuflecting before my might, my Pharaohnic majesty. Morgan Wenlock was but an afterthought, a footnote in my all conquering glory.

Ravenski strolled over from the corner of the room, where she had been watching, and leant against the wall, her arms folded. "Not bad," she said, "for a new boy. We should meet up to discuss the matter further." She tossed the end of a silk scarf over her shoulder.

"I'd like that." I tried to smooth my hand through my hieroglyphic hairpiece but my fingers slipped, frictionless, over the top.

"Tomorrow. My Office. After work."

"Great."

"Good."

She left the board room and I daydreamed us together; the great and the good, with ranks of executives and snails and dogs on springs, bowing before our padded thrones. I pushed back with my snooker cue staff and fell through the concealed door into the executives toilets, smacking my hieroglyphic hair wedge on the ceramic. I looked up, dazed, into the face of the toilet attendant sitting in his chair by the entrance.

"So it worked then, did it?" he said.

"What?"

"My idea."

"*My* idea," I said indignantly, and tried to get up but seemed to be anchored by the weight of the papier-mâché helmet.

"Remember," he put his hand through slicked black hair and then made a curling motion with his finger, "the spring."

I managed, with a degree of effort, to roll onto my side and then push myself up to my knees. "But the spring was just a springboard the whole idea was mine."

"What is a spring board without a spring? It is just a board, a dull executive unexecuting board. A spring is a spring is a trickle of fresh water. And my biro and I are the source of the Nile." The latrines gurgled and flushed behind him.

"Who do you think you are?"

"A toilet attendant, but a toilet attendant with a biro," he said.

I got up by holding onto the grouting between the tiles.

"All I ask," he went on, "is that I get a payment for the next idea and in the meantime I've got these friends in a performing mop squad and…"

"Yes I know, they want ratchets and mop strings."

He adjusted the cuffs of his janitors coat and I noticed he was wearing a gold bracelet. "I can see," he said, "we're on the same wavelength."

"Perhaps."

"Would you like to freshen up, spit out a few cotton wool balls?"

I narrowed my eyes and he smiled. "I know," I said, "frowning doesn't suit me."

"You look perfectly movie star, Mr Velour." I motioned to leave. "Remember," he called after me, "there's a bill for the next idea."

"I don't need your ideas," I said. The latrines hissed as I slammed the panel door shut.

"I hear you're a big cheese," said Abel when I walked into the office.

"Yes, the presentation was a moderate success." I lifted my chin.

"All the secretaries are saying you're the talk of the elevator, a real bull in the china store and you were only meant to be a mop head, that sounds like a promotion to me."

"Aren't you mixing your metaphors?"

"How dare you accuse me, a writer, of mixing my metaphors? They are hybrids, neologisms of the highest disorder. I am the author, lest you forget, of the greatest work of this century."

"But you've only written two syllables."

"Three actually but I've started designing the book jacket."

"Don't books have to contain words?"

"I suppose, but all the best writers write from the outside in. I've decided mine will be bound in vermilion and the title will be 'Tantric Kant - Sex in the Age of Wonder', with a Geneva font and the subheading: 'Fuck right and wrong, let's fuck.'

"Sometimes I wonder," I said and made circles with my snooker cue like a magus summoning the gods.

"You really shouldn't wonder," said Abel. "It doesn't suit you. You narrow your eyes too much."

"I think I look like a movie star," I said and lifted up my hairpieced head as I stepped through into my office. "I'll make a movie," I announced. "If Abel can write a book then I will make a film, Anthony and Cleopatra."

*

The next day I was overtaken by a driving funky rhythm. I was sat at my desk but couldn't help but twist to its insistent beat. "Restless movement, yeh, yeh. Restless movement, yeh, yeh." The words insinuated themselves into my head while the beats of a dancefloor funk rallied along the corridor by the lifts. I ran from the office, past Abel and pursued the sounds to the back of a young dancing girl, complete with personal stereo, overamplified earphones and hip switching body. She was wearing big trainers, hipsters and a small pink T shirt. I ran ahead and then jogged backwards in front of her. She had her eyes closed and didn't notice me. She had short brown hair, a tiny ski jump nose and petulant red lips, closed so I couldn't see the teeth. The music fizzed out of her stereo with the same insistent repetition; "Restless movement yeh, yeh. Restless movement yeh, yeh."

I was just about to tap her on the arm, to rouse her from this reverie, when Abel appeared and pushed me to the wall. The girl continued past us down the corridor. "Don't touch her," said Abel, "and don't ever, ever, speak to her."

"Who is she?"

"That," he replied, "is the beautiful dancing French girl and you must never touch or speak to her."

"Why?"

"It's written down in the unwritten lore of the building. If you speak to her, she will leave, never to return, bringing bad luck to all those she once blessed with her legion beauty."

"Sounds like an Old Wives tale."

"It's the truth. In fact it's in the company statutes, the other secretaries told me about it, I can show you if you …"

"No, no, it's alright." I watched her dance away along the corridor. "Maybe she's lonely and wants a chat."

"No ones ever dared ask. And that," he nodded at me with furrowed brow, "is how it should stay."

I returned to my office and watched a litter sweeping machine chunter across the forecourt below. Its brushes went round and round scooping up bits of rubbish. A man followed behind using a grabbing instrument to pick out the remnants. He made jabbing movements with the pincer and then transferred the cans and crisp packets into a bin liner.

Eventually the man arrived at the side of the forecourt and tipped his refuse into the river. The rubbish joined together into a single black mass, which then fragmented and dispersed along the river. The litterpicker stopped, mopped his brow, and continued on his litter picking way. I bit at my nails one by one and spat them onto the desk.

Five O' Clock came in a joyous rush and I sprinted for Ravenksi's office. She was sitting behind her desk in a grey business suit and cream blouse, nibbling absentmindedly at her fingers. She hid her hands as I made my presence known.

"Take a seat." I sat in the chair to one side of her desk. She offered me some Bombay mix and I took a handful to munch on as she smoothed out a clean sheet of paper.

"Right. I've flagged the points we need to discuss. Number One… Your Project. I thought the ideas you brought forward at the executive meeting were mighty impressive for a new man. Number Two…Future Strategies. In terms of long term planning I think we…" Ravenski had chestnut eyes. I admired the layers of colours as her pupils moved along the page. "…. should begin to draw up revenue profiles…" And then I followed the clear whites of her eyes, like a pulp, a chestnut's sweet. "… in the first instance and then set up further strat…"

"Chestnut," I said.

Ravenski stopped in her flow, the pen dotting on the checkpoint which blotted, spreading darkly.

"What?"

"You have eyes like chestnuts."

Ravenski pulled the blot into a tick. She looked up.

"Your eyes make me think of chestnuts," I said, "of autumn mornings."

"And does this have any bearing on…"

"I'm sorry."

"Point number three. Priorities…" She pulled her tick into spirals making a galaxy of them. "You know," she looked up again, "when I was younger I used to go to a market."

I nodded and watched the eyes that blinked back at me, the widening pupils.

"We lived in a village and on the way to the market, in the next village, by the wood, there was this gypsy who sold chestnuts in a brazier, and…and I can't understand why I'm telling you this." The neckscarf she was wearing had fallen down and one end hung alongside the parting in her blouse.

"I'm all ears." I dropped the Bombay mix and it scattered.

"We would dance over the fallen leaves from the forest and, as we ate the chestnuts from his stove, it felt like we were eating the forest, eating the fire that burnt with the wood of the forest. We used to make hideouts in the leaves, for hide and seek, until, until…." She looked at her nails and then hid her hands under her thighs. "I don't think any of this is appropriate…"

"No," I said, "I mean, yes, yes it is. I liked the story. Look…," I brushed the Bombay mix scattered on her desk into a bin where it made a brief shower on the tin, "…Why we don't go out for a meal and have a chat? We are business partners after all and it would be good to forge… links." I meshed the fingers of one hand with those of the other. "For business purposes of course. The business of pleasure."

She held onto the piece of paper. "I don't like eating out," she said, resuming her sternness. "But I do sometimes have a power supper."

"A power supper?"

"I stay after work and have a few pretzels."

"Oh."

"Tomorrow evening then. A planning meeting." She returned to her files indicating our time was over. I noticed a yellow post it note had attached itself to her elbow like a geometric butterfly. "BANG", the plumbing jolted from behind the walls and I jumped from my seat. Ravenski carried on working and shivered, so the post it note fell and fluttered to the floor.

*

The next day, I gave a fake national insurance number to Frances Blencoe the personal officer. Frances had long black hair and black lipstick. Her teeth had a line of decay marking out the edge of her gums but were otherwise unremarkable. "This isn't a real National Insurance number," she told me. I ate my last remaining fingernail. "Don't worry," she continued, "we'll pay you in cash. I don't care who you are. Mr Mantle likes you, and if Mr Mantle likes you then everybody likes you, including the finance department. You'll receive your first envelope next Wednesday or would you prefer your own Dog Card?"

"Dog card?" I took the nail rim out of my mouth in an attempt to reattach it to its source.

She produced a credit card with a dog hologram on it. "Direct debit to your own account. Digital transfer. Automatic debit."

"Well that seems like a good idea."

"Here, have this one. Should start working by next week. You whistle through that slit to withdraw cash." She noted down the card number.

"Whistle?"

"Regard the hole," she indicated at a small notch by the dog hologram. "Give it a blow and you'll produce a suprasonic pitch at the exact same resonance of your bank account identity. You can use it in shops with swipe machines. Marvellous don't you think?"

"Magical," I said and turned the card so the dogs head moved up and down howling into the light.

"I have to tell you Telby, a favour demands a favour"

"Yes?"

She stood up and undid a few of the buttons on her blouse, sucked in her black lips and then pouted.

"Oh, right," I kissed her and stepped back. "While we're here could the mop team be supplied with any materials they might require for a professional mop dancing troupe."

She undid another button on her blouse. "I'm not quite sure what you mean but if you write it down I'll see what I can do."

She leant forward and we kissed again.

"Do all business relations work at this level?" I asked.

"Oh no, they go much deeper," she said and padded her lips with a piece of tissue.

*

That evening, I skipped up to Ravenski's office. She had her pretzels wrapped up in a napkin front of her.

"Sit," she said, and pointed out the chair on the other side of the desk. I perched there awkwardly. "Would you like one?" she unfolded her napkin and offered a stick across the desk. I took it in my teeth. "Nice huh?"

"Lubbly," I said, munching, my head crooked over the blotter.

"I thought we might look at the revenue figures first."

"Mmm the revenue figures." I wiped a bit of Pretzel from my lips and sneaked a glance at Ravenski's brown eyes. "Pudding," I said.

"What?"

"A mango," I lifted up the carrier bag I'd been keeping under the chair, "after we've finished the pretzels, of course."

"We're here to talk business Mr Velour, not fruit."

"Of course business, though I did wonder if business and pleasure could mix." I meshed the fingers of one hand with those of the other. "So we can, you know, forge links."

Ravenski gazed at the outsized mango that now lay on her desk, tumescent through the plastic bag.

"You know, I've never tasted mango," she said. "Isn't that mad?"

"Insane."

She snapped off a Pretzel in her teeth. "So what do they taste like?"

"You know, sweet, juicy, tropical."

"Then show it to me, reveal it." She showed again her pristine white teeth and I noticed for the first time that the gap between the top two made a faint whistling sound as she spoke. "Reveal," whistle, "it," she said.

I took out the mango from the carrier bag and let it fall onto the table between us.

"They're big," she said.

"Succulent," I said.

She handed me a paper knife and I cut the fruit from the stone. And then we each took pieces and watched the other bite and suck as the juice dribbled between our fingers and soak into the blotter.

"It's such a liberating food," said Ravenski.

"I'd love to feel liberated," I said, "but I feel so hemmed in." I squirmed in my basque.

"Pity." She teased out ribbons of mango fibre through her teeth.

"Would you like to come back," I said, "to mine, for a cup of tea, for a, you know, chat."

She put down her slice of fruit, reached out with a bitten fingernail through my lips and eked out a bit of mango fibre, teasing it straight. The strand wouldn't release so she lifted me up with it as she stood from the desk.

"Why?"

"To look at the design revenues," I added hurriedly, still dangling from the mango strand.

"No I think we'll go to your office," said Ravenski, "you can show me your design ideas there." The fibre snapped and I fell forwards, hitting my chin on her blotter.

The lift was finally working again and Ravenski let her fingers play up and down the buttons. Her bitten forefinger traced the perimeter of a button before pressing the centre in a firm slow gesture so the final joint flexed back and the tip drained a bloodless white. The hem of her jacket brushed lightly against my wrist as the lift slipped down in its rails. "Designs," she said softly.

When we arrived at the twelfth floor Ravenski forced me through the sliding doors, against the foam tiles of the corridor, held me by my tie and kissed me. I spluttered as her teeth became toiled in the mango fibres still threaded in my own. A cleaner went past mopping the floor in great slops of black water that collected into dips in the lino. He looked up at us briefly and then continued on his way pulling a murky trail behind him.

Ravenski dragged me to my office.

"You know," I started to say to her, "you mean so…" She pressed her hips to mine against the desk.

"Kiss my teeth," she said. And as I did so some of the blackness of Frances Blencoe's lipstick printed there, a gothic decay to Ravenski's perfect enamel. "Again," she said, "again." She closed her lips and held onto my hieroglyphic head piece.

"This isn't right," I said and pushed myself away.

"Why?"

"It's my hairpiece," I said, "this thing." I rapped on the printed hive. "It scratches, it itches, it weighs me down."

"Then take it off."

"I can't. It's glued, it's fixed into the hairs of my scalp."

"Well I'll take it off then," she had caught sight of the broken staff in the corner of the room, "I'll use that pool cue."

"What do you mean?"

"Use it to beat the paper off."

She put her hand on the back of my neck and forced me to kneel on the floor and then swung the cue backwards and forwards, lining it up with my head. "Don't worry. I can practice. It's like a golf stroke, like a fairway drive." She raised it a few times swishing the weighted end of the snooker cue through the air.

"Hang on a moment…" but before I could continue she had raised the cue above her head and then swept it down so it smacked into the papier-mâché headpiece. The whole thing cracked and fragments of pulped world news flew across the office.

I rocked back, dazed but she continued smacking the snooker cue against the congealed hair so it demented into pieces. I keeled over beneath the force of each blow and then righted myself for the next; bouncing as if on a spring until my scalp was exposed to the air. "Wait," I said. I put my chin to my chest. "Just pick off the paper now, with your hands."

Ravenski faltered for a moment and then let the cue fall from her hands. Her cheeks were red and her eyes sparkled. It was like the first time we met so many years ago. She picked the remaining paragraphs between thumb and forefinger; levering the flakes from the skin with her bitten nails, prodding and peeling, underneath and between. And then she came to the paste close to my skin which she couldn't scratch away. And so we went outside to the reception and she held my head under the water cooler. She played her fingertips in the stream of water and then over my scalp, encouraging the fluid to seep in and distract the last layers from their close attachment. Artificial tears ran from my eyes and over my mouth so I could taste resin and thin carbons of ink. She put her fingers to my tie and undid it. She unbuttoned my shirt and pulled it off by the sleeves. She let her hands drift to the side of the pectoral Basque, which she unbuckled and unhinged like a shell. And then she ran her fingers dark with the newsprint over my chest, taking the ink into the crevices and shallows so my ribs rose and fell in definition. She raised her lips and we kissed with our hands upon each others chests, my fingers winding through a parted clasp in her blouse, pulling her bra strap over her shoulder. I brought my hand back to the smooth beginnings of her breast and we tilted so our heads touched, forehead to forehead, so our lips parted from the pivot of our brows and our noses touched, side by side, pulling with the barest surface tension, the thinnest films of ink and sex.

"Now that's better than a cup of tea," she said.

In the distance trains rattled on monorails like spoons against china.

Chapter 6

THE WHITE ROOM

We went back to Ravenski's apartment. She lived in a studio development on the top of a hill in a small suburb called Addlebury, some miles outside of Lydon. The building was a square block three storeys high, made of red brick, and it had a grey stone tower in the middle. Ravenski told me that the apartments had been built from the foundations of an old bakery and the grey tower in the centre was what was left of it. Ravenski's flat was on the second floor of the apartment block and had a view overlooking the suburbs. We walked through a patch of green lawn to get to the entrance. Ravenski said that the grass added more to the rent than the studio itself. I listened to her descriptions as I tried to kiss her. She paused and nibbled at my lips with the tips of her square teeth. Over her shoulder I saw a darkness creep amongst grass like a mould.

The studio was the usual array of severe designer furniture and electronic durables. The colour was a nondescript gun metal grey with the occasional black for the television or hi fi. Here and there a pot plant hung awkwardly above the metal chairs and tables, slightly gnarled ferns trying to grow in the central heating. Among the monochrome prints and etchings was the odd frantic watercolor of autumnal forests, windblown, and feverish with colour.

"They're nothing," said Ravenski, "youthful fancies."

She threw her coat over a chair, pulled my sore red scalp towards her and poked at it.

"Ouch."

"Does that hurt?"

"A bit."

She pouted, raising her mouth to mine but as I went to kiss her she stepped back and laughed. As I reached out she turned from me and ran into the adjoining lounge. I followed, tackled her about the waist and we fell with a thump on the tiled floor.

"Ouch," she said, rubbing her knee.

"Sorry."

She pulled me over by my tie and together we leant by the grey skirting board.

"Are you sure you're O.K?" I touched the mark on her knee, just below her skirt.

She looked across the room to a glass tabletop reflecting the rectangular light shade above it. "Sometimes this flat seems so strange."

"Flatness is so strange," I said.

"And what does that mean?"

"I'm not quite sure." I took my fingers from Ravenski's knee and trailed them over the cracked glaze of the floor tiles where they made crab like reflections. I imagined I could see swirls of words, veins of sentences in the patina.

She put her hand over mine and pressed it to the floor. "Would you like to see the White Room?"

"What's the White Room?"

"I found it a few weeks after I moved in. One wall was a different colour and so I picked away at the paint until the plaster came away," she showed me her bitten nails, still with bits of papier-mâché newsprint underneath, "and then I found this…hole." She pointed across the room, next to a streamlined charcoal coloured sofa, a foot above the skirting board, where I could make out an irregularity, a sore in the otherwise smooth surfaces. Ravenski seemed embarrassed. "It was an itch."

I went over and had a closer look. Ravenski had pulled away the plaster and the brickwork behind had crumbled to reveal some loose wooden slats and a hole leading to another room.

It was just big enough for my head and I knelt down and peered through. On the other side I could see a room about the size of a squash court but absent of any defining features save the whiteness of its walls. They glowed with a brilliant crystalline purity, lit from a single window high in the ceiling.

I retreated into Ravenski's apartment and pulled at the edges of the hole, snapping off wooden slats, breaking off bits of plaster and throwing back bits of old newspapers in the cavity, until the gap was just wide enough to fit one person.

I tried to wriggle through but my belt and trousers got caught at the hips. So I took off all my clothes and, with Ravenski gazing at my bare white arse and balls, climbed through.

"Come on in," I said, "the light's lovely."

She eyed me warily.

"No one can see us."

She turned her back to me and undressed. She took off her jacket, her blouse and her skirt, and then her bra and knickers and folded them, one by one, on top of the pile of plaster, broken wood and old newspapers. She had a smooth, pale, supple body and I felt shivers run to my groin as I looked at her. Then she climbed in to join me and we lay on the floor, side by side, soaking up the pure white glow. There were no blemishes, no spots of black or streaks of grey.

"This is the room inside the tower," said Ravenski, "the turret you can see from the outside. It was all that remained of the bakery before they turned it into flats. They must have made bagels here," she meshed the pale fingers of one hand with the pale fingers of the other so her joints turned white.

I put my hand to a wall and felt out the cold stone and then walked along each plane, feeling out the minutiae that you couldn't see; the plaster over the blanked off windows, the pointed cement between the stones, the slabs of the floor closely laid with their separation as fine as the edges of a page. And here I returned to Ravenski's side and drew my fingers along her arm and towards her chest. I touched the crease inside her elbow, tiptoed around a small brown mole, and past the curve of her armpit to her breasts. I felt her own hands exploring me; around my scars, my ribs, the peak of my shoulders and down to my thighs. I kissed her and put the tip of my tongue into her mouth and she bit it with her sharp teeth. I held her hips and pulled them towards me but she pulled away.

"Not now," she said.

And so we lay side by side staring at the skylight. The sun had started to set and the window made a square of orange heat between us. I held my palm under the light, in front of her mouth, as if it was something physical, a mango prism, and she held the haze up to me also and we moved our teeth in synchrony till the light became red and then grey and our palms became empty saucers and our fingers relaxed into the half cups of sleep and then darkness.

*

In my dreams, Morgan Wenlock remained pinned to the gallery wall. The executive board filed past murmuring approval. Mantle reached up and pulled adoringly at the red pearl necklace until it broke and the beads floated towards us like drops of blood in freefall. I opened my eyes.

"Ravenski?"

"Uhuh?"

"Do you remember Morgan Wenlock?"

"Uhuh?"

"He was riveted to the wall of a Soho…"

"Forget it, Telby."

"But don't you think it was strange…"

"Put it to the back of your mind." She turned away and I gazed in silence at the perfect white walls at that surrounded us.

The alarm went off in Ravenski's flat, converting to the radio. "Bleat, bleat, bleat. The news now at seven o' clock. In response to mounting criticism there has been…." I followed her through the hole in the wall, out of the White Room, and we dressed in her flat, listening to a crisis somewhere important. Ravenski offered me a lift to work. But I took the bus as we agreed that the elevators were already too freighted with gossip.

I wondered if I should tell her about my fling with Ibore but she kissed me before I could speak and I was left to ponder the White Room alone. I looked out of the bus at the scurrying people who would forever be outside its walls. I wondered if they had their own White Rooms and, if so, whether they had ever returned, or if they had had them sealed long ago with wet plaster and newspapers and old letters smeared with fading inks.

Chapter 7

Lives Go By Like Weapons On Skateboards

"Hello Baldy," said Abel.

"It's a new style."

"Baldy with scabby bits?"

"Now listen here Abel, we're going to clean up this office."

"I, Mr Velour, am a writer; that is all I do, write. My hands have, and always will be, unsullied by manual labour of any kind. Good day to you…"

He returned as I was brushing the last bits of screwed up paper from my desk and this time he held a vermillion, leather bound, manuscript holder. "I thought you might like to hear the introduction to my latest opus," he said.

"Not now Abel…"

"Tran!" he shouted.

"That's it?" I said. "That's your introduction?"

"What do you mean '*Is that it?*'?"

"I thought you'd have written, you know, a few words."

"I'm serialising it."

"Serialising it?"

"One syllable at a time. I will reveal its storyline in a tumbling momentum that will thrill you to your plebeian core." He snapped shut the folder and looked at me, expectantly.

"I suppose *I* will have to tidy the office," I said and scooped up some pencil sharpenings as Abel watched me, arms folded. He prodded around the circularity of his unusually large nostrils. "I love watching other people work. I find it so energising."

"I'd rather you didn't watch me."

"Oh, you're so delicate," said Abel and yanked a clockspring of a hair from his nostril and brought it up to his eye. "To see the world in a grain of sand, a universe in a…"

"Leave!"

"I suppose you've heard?"

"Didn't you hear *me*? I said Leave."

"Poor Mr McCloy."

"What?"

He turned to go.

"What about McCloy?"

"I thought you wanted me to leave. One minute you want me to go and the next moment you hang onto every word like a sloth. Isn't that some kind of harassment? I ought to sue you. I ought to sue your balls off."

"Just tell me what happened to McCloy."

"Mr McCloy, one of your colleagues I understand, was riveted to the wall of a restaurant. Nouvelle Burger Art."

"When?"

"It was all over today's papers, like ketchup at the chip shop. Not that I looked of course. It might have sullied my imagination. I have a very delicate imagination."

"Who...how?"

"I don't know Mr Velour. I am not an oracle. Though I am, I think you'll agree, one of the new literary prophets."

"And what did the papers say?"

"They said it was Garrick, the Animal Liberation Liberationist."

I steadied myself against the desk and Abel, happily impressed with the impact of his news, left the office. I continued to tidy, if only to take my mind off McCloy's violent demise.

I began to pick up bits of bauble from between the threads of synthetic carpet, using my bitten nails to prise them from the close weave. And as I did so my scalp began to itch and bite as if ticks were gnawing into it. I put my hand to my head and felt another hand alongside mine. I screamed.

"Stop being so sensitive," said Abel.

"What are you doing?"

Abel continued to pick away at my scalp. "I'm pulling off type. Did you know you have bits of Geneva font glued to your scalp? Anyway, I've got a memo." He held up a piece of paper.

"I thought I'd scrubbed it all off."

"Clearly not. Especially here, just behind the ears."

"Ouch."

"Do you believe in synchronicity?" he said.

"Will you just get off me?" I flapped about my head.

Abel bent over, put his cupped palm in front of my face and pointed out the torn scraps of newspaper as if they were lichen.

"Look at that; vowels and consonants, I can paste them together and make a few more syllables for the great novel. Oh look, an 'L'. Do you know what Mr Wenlock's 'L' stood for? Poor Mr Wenlock."

"Will you leave?"

He gave me the memo and skipped out, prodding at his plundered type. The memo read; "All memos shall be short and to the point. They will be written on recycled paper and the recycled paper will be recycled. This will prevent a cycle of waste and allow waste to be recycled." I crumpled it up and threw it in the bin.

I was harvesting the last paper clips from my desk when Abel broke the silence with inevitable irrelevance.

"Mere Rov," he shouted at me through the door.

"I'm warning you, Abel."

"Those are my next two syllables; aren't they enchanting? See, it's 'Tran-mere-Rov' altogether. Aren't you drawn inescapably into the plot? I should have the next two diphthongs by teatime."

I decided the only way to escape Abel's book was to get someone else's.

The library had a pleasing architecture; an abandoned emptiness after the restless corridors of Priscilla. The place smelt of the dust of hundreds of human beings and fingertips scraping across type. At the unpainted enquiries desk, they had some idea of what I was talking about.

"Morse code, that's an outdated form of communication isn't it?" My assistant was an unshaven young man in jeans and t-shirt with just enough stubble to pick at with his well groomed nails.

"That's why I've come to get a book on it," I said and dropped the bags by my feet.

"Have you thought about using our computer information database?"

"No, I want a book, a book I can hold in my hands."

"Well let's have a look in the catalogue." He tapped away on his keyboard. "Da, dee, da, dee, da…memories, menarche, morphine…," I rubbed my bites, "morose...morris dance, Mors gods…*Morse Code*: A Practical Guide For Beginners. Republished 1948. Still want it?"

"Of course."

He tapped away some more. "It's in the reserves section, been cordoned off; all the books got sprinkled in rat poison during an infestation last year. Can't get at it, I'm afraid."

"What's the point of having a library if you can't get books out?"

"Rules. Who wants to be covered in rat poison anyway?"

"I really need that book," I said, "I really need to have it in my hands." I opened my palms side by side.

"Sometimes we do go down to reserves," he cleared his throat and looked behind him, "for a price…"

"How much do you want?"

"How much have you got?"

I handed him a sheaf of notes. He inspected them, incredulous, and then stuffed the bunch in his back pocket.

"O.K. I'll be about half an hour. I have to put on the boiler suit and the respirator mask." He glanced each way, turned the cardboard 'Open' sign to 'Closed', and disappeared through a gate behind the enquiries booth.

When he returned he was still half dressed in his boiler suit, a gas mask hanging from one hand and the book from the other. The pages were dripping. "I had to wash the rat poison off so it's gone soggy. I'd leave it to dry on the radiator, on a low heat." He spent some time looking for a rubber stamp. "Not databased, you see. Don't often get a chance to use the inks." He smeared the date onto the first page. "I did enjoy that." He looked up and then showed me his violet rooted fingerprints.

"I'm glad."

"Any other obscurities you'll be wanting?" His gas mask dripped black onto the varnished desk.

"No, that'll be all. Thank you."

When I got back to Priscilla, I hid from Abel in my personal toilet, just off the main office; a casual and luxurious apportment behind the hat stand. Lucky enough to be based on the twelfth floor I had access to its elusive plumbing. I wiped my arse with memo toilet paper; "Ties should be worn at all times, the knot two millimetres above the collar bone; always tear along serrations to prevent aggravations".

"BANG" I jumped off the seat with my hands clasped into a fingergun. But there were no further eruptions, merely a dull clank from the pipe that led from the cistern. I was listening to Abel experiment with new sentences through the walls when the tapping sound returned, a distant echo, behind and then in front of me, like blunt typewriter keys. I waved my hands in front of my eyes but it soon became clear that the tapping was coming from the walls, the tapping of the plumbing returned, its echoing rally from one side of the office to the other.

I pulled up my trousers, laid the morse code book on the office floor, and set about deciphering its transmissions. "Tip tap, tip, tap, tip, tap, tap." Soon I was able to decipher letters, and then syllables, and finally words. I could hear it best with my ear right up to the wall. I tiptoed to the side where the Turner print was and started to transcribe the tapping, pen to paper.

"There is a poet in the galley of the ship and his wrists are handcuffed to the oars so the blisters do not slip." I looked at the words, startled; startled that they made a sentence and then startled that the sentence did not make sense at all, at least not from a pipe. I went to the other side of the room and translated the tapping from below the Marilyn Monroe print: "Journalists are the pimps of popular culture, pointing out the public to the latest sensation to be fucked of all its youthful zest." This was far too confusing. I decided to scamper between the walls and record each sentence in turn to see if there might be some kind of coded conversation in progress.

"So you think the secret of prophecy is to be profane?"

"No I think it is to be articulate without being archaic."

"And poetry is not articulate?"

"My right leg aches you know."

"I thought you had no leg?"

"Well I must do. If it aches."

"It's probably phantom limb pain."

"I don't subscribe to the theory of phantom limb pain."

"Not factual enough for you? Too poetical?"

"If my right leg aches it must, by definition, be in existence."

"Well my left arm aches and I know its not there."

"How can you tell?"

"Once they knocked off those reflective glasses, by mistake, and I saw that my left arm was definitely without presence… but still it pains me."

"You must be mistaken."

"No, I saw it, or rather I didn't."

"You need more proof."

"Be done with proof, use your instincts to guide your fleeting perceptions."

"English life is vast tracts of politeness with punctuations of extreme violence."

"I'm tired of your aphorisms."

"I'm tired of your poetry."

The tapping stopped. I stared at the dialogue, breathless from running between the two walls but certain that I had stumbled onto a transaction of some crazed importance. Who, I wondered, was conducting this conversation? Who was tapping on the pipes and where did they begin? I looked at my feet and imagined the plumbing springing up from many floors below, from who knows what underground source. I knelt and put my cheek to the carpet but all I could hear were the sounds of the office workers below; the dull platitudes of the clerks and the clunking of the photocopier. And then I caught a waft of something putrid. Its odour was strongest below the Turner painting, nearer the skirting board. I got down on all fours and sniffed.

There was a sudden stutter of knocks on the office door and Strachen, Head of Product Enquiry, put his gaunt face round. He looked like a dried out coconut at a run down shy. "I wonder," he said, "if I could have a word with you…"

"Sniff this." I urged him over to the Turner print and pressed his face against the wall.

"I'm sorry I can't smell anything," said Strachen.

"Mmm, seems to have gone," I said, "very curious."

Strachen was a spindly man who seemed to fit uncomfortably into his seat, it being both too wide and too short at the back. He crossed his legs, put his arms on the desk and leant forward slightly, as if he had to create new architectures to remain upright. His shirt was too small and his thin wrists and arms emerged from his sleeves like birch saplings from protective pipes. His teeth were crooked and the top two incisors overlapped. He pushed his half rim spectacles up his nose.

"Interesting haircut," he said, nodding at my baldness.

"Thank you." I drummed my biro on the desk.

"I suppose I ought to get straight to the point." He leaned even further forward and then shuffled to the edge of his seat. I tilted to join his confidence.

"I'm a bit washed up," he said, "I haven't had a good idea in years… I think *they're* thinking of "LETTING ME GO" …And I can't afford that. I've got a family, two kids at private school and a wife who wants holidays in exotic, EXOTIC, places. Do you understand me?"

I nodded, pretending to. His glasses fell down his nose and his chin hovered just above my blotter. "I was wondering if you could, you know…," the man was so close I could smell tuna on his breath, "give me an idea."

"Idea?"

"Yes, one of those bull in the china shop ones."

Black spots floated between us, joined into bloated amoeba and then slipped down the sides of his jacket. I rubbed my eyes and they disappeared. "You're Head of Product Enquiry. That's market research, isn't it? You don't need ideas."

"But I do, I do. Market Research ideas; clever questions to ask, clever ways to ask them. And I need them now."

"O.K., I'll let you in on a secret. The toilet attendant."

"What?"

"The toilet attendant. The man in the toilets off the executive boardroom. He sells ideas, for a price."

"Don't play with me, Velour."

"No it's true, I swear it is. Of course, I don't always use him." I tried to appear nonchalant.

Strachen slid his glasses down his nose as if to allow the full directness of his rather weak and beady glare. "The toilet attendant?"

"Absolutely."

"If you're playing tricks with me…"

"No. I promise, it's the truth." I made the Scout sign, stood to suggest the interview was over and offered him my hand. He shook it warily.

"If this is some kind of practical joke…" He released his grip.

"No, of course not." I looked at my watch as he left. It was getting late and I desperately needed a PRAXIS injection.

The injections were becoming more and more important to me. The bladder stone colic had faded but the Pethidine still offered that vital little break to the endless continuum of the day. "Like a good cup of tea," I thought as I got home and tapped the syringe. I attached the tube to the sideboard and brushed my arm against the needle until it punctured the skin and let the flavour flood through. I fell into a delicious sleep and forgot about Ibore and Ravenski and McCloy and Wenlock and all the echoing transmissions of the day.

The following day there was a letter on the mat from the doctor's surgery. 'EMERGENCY RECALL', it said in red type. 'Please make an appointment to see your doctor as there has been a problem with your prescription.'

I grappled the phone and got a last minute appointment at the morning clinic.

"Mr err, Velour." The doctor looked at his notes and flicked between his decaying teeth with his tongue. He found a bit of watercress between the top two incisors and returned it into the pink fold of his mouth. "So how are we today?"

"Much better, thank you, but I got this letter about my prescription and the thing is I need that Pethidine. I really need it."

"Forgive me if I don't understand but if the pain's improved, you won't need any more injections. We could, however, swap to tablets."

"But I need those injections," I said, "so much, oh so much."

The doctor raised an eyebrow. "You do?"

"The pain is still quite bad, tortuous, endless…"

"It appears you might be quite dependent on those injections, Mr, err, Velour."

"That's not true, I just need them all the time."

"I was hoping I wasn't going to have to tell you this, Mr Velour, but," he sucked at his brown molars and dropped his notes to the desk, "those injections…"

"Yes?"

"There was a mistake with the prescription. Somehow, in a quirk of fate, and perhaps, just perhaps, a peculiarity of my own handwriting, you were given the wrong injection by the pharmacy."

"What?"

"I don't know how to break this to you Mr Velour but I've been told you were given a batch of Rabies vaccine instead of the Pethidine."

"I don't follow…"

"Those weren't Pethidine jabs you were giving yourself Mr Velour, they were Rabies vaccinations."

"But those injections stopped the pain. I need them, I just need them."

"The mind is a wayward thing, Mr Velour. Sometimes it is more, sometimes it is less powerful than the forces of the body." He rolled his tongue into a flute, blowpiped the watercress onto the ink blotter and then smeared it under his thumb. He looked up and smiled. "Egg and watercress sandwiches, homemade. My wife makes them for me."

"The injections, doctor?"

"Oh yes. I suppose you have a psychological dependence on them. You imagined they took the pain away and they did, you imagined they brought you relief and so they did..." He looked at the imprint of the cress on his thumb. "Do you think there are such things as lucky four leafed watercress? Because this is most fortuitous…one, two, three…"

"Don't you understand? I just need those injections."

"I'm sorry Mr Velour." He wiped the cress on the side of his jacket. "But I can hardly prescribe you Rabies Vaccine because you are addicted to it and perhaps not even that, perhaps you are addicted to the masochistic pain of the needle itself." He picked off the watercress and flicked it into an enamel bin, where it made a tiny but perceptible 'pling'.

"So what do I do? I *need* those injections."

"Well, we have this psychologist who has just done a course on the ritual enforcement of painful pressure." The doctor spread some drawing pins out on his desk. "Now," he held one up, "I'm sure we can teach you to be *afraid* of the needle. All you have to do…"

I jumped out of my chair, "I need those injections, don't you understand?"

"Well, you can't have any." The doctor picked up his prescription pad and pressed it to his chest.

I ran for the bus. I was sweaty and perturbed. "I needed those injections. Couldn't he understand…?" I didn't take the number thirty two though, not the bus to Priscilla, I couldn't go there. I had a board meeting at midday but I couldn't face missing another PRAXIS injection. Instead I went to the Dogs Home on the outskirts of the docklands. It was on the banks of the river, in a plateau of concrete, fenced off with wire, and divided into corrugated steel pounds.

I told them at reception I was looking for a pet. A man in a black uniform studded with silver buckles made me fill in some forms and asked a few questions.

"Can I confirm that you are not intending to use your dog for domestic purposes?"

"Yes, yes of course."

"You don't intend to make it into a sofa or a coffee table? Some people do try, without going to the established companies, and you can appreciate such conversions can be very distressing for the dogs, in the wrong hands."

"Absolutely."

"Will you pledge to look after the animal as if it were your own?"

"Look, do we have to go through the whole of this form, I'm very busy."

Eventually he led me from the reception to the corrugated pounds. As casually as I could I asked: "Do you have any quarantined dogs here. You know, from more exotic countries?"

"Oh yes we have a lot of dogs that come straight from the airports."

"Might some of them have Rabies?"

"Quite possibly sir but that's why we quarantine them. Needless to say all our other dogs are nationals of this country and demand a clean bill of health before we pass them onto their owners." We walked past a few more cages.

"If you don't mind," I said, "I'd like to spend some time with these dogs by myself, so I can get a feel for the right one."

"That's not a problem Sir, many people feel the same way."

He left me alone and I quickly hurried to find the quarantine area. At the end of a wooden walkway I came across a steel door that had 'Restricted Entry' stencilled in clear red letters. I climbed over it and moved on to the next part of the compound. It had similar corrugated kennels but with chicken wire at the front, so you could see the hounds barking in their cages and there was an air of neglect here as if the dogs weren't being treated in the same way. Black marks dimpled the concrete floor and here and there had aggregated into patches, of piss or shit or blood I wasn't sure. I came to 'Kennel B 32. Rabies Exclusion' and peered through. The beasts seemed docile enough and a few stretched towards me, tails wagging, as if expecting food. I peeled a gap between the chicken wire and the corrugated roof, looked both ways, rolled back a sleeve and shoved my arm into the cage. A mongrel sniffed at it and then limped away.

"Come on you bastards, you bitches," I shouted, "bite it."

The assorted pack slumped on the floor, ignoring me. I waved my arm about.

"Come on, come on." I tried to harangue them. I expected potentially rabid dogs to be more, well, rabid.

I looked about for incentives. There were a couple of licked out bowls with a nearly empty can of dog food beside them. I scooped out the remaining chunks and smeared them over my arm. I pushed my newly garnished muscle back into Kennel B 32 and waved it about. Eventually the hounds hoisted themselves from their reverie, sniffed at my arm and barked. "Go on take a snap." The tallest dog was a handsome greyhound with a black pelt and a silver stripe between his eyes. He stretched his narrow muzzle towards me and licked an arm. "Don't slurp, bite." I knocked my elbow against his nose. He looked at me curiously. "Go on." I knocked the dog again. It had dark, sad, brown eyes. "Bite me." He barked three times and on the third yap I inserted my forearm between his teeth and he bit down into the flesh, puncturing it and leaving six bloody notches. He released his grip and backed off, looking, I thought, regretful; he turned his head and the spidery lashes of his eyes closed.

Anyway the bite did the trick and I felt a ripple of pleasure tingling along my arm and through the rest of the body before finally arriving as a warm glow at the back of my head. This sensation was more than compensation for the pain the bite had wrought. I patted the dog on his head. He wagged his tail and sniffed as the blood welled on my arm.

"You…Hey you?" It was the uniformed warden, turning a corner a few kennels along. I withdrew my hand, jumped onto the corrugated iron roof, clambered over the wire fence and into the side streets before he could call for help.

I ran and ran and then leant against a wall, panting. A single raindrop hit me on the forehead. I looked up and saw the sky was heavy with clouds, black at the horizon like the smear of last nights mascara. Bits of black sloughed off and seemed to drift away, tumbling into the light. I closed my eyes allowing the darkness to become all, put my hands to my eyelids and pressed, and when I looked again the blackness had gone and the clouds had returned to their grey canopy.

I stopped off on the way to the board meeting to buy some sterile bandages and spent some time in a public toilet cleaning and dressing the wound. The punctures were arranged in two lines of three, like a six of spades. Every time I touched one it brought exquisite pain but also an enormous pleasure. I felt peaceful as I dressed the bite and, when I had buttoned up my shirt and jacket, nothing showed save a bump in the sleeve.

There was a buzz at the board meeting. Word had got round that Mantle wasn't happy. I wondered if they were finally going to raise the assassinations. I looked along the table, there was Morgan Wenlock's empty space, and then Denis McCloy's vacant chair and, immediately to my right, Ibore Davidson, still very much alive and applying a bronze blusher from a compact. In front of the spaces left by McCloy and Wenlock were small piles of nail clippings.

Ravenski, to my left, pinched me on the thigh. She was wearing her leopard spot silk scarf and had stuffed the end into the gap in the front of her blouse.

Biros began to tap nervously. I noticed that the executives on the other side of the table had completely turned their backs to the spaces left by McCloy and Wenlock, the dismembered corporate body. I bit at a nail and turned to face the chairman.

Mantle was a man borne down by gravity. Presumably never very tall, his advancing weight had pulled him ever earthbound and his belly ballooned at the waist. His teeth were paradoxically thin, brittle and chipped at the edges.

"I have one thing to say and then I shall leave you to proceed with the agenda. It has come to my attention…" The boardroom took a collective breath and Strachen's glasses slipped a few more freckles down his nose. Mantle croaked and patted his chest. "Bring me some milk." His assistant shuffled off and brought him a saucer into which he dipped his fingers and flicked the milk into his mouth. "Hmm. Where was I? Oh yes, it has come to my attention that certain members of the executive board have not been fulfilling their duties. He turned to his assistant. "Sandra, bring down the screen."

Sandra, his black suited P.A., retreated to the wall behind Mantle, pressed a button and some of the panels slid back to reveal a flat screen television. Mantle swivelled in his chair. "Here we have the evidence."

I squeezed Ravenski's calf as the screen brightened into life and the lights of the boardroom dimmed. Ibore snapped shut her compact. The screen detailed the inside of a house. There was a sofa, the silhouettes of two figures and a strange object swinging towards the top of the frame. The camera zoomed in and I saw, to my dismay, that it was Ibore and I during that evening at her flat. We were at the point of tearing off each other's clothes. I took my hand from Ravenski's thigh and made a cage of my fingers over my eyes though I could not help but follow the carnal progress on screen; Ibore in her lingerie and I in my boxer shorts.

"Here," shouted Mantle and the camera focused on our crotches, me clearly protuberant through the material of my briefs and Ibore tilting her hips towards me in her frilly, bronze knickers. I looked across at Ibore. She continued to look bored and was inspecting her fingernails. Ravenski however was developing a torrid flush.

"See," Mantle prised himself from his chair and went over to the screen, his eyes now finding a luminescence from the reflected images. He prodded with a stubby forefinger at the groins. "Are they wearing the regulation underwear? Are they?" He turned to the executives and they concurred with an outraged chatter. "How can we expect to maintain a corporate identity," he went on, "without a bit of cohesion, COHESION?" He dribbled in his fury. Strachen was sitting upright and nodded approvingly.

Mantle returned to the board table. "Everyone up." Everyone stood. "Lights on." I stared at my shoes. "Trousers, skirts down." I heard rustles and thumps. "You as well Velour." I unstrapped my belt, and looked across the board table, but only with my eyes, my chin pressed to my chest in humiliation. Everyone displayed their knickers, pants and boxers, and I could see the underwear, without exception, was manufactured from the same red coloured material with the identical 'Pet Furnishings' logo printed on the groin. The design was the profile of a toothless dog with a front-on elliptical eye, an ancient Egyptian hieroglyph. And all were showing it, except myself and Ibore. I wore a pair of plain black and rather destitute boxers, while Ibore displayed some azure, frilled panties.

I heard Strachen snicker and saw him in a pair of loose red Y fronts, his legs two sickly poles in the artificial light. Even Ravenski whose gaze I dared not join was wearing a pair of crimson, Pet Furnishings knickers. Despite my anguish I could not help but appreciate the sensual swell of her calves. Behind Mantle, the screen continued to play out the sweaty intercessions of Ibore and I.

"Trousers up," said Mantle. "Any further indiscretions will result in immediate dismissal of these individuals." The television screen showed us doing it doggy style, our faces lifted up in agonies of passion. Ravenski had turned her back to me but beyond the edge of her black bob I could see the progress of a tear, the oily trail of a mascara tadpole.

The boardroom emptied quickly, Ravenski striding off before I could speak with her, all reluctant to fraternise with either myself or Ibore. I held Ibore back by her shoulder pads.

"How did they get that film…? How could they show that in front of Ravenski, in front of all the other executives?"

"Every screen is a screen, darling."

"What is a what?"

"The window in my flat, it looks in as well as out; it's a two way thing."

"How could you let them film us like that?"

"I have no secrets, my petal. How about you?" She fluttered her lashes and walked away with a stern upright poise, still in her lingerie, seemingly seven foot tall in her orange high heels. I followed her across the empty boardroom with its litter of biros and blank blotters and as my elbow brushed Ravenski's seat it seemed to conjure her perfume anew. "How could she ever trust me again?" I paused and wiped away a slow tear. Ahead were the empty spaces of McCloy and Wenlock with their piles of nail clippings, as if this was what they had been reduced to.

"BANG." The walls shuddered. I made a fingergun with my hands and found myself pointing it at the pile of nails. Was this my destiny? The bitten trails of my own worry? I took out a piece of cotton wool from my mouth to mop away the sadness and sidestepped into the executive toilets.

Strachen was inside, arguing with the toilet attendant. "This isn't an idea," he waved a napkin under the attendants nose, "this is a full-stop. In fact it looks more like a piece of dirty snot."

"You'll have to pay for the next one," said the man. Strachen left without bothering to acknowledge me, his skeletal frame hunched over. The attendant turned my way with a tissue. "Don't worry Sir," he said, indicating my damp cheeks, "women are strange creatures."

I took the tissue indignantly. "It's hayfever, very bad at this time of…"

"Perhaps Mr Velour would like a fresh piece of cotton wool, for the mouth." He took some fluff from a polythene bag. "Women are both more strong and fragile than we could ever imagine, aren't they sir? But I was glad to see that my idea was a success; the dog in the box."

I spat out the old cotton wool and slipped the new stuff into my cheek, "That was my idea."

"You will of course have to pay for the next concept. I hear the mop dancing troupe have finally got their ratchets; truly multidirectional I understand." His wrist flopped backwards and forwards and the gold chain he wore slipped up and down.

I finished mopping away my tears, adjusted the cotton wool balls, and smoothed my cropped scalp before leaving.

"Your flies, Mr Velour," he called after me, "they're undone… be careful of the spiders." I felt out the Braille of the credit card, loose in my pocket, and wondered if the embossed numbers had some special meaning.

Back in my office I sat in the swivel chair and gazed out across the wharf. A toddler was playing with a tiny kite. It fluttered in the air a few metres above him as the boy's father tried to drag him back across the vast plaza. The boy managed to hold his ground, gazing up at his plastic toy as it rose and fell in elevator shafts of air, until eventually it plummeted and was consumed by a puddle. The boy was carried off, sobbing, and disappeared from view. The puddle seemed to grow black and spread towards Priscilla before recoiling to its original, ragged dimensions.

Abel arrived. "You will be pleased to hear," he said, snorting down his turbine nostrils, "that I have completed the first sentence of my book. In fact," he paused for dramatic effect, "I have completed the first one and a half sentences."

I traced two fingers about the blotting paper, so they made slow turns like the maudlin arcs of a defeated speed skater.

"So you don't want to hear it then?"

"Uhuh," my fingers collided listlessly with the edge of the telephone.

Abel raised one hand dramatically in the air. 'Tranmere Rovers were the team to beat. Roy was…'" He left the 'was' hanging in the air like a trapped insect. "So what do you think?" He snapped shut his folder.

"Uhuh."

"What do you mean 'Uhuh'? Do you know how many hours that took? How many sweeps of the clock? How many grains of the sands of time? Perhaps you didn't hear?" He opened his folder and repeated his sentence with its hanging clause. "'Tranmere Rovers were the team to beat. Roy was…' He 'was', did you hear me, he 'was'?" He fixed me with his questioning gaze.

"I thought it was called Kantric Tant," I said, "or something like that."

"It used to be called Tantric Kant but not now, now it is an Epic of an altogether different nature. Now it is called; 'Roy and What He Does'."

"Beautiful."

"And this is only the first incendiary sentence in a powder keg of prose."

"I'm gripped."

"You are?"

I let my hands fall loosely to my side. "Absolutely."

"Good to see you still have some artistic bones left in your body. I shall reveal the second sentence as soon as I am enlightened."

"I look forward to it."

Abel packed up his novel. "You don't seem so bright," he admitted, "worn out by shagging rusty busts? What you need is more of the same. You need some lumpy pumpy."

I offered him a questioning eyebrow.

"It's like rumpy pumpy," he said, "except you do it on a bouncy castle."

"Out."

He left with his manuscript, and I was abandoned to my blotter and the bitten trails of my worry.

I sat for an hour staring at my lap until an insistent funky beat returned, as if present in my middle ear. "Restless movement, yeh, yeh. Restless movement, yeh, yeh." The sound of the dancing French girl and her pervasive rhythms. "Where are you?" I stood up and accused the walls. They in turn offered a different response, a rally of tapping from under the Marilyn and the Turner painting; "Tap, tap, tappety, tip."

"Restless Movement yeh, yeh. Restless movement yeh, yeh."

"Tap, tap, tippety, tap, tap, tip."

"Shut up all of you. Shut up." I ran from the office and the tapping faded but the funky beat carried on. I hurried past a typing pool and saw her again, the mysterious dancing French girl. She was wearing a bare black top that revealed a gyrating lower back and her headphones mashed out the addictive funky beat that made me rock in time behind her. "Restless movement yeh, yeh. Restless movement yeh, yeh." I ran up and was about to touch her on the shoulder when Abel reached his arm across my chest and held me back. He looked down his nose with disdain.

"I told you didn't I? You must never touch the beautiful dancing French girl or she will you bring bad luck. Curdled karma."

The girl bodypopped into the distance.

"Let me go will you; all of you." I wrestled myself from Abel's grip and ran away; away from Abel, from the dancing girl, from the printed underwear, the violent rivetings, down the lifts and out of Priscilla.

Chapter 8

Do you Really Know me?

I waited till night in a bus stop and then went to find Ravenski. I made my way to her studio development, perched at the top of a hill, its central stone tower iced by floodlights into a monolith, a monument against the dark.

I walked around the lawns of the complex looking for a way in. But every door had its own security code and there were double locks on the windows. So I climbed up a drainpipe on the side. I couldn't see through the windows, but I could hear the faint tinkling of wind chimes and water music. I waited for a moment and then continued up to the roof and the stone tower in the centre. I found an old service ladder on the side, climbed to the top and then over to the skylight in the middle and looked through. The White Room was featureless in the dark and seemed impenetrable, unknowable. The skylight was locked with a rusty clasp but after some pulling and shoving I was able force it back. I tied the jacket I was wearing to my shirt, knotted this to the clasp and then dangled by the cord into the room so I dropped down the last few metres to the floor, escaping with only a bruised ankle.

I sat in the darkness and felt out the bandage on my arm. I unravelled it and pressed the six bite marks. They were beginning to heal but still allowed little thrills of pleasure.

I played out this delightful tune until I found the strength to crawl, carefully because of my ankle, to the walls of the White Room. I felt along the cool smooth surfaces to the broken entrance to Ravenski's flat. Bits of plaster and splinters came away and I found the back of the charcoal coloured sofa that Ravenski had pushed across to cover the hole. I put my ear to the upholstery and could just make out the chiming of relaxation music and, I thought, the soft putt of footprints on the floor.

I pressed against the settee with my shoulder until I emerged halfway through the hole, trapped at the waist by my belt and trousers. Unable to press any more because of the pain in my ankle I languished there, caught between rooms, a miscreant pollution of the partition.

Gradually my eyes began to adjust and I registered the familiar severe designer furniture, the grey paint and the odd watercolour of autumnal forests. Every now and then I caught a glimpse of Ravenski's passing calves, smooth and muscular below the edge of a dressing gown.

"Hallo" I said, quietly at first, and then with more confidence. "Hallo, it's me Telby, I'm behind the sofa."

I saw Ravenski's legs stop and then scissor backwards to the stereo. She couldn't see me, hidden as I was behind the settee, and turned the music up.

"No honestly it's me, Telby, behind the sofa." I splashed around like a fish out of water, trying to push myself from the hole, pummelling my fists against the floor. "Over here. I'm over here."

And then Ravenski's calves advanced. She stopped by the edge of the sofa. The music tinkled and chimed and my anticipation seemed to magnify these pretty sounds into a clamour. I lunged at her legs and clamped a hand around an ankle. She fell with a thump and screamed, as I dragged her kicking across the tiled floor and towards the hole. But it wasn't Ravenski. It was a woman with a mud face broken only by a pink astonished 'O'. I pulled at her chin and the mud came away to reveal a whiter skin. It was Ravenski but she was concealed beneath the thicker mask of a facepack. "Ravenski," I shouted, "it's me, your hope, your common chalice."

She stopped struggling and fixed me with brown widening eyes, the mud was deep and black in the sockets.

"What did you say?"

"It's me, Telby."

"No before that, you said something else."

"We have to talk," I said, "It was a mistake, Ibore and I; it was just a fling, an inconsequential fling."

"Just then you said to me 'Your hope, your common chalice.'" Her mudpacked face cracked and fissured. "There was only one other man who said that to me and it wasn't you, or was it? All those years ago outside a Pet Furnishing's warehouse. Who are you?"

"Telby." I reached out towards her mask.

"How can I be so sure? Maybe you're not Telby, maybe you're someone else."

"No look, touch…" I took her hand and let it trail it over my face, made her touch the goatee and the sideburns and the jowl of my cheeks.

"How things look, isn't always how they are," she said.

I bit down on my cotton wool. "I just want to talk to you, honestly."

"I thought you were the assassin."

"What assassin?"

"Ibore's been killed."

I had to do a press up on the carpet to stop the plaster and timber cutting into my stomach. "What?"

"She's been crossed off," said Ravenski, "nailed, pinned, gunned down."

"Assassinated?"

"She was riveted to her floor by her hands, feet and," she gulped, "chest."

I returned to my press up position. "Christ."

"They say it's Garrick. You're not Garrick are you?" She looked at me nervously.

"I'm Telby," I said, "Terribly Velour."

"You're not Garrick. The Animal Liberation Liberationist?"

"Of course not," I said. "I'm Telby."

"They say Garrick's going to wipe out the whole board. Garrick thinks that we're cruel to dogs."

"That's nonsense. Dogs are just furniture with pets attached."

"Ok," she said, widening her eyes and letting the mud crack some more, "If you're not Garrick come to rivet me. Who are you?"

I chomped on my cotton wool. "I'm Telby, your one true love, who else could I be?"

Ravenski was silent for a moment. "I suppose you are. But even if you are, you're not the man I thought you were."

I prodded my cotton wool balls nervously with my tongue. "I'm not?"

"You're the slut who screwed Ibore Davidson, just like every other sleazeball in P.F. and now Ibore's gone and we're next on the list." She started to cry. "I thought you were someone special, someone I could rely on."

"Don't cry Ravenski, I can explain." I made a lunge for her calf. She stepped away. "Please Ravenski."

She hesitated. "Five minutes," she said, "that's all." And then she bent down and tried to drag me out but I was firmly lodged by my belt in the fixtures of the wall and couldn't find any leverage with my bruised ankle.

"Hang on." I wormed my way back into the White Room, removed my belt and trousers, and tried to return back through the hole. I was up to my waist but still couldn't find a way in.

In the end she undid her bathrobe and I pulled her naked body into the shadows of the White Room. I put my arms through and hauled the sofa back across the hole. The moon retreated behind the clouds and we were left alone in darkness.

"Let's make a new start," I said and reached out towards her mudpacked face.

"Careful, that's my eye."

"Sorry." I followed the cracks of earth, the dusty lines and tributaries to her mouth and let my fingertips rest on her lips as she spoke, rising and falling, like the conductor of a diminuendo.

"You don't know me," she said, "you think you do but you don't. You've made me into the kind of woman I'm not."

"Which is?"

"Everything that Ibore isn't; gentle, perfect. Some kind of buttercup girl."

"That's not true. You're so precious, so real to me." I pulled off a flake of caked earth next to her mouth.

"I'm not a tart," she said, "but I'm not a pussycat either," she pushed my hand away, "I came from an orphanage, from Romania, I was brought up in the mud."

"I know."

"How?"

"Gossip."

"What kind of gossip?"

"The elevator kind." I returned my hand to her cheek and she let me keep it there, next to the workings of her molars.

"You could never know what it was like back then, in the mud, in the dirt. It was everybody for themselves, everybody eating hand to mouth. You were lucky if you got the slops at the bottom of the pan. So I ran away. I ran into the forest. But they found me and punished me and

I was bought in this package deal by some rich Americans." She shook her head in my palm and a fragment of the face pack fell away. "I want your sex." I felt her hot breath on my hand. "But I want power, I want money, I want real estate. I want to consume as I am consumed." She bit my dusty finger. "I want to make a forest."

"What, in the garden?"

She pointed at my stubbly scalp. "In our minds."

"What, through making pet furniture?"

"I want to create my own wealth. I want to create my own lifestyle. I want to be the leader of the pack."

"Oh I think I see," I said, not quite able to see her in the night. I took my hand away and we tried to make out each other's shape. Then she lay down and we slept until I awoke with moonlight filling the room.

Ravenski lay on her side, naked on the floor. The remnants of her mudpack had become silver in the moonlight. She appeared as a sculpture might, breaking from its mould, waking into shape, the alchemy of dreams.

I lay watching this half fragmented cast and then I put my hand on her cheek. She opened her eyes and then her lips, revealing her symmetrical teeth one by one, from the central gap to the pointed incisors. She snarled and shook her head.

"Sometimes I think I'm in the forest, in the trees." She sat on her haunches and the remains of the face pack fell away, leaving only a band around her eyes. "Tell me about you," she said.

"You know me I'm Telby, Telby Velour."

"Who is Telby Velour?"

"It's short for Terribly, Terribly Velour."

"And you were an executive in the Middle East?"

"Yes"

"Where?"

"Dubai."

"Who for?"

"Do or Die inc."

"What did they do?"

"They developed lifestyle packages for the over seventies. You know cruises and stuff. I made motorised scooters with roll bars, for the aged."

"Oh."

I noticed Ravenski gazing over my body. I followed her eyes across my chest, the scratches of the basque, the penny brown coins of my nipples, the lipped punctuation of my navel, the fur of pubis, the closed anemone of my penis.

"But who are you really?"

I reached out to pull the last bit of mud from her eyes. "Does it matter?"

She blinked and smiled.

"That mud itched," she said. She pointed at the bites on my forearm. "Is that a tattoo?"

"It's a scar."

"From what?"

"Nothing."

"You're not being honest with me Telby and how can I trust you after doing it like a dog with Ibore?"

"Isn't this honest enough, us lying together, naked, in the white room?"

She said nothing. The dawn was breaking but with no sunrise only the cold rind of a clouded morning.

We closed our eyes and slept until the growing dawn would let us sleep no more and we woke into the day that was diffuse, uncertain, scratching into our lives.

I made a sundial by standing in the middle of the room and a shaft of light from a gap in the clouds cast a morning shadow, my penis a second hand on the clock. And then we left the White Room, squeezing back through the gap into the crisp, monochrome flat.

We went our separate ways to Priscilla. Ravenski said she was prepared to give me a second chance but wasn't about to let the rest of the company know. I climbed the reception steps, weary, but content that I had made some kind of peace with Ravenski. The day remained grey, the clouds low like lids above the earth.

Getting through the revolving doors of Priscilla wasn't easy. There were guards posted at every entrance. They swept everyone with magnetic loops, looking for guns and knives. "Safety sir, after the assassination." But this was nothing compared to the wrath of Abel.

"They've been looking for you all over the building," he said. "They thought you'd been assassinated. I knew you hadn't… You're just a lazy schmuck."

"Hang on."

"And what's worse I spend all day fending off these calls from security, waiting for you to turn up, and when you do you don't even have the decency to ask me how my book's going."

"How's it going?"

"I," he announced, "have finished the second sentence."

"I'm pleased for you."

"Would you like to hear it?"

I gazed through the window.

"So you don't care about my second sentence then?"

"Ibore's been riveted."

"Who cares about Ibore? The woman had no appreciation of art…"

"She was riveted to a wall."

"The only true rivets are the punctuations of the page."

"Sometimes you take your writing just a bit too seriously Abel."

He rested his elbows on the desk and bent his long body over it, so I could see the grey shotgun peak of his quiff.

"I don't take it too seriously," he said, "I don't take it seriously enough. And," he made his hands into fists, "isn't the world frivolous enough?" I waited for him to move but he continued glaring like some kind of aesthete gorilla. I played nervously with the fringes of my goatee.

"I never said your writing was frivolous…"

"Yes you did."

"I'd really like to hear your sentence…"

He straightened from the desk. "I'm not sure I want to tell you now."

"Go on, tell me."

"It's not a sentence anyway. It's two sentences; it's getting on for a paragraph…"

"I'd love to hear your sentences, your getting on for nearly a paragraph." I tried to smile.

"Very well." He opened his vermilion bound manuscript holder and jutted out his chin. "'Tranmere Rovers was the team to beat. Roy was.. he left the 'was' hanging in the air and then continued,"'… anticipating the next game even though he had never scored away from home and they had three injured players and the rest of the team was getting nervous. How could they maintain their unbeaten record and stay at the top of the league?'" Abel snapped shut his manuscript with a flourish.

"That's three sentences."

"I thought I'd surprise you with my productivity."

"Well, I'm surprised."

"That's all?"

"Overwhelmed."

"A message from Ravenski Goldbird," Abel added, "she'll meet you at your flat at six. Sleeping with Miss Goldbird now are we? A real corporate toy boy."

I reached out and pinched Abel's exuberant lips. "Shut it."

"Don't manhandle me," he puttered through his closed lips, "my man is not for handling." And then he wrenched himself free and fingered his lips; "flubba lub a dub," he said, before adding; "how dare you touch the mouthpiece from which such beauty soars?"

"Shut it, big nose."

"I've finished the next sentence," he called out as I left the office, "and it's quite brilliant, extraordinary and I haven't got a 'big nose', it's a proboscis, a Caesar of the Gods."

I had to make a diversion to the dog's home before I went to Ravenski's. The punctures on my forearm had healed and no longer provided me with the same waves of relaxation and pleasure as before. I was beginning to experience a certain craving and, I suspected, withdrawal. The security guards at the exit of Priscilla regarded my tremor with suspicion and I was reminded of Ibore's assassination. I kept to the walls and shadows and sized up the bus queue for its murderous intent. It was only when I was safely in my seat that I was able to relax, as much as my craving would allow.

I got off at the stop before the dogs home and walked the rest of the way by foot. I couldn't go through the main entrance, given that I had been caught in the act of dog baiting, so I wandered around the perimeter. I could see Kennel B 32 from the road; its lackadaisical hounds sprawled on the concrete floor. I checked to see none of the staff were patrolling, scrambled over the wire fence and crawled over to the kennel, my belly scraping against the crusts and smears of the concrete pathway. Blacks spots appeared before my eyes, dissolved, fragmented and then joined themselves together, like a dot to dot drawing. Then, all at once, they swarmed apart and I was left facing the crusted concrete and the kennel with the slopping hounds.

The greyhound with the silver streak padded over, sniffed, and began to bark loudly. I rolled up a sleeve, put my unbitten arm through and without hesitation he gnashed into it, giving me that sudden rush of pain and wellbeing; the strange vitality sizzling along the nerves, through the armpit and thence into the brain. The dog released his grip and turned his doleful, brown eyes on me. I patted him. "Don't be stupid," I said to myself, "it's a dog, a mutt." I withdrew my arm from the cage and climbed over the perimeter fence to dress my bites in the nearest convenience.

Ravenski was sitting cross legged on the lawn outside her studio apartment, looking over the streets of terraced houses that ran down from the hill from her flat, reaching into the city. I sat alongside her and we gazed in silence over the ranks of houses. The clouds were all enveloping and here and there I could make out the black sinews of a storm. A squeak interrupted the distant traffic hum and I saw that one of Ravenski's neighbours had wheeled out their pet furniture for its preset ablution. It was a Great Dane that had been crafted into a lover's bench. It had just enough room for a couple to sit down side by side with arm rests bolted into the animal's reinforced spine at neck and tail. The Great Dane's castors squealed as the owner pushed it along the lawn to a flower bed. I pointed and nudged Ravenski.

She yawned. "One of the old designs; 'Classic' they call them. We still sell thousands. There'll always be a market for love furniture, that's what Strachen told me. But I don't trust his numbers; he's getting out of touch. Love furniture is outdated in my opinion. Personally I think there's a real market for lust furniture, fetish furniture. What's your take?"

"Well I'm not sure. I mean," I reached out for her hand, "there'll always be a market for love won't there?"

"I suppose," she said and left her hand under mine. There was a hiss from behind us as the Great Dane pissed into the flower bed. The owner fiddled with some buttons behind its collar and it let out a plaintive howl.

"Just think," continued Ravenski, nodding at the terraces below, "all those households, with their own pet furnishings, bringing comfort and practical support twenty four hours a day, without," her smile tightened, "…causing any threat, to anyone."

"Wonderful," I agreed and we kissed as the creaking Great Dane was hauled back to its flat. We watched the sky bleed black into the night. Ravenski knotted her scarf around her neck and then tucked the loose end into the front of her blouse and we took a taxi into the heart of Soho.

The area had a harmonious rhythm, lilting with strolling couples, seeing and being seen on their way to pre-show meals. Some of the paved streets were dotted with buskers. Ravenski and I dawdled up to a band that already had an audience. From one side I could see they were being interviewed. A young woman pointed a foam tipped microphone towards one of the singers while her assistant focused a camera on his face. The band consisted of five or six men, each holding classical guitars. The men were extraordinarily ugly; each had a contorted feature such as an overdeveloped chin or a hairy mole on their cheek that seemed to characterise their grotesqueness.

"Oh yes," said the man being interviewed, who had terrible teeth, "we're called the Ugly Guitar Band."

"But," said his compatriot with the over-evolved chin, leaning his stubble into the interview, "we play beautiful music."

The man with the hairy mole on his cheek intervened. "No we don't."

"Oh no, sorry," Big Chin checked himself, "we don't."

"But we have a good time," said Hairy Mole.

"That we do," said Bad Teeth.

"Let's hear it then," said the glamorous interviewer and stepped back as the camera zoomed in.

The lead singer started to wail, as if at a beloved's funeral but through a big toothy smile. The others joined him to make a screeching pack and then plucked at their guitars, out of synch, adding to the cacophony. The interviewer retreated and the cameraman covered his lens. But I was transfixed. I could discern an insistent rhythm within the music; the irreverent joy of a country hoe down. I took Ravenski into the small space in front of the crowd and started to spin her round to the beat.

"What do you think you're doing?" she said, her black bob flailing.

"Dancing," I said. The crowd looked on incredulous.

"You're hurting my arm."

The Ugly Guitar Band, who had sensed that someone might be enjoying their noise, cranked up the volume and played with ever more ferocity. I let go of Ravenski and did a little skippy dance as the crowd dispersed. Ravenski glared.

"You can't do that."

"Why not?" I said, wilting slightly.

"You look like a peasant at a barn dance," she lowered her voice, "and it's a terrible sound."

"I think it has a savage ecstasy."

"It's the sound of dogs drowning," she said and walked away. I dropped some coins into the Band's bucket, picked up their business card and gave them a wink.

"We do weddings you know," shouted bad teeth as I hurried after Ravenski.

"So you didn't like it?"

"No."

"Not even bits of it?"

She hesitated. "Mostly I thought it was terrible."

"But?"

"Perhaps, in places, it did have a certain passion." I squeezed her hand. "But generally," she pointed out, "it was terrible."

Eventually we found a tiny restaurant, away from the main drag. It was quiet and unpretentious, serving simple food to relaxed couples. There were candles on the tables which reflected a warm light off the orange brick walls.

"A themeless restaurant," said Ravenski, "how original."

We went in and took a table just next to the bar as the tidy, well mannered waiter took our orders. I looked over at Ravenski, whose pale face was now gold in the candle glow.

"You look prettier than ever," I said and took her hand. Her brown eyes waltzed with the flame. She said nothing and looked at the menu. The shadows around her twisted in the candlelight, snaring, joining, spreading, weaving into a black cloth, until I blinked them away into the half light.

She let my foot rest against hers and at that moment the background music in the restaurant lurched from a classical track to a loud Hawaiian chorus. There was an immediate confusion as a line of busty women in grass skirts and bikini tops bustled in, one carrying a stereo on her shoulders that played out the Polynesian riff. They shook their hips and Hula danced to the music, making the traditional Hawaiian signs of sea waves and birds with their arms and hands. They knocked the tables as they did so, spilling red wine from half raised glasses and astonished mouths.

The women had a Botticellian plumpness, pronounced by their skimpy, flower graced costumes and long dark hair that fell about their shoulders. They turned off the stereo and the group stopped dancing to survey the baffled silence.

"We," shouted the first in the group, "are the Gender Go Go Girls, a group of situationist guerrillas, and you," she pointed at the diners, "are guilty of the myth of Romantic love. This, all of this," she tried to grasp the candlelit atmosphere in one pink hand, "is the programmed dissolution of ego boundaries between naïve women and self deceiving men. You must be retrained. And this man will be our first design." She held me by my neck and the Gender Go Go Girls bound my wrists and applied a blindfold. Ravenski tried to protest but was held back by a busty woman in a pink garland. The stereo kicked into life and I was led out of the restaurant in a huddle of dancing Hawaiian girls.

"For god's sake don't rivet him," Ravenski shouted as I was bundled into the street. I was dumped in the back of what I took to be a van and driven for miles as the women sang Polynesian chants. My backside hurt as I bounced on the metal floor and they pressed their fleshy arms about me.

Eventually we stopped and I was led out of the van and down some steps. The blindfold was removed and I found that I was in a room with damp stone walls and no windows, illuminated by a single lightbulb. In the centre of the concrete floor was a wooden prop table. Two Go Go girls, still dressed in their Hawaiian costumes, strapped me face down with strands of plaited grass. Their leader, whom the others addressed as Penelope, stood at the foot of the table so I had to crane my neck up to see her. She had very white teeth.

"You," she said, "are the first of many. You will be the first lesson which brings harmony to the riven waters of the sexual divide."

"Honolulu," shouted the others.

"Let us sing the chant of the seas of the mother pearl." Penelope started to sing and the others joined in, a wavering song about the oneness of the oceans of the world, and how all wombs were attuned with its feverish fertile energies. They swayed, harmonised, held hands and danced in circles around me until Penelope shouted "Pull down his trousers."

One stepped forward, unclasped my belt and pulled. There was a sharp intake of breath as they saw my newly acquired Pet Furnishings underpants, which were round the wrong way with the toothless dog logo gaping on my rear.

"He's from Pet Furnishings," someone ventured.

"Don't rivet me," I murmured in my grass plaited bindings.

"We have no intention of "riveting" you," said Penelope, "we are here to educate you, to imbue you with the harmonies and resonance of the earth, to teach you respect for the wombman that lives within the man…Pull down his pants." My briefs were hauled to my ankles. "Nice arse," said Penelope

"Nice butt," agreed the others.

"I prefer it when the cheeks are a bit harder myself," said one and the woman next to her concurred; "a bit firmer nearer the hips."

"Enough," said Penelope, "let us sing the song of the waves of the earth's turning centre." And they sang in close harmony, a swooning hymn of how the coconut seeds are carried far across the islands to bring the palms of life to foreign shores. And then each of the women, gently swaying their blossom garlanded hips, Hula danced past and took a firm pinch of my arse.

"Oy," I said, "I'm bit bruised from that ride in your van." They stuffed a gag of blossom petals in my mouth.

"And the coconut shall caaaaarry far and wiiiide, till the palm will find its earth, its wife."

"I reckon he could do with being a bit firmer in the thighs," said a passing Go Go Girl.

"Shush."

"And the coconut shall caaaaaaaarry far and wiiiiiiiide."

They came, eventually, to the end of their reprise and Penelope settled in front of me, bringing her swaying hips to a standstill.

"Now do you understand?"

"Humpf," I said through my blossom.

"You will drink of the spirit and awake refreshed." I was passed a small polystyrene cup and the petals were removed, one by one, from my mouth. Then I was forced to drink from the plastic chalice which tasted of strong cider. The Go Go Girls made a chorus line and danced their familiar forms as the spiked liquor in the cup took hold. I closed my eyes as they sang of flaming hummingbirds bringing pollen and nectar from the river flows of plenty.

I awoke alone, on the table, with a blanket over me. The bare light bulb fizzed. I sat up and found I had been sleeping on a bed of blossom. I was groggy and still had the Go Go songs filtering through my mind, "…the coconuts carrying far and wide…"

They had dressed me back in my trousers so I tentatively undid the belt and peeked inside. The Pet Furnishings underpants were still there but this time the right way round, prima facie and there was a peculiar tickling sensation around my balls. I pulled out the waistband to discover my pants were full of blossom. I took a pinch and threw them into the air where they fluttered down, a flurry of silhouettes against the naked electric light.

Getting off the table wasn't easy, my muscles ached from their recent battering, but eventually I slipped off and made my way to the only door in the room. I pulled and pulled but it wouldn't budge. I was leaning against it in exasperation, wondering why I had been kidnapped and had flower petals stuffed in my pants when the door swung outwards and I fell through into a stairwell. A breeze played about my face and some blossom lifted from my hair and pressed against the concrete steps above, confounded confetti.

It was night outside and a few electric lamps marked the road. I turned to face the building I had come from. It was an old warehouse and I had been closeted in the basement. There was a wooden sign hanging on the wall, on which I could just make out the faded words; 'Giuseppe's Cannelloni Pasta.'

The whole district was a run down plot of old warehouses and factories, not far from Lydon where I could still see the pyramid topped tower of Priscilla steaming like an overheated Coptic phallus. I sat disconsolately on the kerb and wondered how I was going to get home. I gazed at my palms, the tributaries of creases, the map of myself, and behind my fingers the slippery shadows of the gutters. There was a soft hiss and a rumble and the shadows slid away. I looked up and saw an articulated lorry by the roadside. It was jointed like a bug with a high cab at the front and an eight wheeled trailer behind. On the trailer's side, clearly stencilled in red letters were the words; 'Ferris Bloom, Romantic Incorporations Incorporated.' The nearside window of the cab whirred down and a middle aged man put his head out. He had striking, long, orange hair.

"Hey boy, where you goin'?"

"Lydon."

"Headin' there myself."

I looked both ways, the road was deserted. "Thanks," I said and got in.

He was wearing a black silk shirt flecked with silver and a pair of denim jeans with an eagle belt buckle. His ginger locks were swept behind his ears and his nose perched on a ferocious handlebar moustache. His teeth were bold and bright and capped. He offered me a hand. "Ferris Bloom," he said, "purveyor of love to the listless." His vowels trawled through a Louisiana accent like a learner swimmer in molasses.

"Terribly Velour, Telby."

"Good to meet you, Terribly." He shunted the truck into gear, the breaks dehisced and the seats expanded and rose as we moved forward. "So what's your line of work Terribly?"

"Bull in the china shop."

"Some kind of rodeo retail?"

"Yeh."

"Me, I got my own company; haul this romance right across the city." He pointed over the steering wheel at the fairy dust of neon. "All them lovers pining for a soulmate and my job is to get their juices flowing like a rattlesnake down a chicken run."

"Isn't love just the pre-programmed dissolution of ego boundaries between naïve women and self deceiving men?"

"Hell no boy, it's big business. There's more heart shaped money boxes in this town than there are pig bellies in pigs. Why the other day I was…"

I nodded, in as much agreement as I could muster, and drifted in and out of sleep as the truck wound its way into the heart of the city. We began to approach the indefinable outskirts of Lydon, the landmark of Priscilla, looming large.

"…so he says that's a dollar to every first born child. And I said if I was actually paid per uterine conception I'd have a whole goddam fleet of these trucks by now, but then it wouldn't be so personal, you know… and that's so important to me; the pers-onal aspect." He blinked. "So how about you, you involved in some kind of pers-onal relationship?"

"I think so."

"What do you mean, you think so? You either know these things or you don't, boy. If you can't see a diamond when you look her directly in the eyes then there's a wronging with your longing."

"This is my stop." Ferris applied the breaks. I thanked him and was about to walk away when he jumped out to join me on the pavement.

"I got something for you, boy." I followed him to the back of the trailer. The truck's tyres reached up to my neck and I could see bits of newspaper print mashed into the tarry tread. "This is what you need, some of my pro-duce. He knocked off a padlock, swung open the doors and a cold mist drifted out, infused with a strip light glow. Inside there was a freezer compartment rammed with thousands of polythene packets, stacked to the ceiling. He wriggled one out and slapped it into my hands. The ice crystals crunched. "Prime romance."

I wiped away the frost and found that Ferris's ardour was a red rose, freeze dried in polythene. "It's a flower," I said.

"It's not *just* a flower boy. It's the finest farmed rose of Kansas fields dipped in my own 'finger licking perfume'. When your lady gets that flicker in her snout, she's not going to be pining for anything else but your rude health. You got me? It's like a viper boy, a viper." He turned the packet over; 'Sweet satisfaction guaranteed,' its label read, 'or your money back.'

"Well…"

"And I'm going to let you have this 'un for free."

"Thanks." He swung the trailer doors closed and it emitted a frosty cough. I tried to fold my arms against the cold but pushed the rose more chill against my chest.

"The love you make, boy," he shouted as he climbed into his cab, "is equal to the love you take. In any transaction." The lorry's pneumatics hissed and creaked and then he was gone.

I put Ferris's frozen rose on the bedside table next to the mango seedling. It looked like a stunned eel; its thorny stem a switching tail; its red bloom the serpent's bludgeoned skull. A dark crimson juice leaked into one corner where it had warmed against my skin. I lay on the bed and tried to sleep but in my minds eye I saw the thing like a worm, a worm that would work its way into the cavities of my body, gestate and then breed. In the end I had to get up, toss it into a microwave and heat it into boiling mulch. I couldn't even bear it being in my bin and I opened a window and spun it out across the carapace of the city.

When I arrived at Priscilla the following morning I was cornered by a group of security guards and frogmarched to the underground boardroom. But we went straight past the boardtable and on through a door at the far end. I found myself in a narrow, dimly lit corridor. The walls had a greenish glow and were punctuated by stainless steel doors stamped 'Restricted'. The corridor ended with a small, dwarfish sized, entrance. We went past the Restricted signs and bent down to go through the oak portal that led into Mantle's office. All four of its walls were upholstered with black leather.

He inspected me from behind his desk with tiny dewy eyes, a smartly dressed bug in the burrow of his room.

"Where have you been?"

"Well I'm not sure if it's a long story or a strange dream…"

"We thought you'd been assassinated."

"No, not assassinated, more…blessed with blossom."

"What?"

"I was kidnapped by women in Hawaiian skirts who wanted to… err… I'm not sure what they wanted, perhaps…" The walls of the room seemed to puff out towards me, like blackened fungi ready to release their spores…

"Wake up," said Mantle, "I have decided to allocate you a private detective, who will debrief you and then stay by your side at all times. I suppose we ought to contact the police but for now, just talk to Daniel Cluff, I don't want this incident damaging morale." He pressed a button under his desk. "Bring me Daniel Cluff."

"I really need to speak to Ravenski," I said, "she was with me at the time…"

"Miss Goldbird is now working at a secret location. For security reasons."

"But she's..."

"These are dangerous times Mr Velour. It is wise that those at the sharp end of our operation do not meet where they could become targets. If you need to communicate with her you may do so through me." A rather plain looking man in a dull grey suit came into the room. He had blue sorrowful eyes, wispy blonde hair and yellow teeth. There was something about his smile that made me uncomfortable.

"This is Daniel Cluff, Private Detective. He will be with you at all times."

"Actually it's Cloff," said the man with a whisper, "Daniel Cloff." He flipped open an I.D. badge in a wallet. It showed a picture of the investigator with the words: 'Daniel Cloff, private detective,' and beneath this: 'Blessed are the Meek For they Shall Be Pounded into the Earth.' He pushed a scrunch of handkerchief under his nose and sniffed.

"Whatever," said Mantle, "You will find out from Mr Velour exactly why he disappeared and then report back to me. You, Velour, will continue with your business but with Mr Cluff's twenty four hour observation. We will await news of your research developments at the next board meeting. That is all."

I nodded at Daniel Cloff. He managed a weak but disconcerting smile. I noticed that his nose had been broken and was twisted a degree to the left and he had a speckling of scars here and there in his creamy complexion. He was a head shorter than me and his frazzled blonde hair was streaked with grey, as if his youth had recoiled suddenly like a fused wire.

"I need to contact Ravenski," I told him as we walked back through the boardroom.

"No executive is permitted to contact another," Cloff announced, "without Mr Mantle's express permission."

We trooped up to the twelfth floor and I tried to engage him in conversation. "So have you always been a detective?"

"No."

"So what did you do before?"

He hesitated and then said, "I was a drunk."

"What was that like?"

He turned to me with his scarred face. "Beautiful." We continued in silence.

Abel was in the office sharpening his pencils.

"Still not dead then?" he crumpled his Promethean forehead, "I'd decided you'd been riveted."

"This is Daniel Cloff," I introduced the pale detective, "he'll be spending some time with us."

Abel eyed him suspiciously. "I suppose you've heard?"

"What?"

"I've started the next paragraph. I may even let you see the first sentence."

"Has Ravenski called, left a message?"

"Yes but I shredded it. I'm under strict instructions to destroy all non approved communications."

"So what did it say?"

"I don't know, I shredded it."

I went into my room with Cloff and propped a chair under the handle of the door.

"There's no need for that," he said, "you're safe with me here."

"It's just to stop Abel getting in," I said, "his writing has a habit of sneaking up on you." I took my place behind the desk.

"You better tell me where you've been," said Cloff, "they want to know."

Half an hour later we were done.

"So let me get this right," said Cloff, "you were kidnapped by a group of Hawaiian dancing gender activist women who tied you down and filled your underwear with blossom petals?"

"Uhuh."

"And your drink wasn't spiked in the restaurant and you don't use drugs?"

"No. But then, you see, strange things happen all the time."

"Mmm." Cloff rubbed his skewed nose.

Abel chose this moment to reveal his new sentence. He rammed himself against the door.

Cloff jumped to his feet and spun around.

"Don't worry," I said, "it's only..."

Abel broke the chair and burst into the room, felling Cloff. Abel stepped over the detective and came to a standstill. He was holding his vermillion bound manuscript folder.

"The start of the second paragraph," he said.

Cloff groaned softly. "You just trampled Mr Cloff," I said.

"Nothing gets in the way of great literature. I reiterate; 'Tranmere Rovers were the team to beat. Roy was anticipating the next game even though he had never scored away from home and they had three injured players and the rest of the team were getting nervous. How could they maintain their unbeaten record and stay at the top of the league?'"

Mr Cloff groaned like a far off train.

"Shhh," said Abel; "'Roy put on his lucky boots with the golden stripes. There was a knock on the changing room door and...'" Abel snapped shut his manuscript holder, took a step back and bowed. I clapped weakly. Abel lifted a finger "Who," he said, "could that be knocking at the door?"

"A writer of genius?"

"I can tell you no more. You must hang tenderly from your hooks."

"Thank you Abel."

"And so you should." He left, stepping over the prone bodyguard.

The walls, as if awakened by Abel, resumed their tapping. I took out the Morse code book from my desk and began to transcribe the communications, running from one side to the other as Cloff watched me from the floor.

"Thank God for the imagination, God who multiplied man in his image. Thank fucking God."

"There is no summer like a thorns heartbeat. There is no winter like a crying rose, singing petals to its death."

"Your poetry's always so bloody miserable; so bloody and so miserable."

"That's because it's so dismal being stuck down here with nothing but a cynic for company."

"How can you call me a cynic. I exalt the imagination?"

"I'm tired of the imagination."

"Ah, coming round to my point of view."

"No I'm just weary of being stuck here, limbless."

"I've told you before; you don't know if you haven't got any limbs until you've seen there are no limbs there not to see."

"I've told you I've got no arm. I saw that when my glasses fell off."

"That was your imagination."

"That was what I saw."

"How can I trust what a poet sees."

"So what do you see?"

"Nothing, I told you, I'm wearing these glasses."

"So what are we doing here, wearing these glasses, seeing nothing?"

"There's obviously some rational explanation."

"I'd like to run through a field of flowers."

"Don't tell me; fields of roses, fields of thorns."

The conversation stopped and I lay down my pencil and rested, breathless. I pointed at the Turner Painting and the Marilyn Monroe. "The walls talk." Cloff nodded sympathetically.

"Right, I'm off to the executive washrooms, I've got a board meeting tomorrow."

"And that means you have to go the washrooms?"

"You'd be surprised."

I left Cloff outside, sniffing into his handkerchief, and sidled through the oak panels into the bright ceramic of the executive washroom.

"I've been waiting for you," said the attendant, who was as usual sitting by the door, holding a towel across the grey folds of his coat.

"I've just come for a pee," I said and went to the urinal. Trying to be casual, I called over my shoulder; "Have you got any ideas spare, you know, the odd one knocking around?"

"A quarter of your annual income." He adjusted the knot of his black tie and his gold chain slipped down his wrist.

"What?"

"A guaranteed quarter of your pay for the next twelve months, that's the deal. First idea free, next idea a quarter of your annual income."

"That seems a bit steep."

"I think you'll find an original idea is priceless. You have to grab the Zeitgeist, Mr Velour, or the Zeitgeist grabs you."

I zipped my flies and had a quick look either way before approaching him. "O.K. I'll take it."

"Sign here." He opened a ledger from under a pile of towels. The last two names on the page were: 'Strachen', head of market research, and, below this, 'Denis McCloy', crossed out with red pen and annotated in brackets; '(Claim back through insurance.)'

I signed as the toilet attendant scribbled something on a paper napkin.

"Here you go. No refunds." The toilet attendant had drawn a curl, just as before, but this time with a circle round it.

"That's what you did last time. It's just you trying to get your biro to work."

"I think you'll find," said the toilet assistant, "that it's got a circle around it."

Cloff knocked on the oak panel door. "Everything alright in there?"

I slipped the design into my pocket. "How do I get out of here without going through the board room?"

The attendant pointed. "Past the cubicles; a fire exit takes you to the basement corridor."

I took the opportunity to escape from Cloff and tried to find Ravenski but her office was locked and her secretary nowhere to be found. Eventually Cloff caught up and snorted his anger into his handkerchief.

"Where have you been?"

"For a wander."

"I thought you were trapped in that toilet. I had to kick in the door."

"I used the fire exit."

"From now on you don't go anywhere without me."

I noticed that he had a swelling above one eye.

"What happened to you?"

"Misunderstanding on the stairwell."

"Misunderstanding?"

"I was beaten up by a cleaner. It's nothing. It happens all the time." He stuffed his handkerchief, now spotted black, into his pocket.

I resumed my place behind the desk. Cloff pulled up a chair and sat beside me. He snapped one ring of a pair of handcuffs on my wrist and snapped the other round his own. "It's for your own protection," he said.

"You can't do that. It's against human rights."

"You're company property now." He sniffed and wiped his face with his coagulated cloth.

I lifted my hands, now three, to my head and gazed at my paper napkin.

"What's that?" said Cloff.

"A china-shattering idea," I said glumly.

"Looks more like a light bulb to me."

"Of course," I said, "you're a genius." And I kissed him on his bruised forehead.

Ballistrade took three hours to get to the office. His white coat was, as ever, fringed with green slime.

"How's the dogs' heads going?" I asked him.

Ballistrade glanced over his gold framed spectacles, as if seeing me from a distance, and then pushed them up his nose. He poked a finger under a lens and wiped away something I couldn't see.

"Are you alright?" I said.

"Oh I'm fine," said Ballistrade. "It's just those things down there, they..."

"So how are the dogs' heads going?"

"They're growing," he sniffed, "slowly."

"Well, I've got another idea."

"Another one?"

"Can't you keep up?"

"Of course I can keep up," he said, hunching forward slightly.

I went on to explain my idea using the napkin. "And I want a mock up by tomorrow. I want it to be to the highest specifications. I want it to be a shining example of my research and development."

"Tomorrow?"

"Morning."

"But I'll have to work through the night. I promised my son I'd take him to the cinema. It's his… "

"The company does not pay for your son Mr Ballistrade. The company pays you for this," I prodded at the napkin, "groundbreaking technology."

He gulped and left with the toilet attendant's design.

Chapter 9

It's GETTING DARK UP NORTH

Dogs With Headlamps in
their EYES)

The next day Abel arrived with a megaphone.

"Second Paragraph; third, fourth, fifth sentences," he announced tinnily through the loudhailer.

"What's with the megaphone?"

"For some people, the only way they're going to appreciate great literature is to BLAST IT INTO THEIR SKULLS."

"What about subtlety?" I said quietly and put my fingers in my ears.

"THIS IS VERY LOUD SUBTLETY." He took a deep breath. "ROY PUT ON HIS GOLDEN BOOTS WITH THE LUCKY STRIPES. THERE WAS A KNOCK ON THE CHANGING ROOM DOOR. Bluff…am…ma…air …ree."

"What?" Abel had begun to whisper and I had to remove my fingers.

"YOU WANT TO HEAR WHATS HAPPENING NOW DON'T YOU?"

"PUT THE MEGAPHONE DOWN ABEL. I *DO* WANT TO HEAR WHAT'S HAPPENING. Honestly."

"Honestly?"

"Of course. I'm always honest."

Abel took a deep breath. "'There was,'" he said, "'a knock on the changing room door. It was…the manager. "Billy's injured," said the manager, "and all the subs are out of action. You'll have to play both midfield and striker. Do you think you can do it?" The boss looked across at Roy.'" Abel looked up at me expectantly. "Do you think he can do it? Do you think so?"

"I'm not sure," I said, "but, you know, I'm gripped."

"So am I," said Cloff, digging his nails deeper into the blotter.

"Well, you'll have to wait till the next instalment."

"I'll try," I said. I widened my eyes in intimation of a greater excitement.

*

Cloff unpicked his nails from the blotter and we went down to the boardroom. It seemed as if there were fewer and fewer people in the building as if the recent assassination had scared everyone into hiding, but the members of the board had gathered and seated themselves around the table. Ravenski managed a tight lipped smile. Cloff uncuffed me and I was allowed to take my place next to her. There were now three empty spaces beside me, Morgan Wenlock, Denis McCloy and Ibore Davidson. I was aware of these spaces as if their absence was a presence, as if part of my newly defined corporate self had been lopped away and I was experiencing its phantom shape. I reached in the other direction and squeezed Ravenski's full, muscular calf.

The remaining executives squirmed in their chairs. They beat their biros against the blotters, scratched the underside of their chins with the caps, nibbled the ends and twisted in their seats like corkscrews.

"I'm glad you're still here," said Ravenski.

Before I could reply the clock struck the appointed hour, the far door opened and Mantle, together with Sandra his black suited P.A., and two bodyguards came through. Mantle took his seat while his entourage stood behind.

"So what have you got to show us, Velour?"

I opened my mouth but nothing came out. I turned to the empty spaces beside me.

"Get on with the presentation, Velour."

The other executives rubbed their hands over their cheeks, tugged at their hair, bit at their nails and beat their biros.

"Have you got anything to show us or not?" he bellowed.

"Dogs," I said, "Dogs with headlamps in their eyes." I summoned Ballistrade and he wheeled in a papier-mâché mock up of a dachshund on castors. Instead of eyes the dog had headlamps. The work weary Ballistrade flicked a switch behind the dog's tail and the bulbs lit up with a 200 watt brightness that made the audience squint.

"This," I said, "is an astounding development in Pet Furnishings security. Dogs with headlamps in their eyes will make midnight walks a real possibility, providing our customers peace of mind, allowing them to exercise safely, warding off intruders and permitting the furnishings to perform their vital functions under the cover of darkness. As winter approaches, and our customers up North receive less and less light, it will brighten up the mood of the market like a portable sun. Everything is transient now, on the move, on the go; this is where the market is heading and this is where Dogs with Headlamps in their Eyes will lead us with their incandescence." I stood and bowed and fell back into my chair.

Mantle burped. "That'll do." The rest of the board clapped hesitantly, a tremor in their appreciation. "It will be ready for Christmas I presume." Mantle turned to Mr Ballistrade who was cleaning his gold spectacles but ended up adding more of the slime that flecked his coat like a whisked sap.

"Who knows? Who knows?" murmured Ballistrade, "Who knows if Christ will be ready for Christmas?"

"What?"

"Everything," sighed Ballistrade, "will be ready." He replaced his glasses and stared at the floor. He flicked a switch behind the dog's tail and the headlamps shut down with a thunk, returning the boardroom to its oak panelled gloom. A sudden black cataract obscured my view of Mantle, and then Ravenski, before draining away just as rapidly into the grain of the walls.

Mantle filed out with his entourage and Ballistrade wheeled away his papier-mâché dog. I wanted to stay and talk and kiss and grip Ravenski's muscular calves. But Cloff yanked my hand up and applied the handcuffs.

"No fraternisation allowed."

Ravenski opened her mouth and I could see her perfect square teeth just parted, her tongue hesitating on a syllable that I could not stay to hear.

After lunch, the tapping from the walls returned. I picked up my pen and Morse code book as Cloff hung his head. "Does anything ever stop," he said, his hand mirroring mine as I held the biro.

I paused in mid air and then returned the pen to the table. "No, it never seems to stop, does it?" I thought for a bit. "When I started working here, for big business, everything moved so fast, accelerated, but now I've arrived at the top I can't help but move at the same pace and it seems that, relatively, I'm at a standstill, even when I'm racing from exciting new project to exciting new project. It's like being in a rocket going through space at a thousand miles per hour and the stars never move; everything close is going at the same speed, everything far away is too distant to touch. Even when I'm sleeping I'm 'power napping'. And when I'm sitting down I'm brainstorming." The tapping continued. I picked up my biro and it followed its own path into swirls on the blotter.

"And that's what you want?"

"Oh yes," I said, "It's what I want. Well most of the time…" My pen stopped at the blotting hole of its solar cavity. "Sometimes I feel a tiny bit alone, just a bit. It's as if at the centre of all these occupations and leisures and restaurants and hobbies is a soullessness and we make for ourselves a whirlpool; a whirlpool around us."

"That sounds profound."

"Oh yes, it *sounds* profound. Now if you don't mind I must write down what the walls are saying." Cloff gazed at the ceiling as I shuttled the both of us from side to side.

"There is a fine dividing line between sanity and insanity, be careful you don't fall into sanity," said the Marilyn print.

"Don't you ever long for escape?" said the Turner.

"Airport check-ins are the fast food counters of the world."

"To run or even limp away."

"Bite sized packages."

"Escape."

"You know, you're a miserable sod."

"You're hardly full of the joys of spring."

"A joy spring. That's what we need, that's what we really need."

"A spring with fresh water, that's what I would like; fresh water."

"We could buy one. Buy a spring. You can buy anything nowadays."

"We can't buy or do anything, we can't leave here."

"We could ask them."

"Who?"

"Them."

The plumbing stopped and I dropped the battered transcript into a bin as Cloff caught his breath.

"Couldn't we just sit down and do nothing?" he said. He propped himself against the desk.

"A power nap?"

"How about a normal sleep?"

We sat behind the blotter and Cloff nodded off. My wrists were grazed from the handcuffs and a drop of blood fell onto the blotter and spread among the dots and swirls. I thrummed at the paper and twisted in my seat. I longed to see Ravenski again but was uncertain how I could achieve this. I wanted to throw myself into my work but my work didn't seem to want me. And then there were the assassinations, the rivets of the Liberationist.

"CORC," I said suddenly.

Cloff muttered and returned to his snooze.

"Corc," I said again and put my fingers to my lips. I looked about the office and scanned the tall windows behind us. There was nothing to see, no palpable design directing my utterances. On the plaza I could just see the outlines of workers enjoying a coffee break, dipping their heads to triangles of sandwiches.

The door to the office was closed but I could still hear Abel rehearsing lines for his book: "Derby County....but...the most important ...game....The crowd..." I turned my head to listen and could just make out the scrape of his pencil.

"Corc," I said, and then, "Orca. Corc. Orc. Orc." I tried to keep my lips closed by holding them between thumb and forefinger. "Orc." I ground my teeth and this seemed to stop the spasm. I held firm onto the edge of the desk. I decided I would focus on the company, on the need for advanced marketing strategies, on the pros and cons of auditing, on what I could be earning, on what I ought to buy, on what I really needed; the apartment, a new dog...

"Orc." The involuntary orcing made my teeth ache. My feet began to dance under the table; a little jig. And I became aware of other sounds; insistent beats. "Restless movement, yeh, yeh,..." "The French girl," I thought, "the mysterious dancing French girl. It must be her; she is responsible for the Orc."

"Orc. Orc." I held on to the desk ever tighter as if this might anchor my jittering feet and stop Cloff from waking.

The tapping from the pipes restarted but this time there was no code. The tapping seemed in time with the insistent beats of the funk sounds; the rhythms of the dancing French Girl, as if the conversation of the plumbing had tuned into her, the limitless reaches of her music.

"Abel," I called out weakly, "Abel. Orc, Orc…"

Abel very slowly put his head round the door. "Can't you see I'm working, I'm thrilled to my art."

I nodded down at the handcuffs chaining me to the sleeping Cloff. "Orc."

"What?"

"Orc. I mean Corc. I mean can you unpick these handcuffs, like you can do with the door. Please, Orc?"

"Hiccups?"

"I think Orc so."

"Well I'm afraid I can't let you have a glass of water because the cooler is empty and all the fish have died."

The beat went on, louder and louder. "Restless movement, yeh, yeh." The pipes carried on knocking, as if in time; "Tap, tap, Tap, tap. Tap, tap." "Just unlock the handcuffs." Cloff began to snore.

"Why should I?" said Abel.

"Restless movement yeh, yeh."

"Because Orc, because I want to read your book, to experience its true and shining glory in my hands; to feel its radiance pouring upon and through me."

"Well, if you put it like that." He returned with his manuscript holder.

"Restless movement, yeh, yeh. Tap,tap. Tap,tap. Restless movement yeh, yeh." I nodded at the handcuffs. "Unpick the lock, so I can Orc, read the book, Orc."

Abel took a paper clip from his shirt pocket, inserted the end into the lock and prodded about till I was free. Abel offered his manuscript but I knocked him to one side and ran from the office.

"What about the radiance of my prose?"

"Corc," I said "Orc, Orc, Orc," and swerved into the corridor, my body jerking to the beat. "Restless movement yeh, yeh. Restless movement yeh, yeh."

I found the French girl as she was turning a corner. Her pale back gyrated beneath the few black straps of her dress; her headphones were clamped to her ears but the impetuous funk broke free. I didn't touch or talk to her, just followed, dancing down the synthetic carpets, moving in my ill fitting suit to the sublime beat of her disco blues. "Orc," I said, "Orc, Orc, Orc."

Chapter 10

THE FALL

The French girl danced past the lifts to the stairwell and I followed her switching hips down the stairs, through the reception and across the plaza. There was a light wind and I was close enough to see her flesh leavening with goose bumps but onwards she danced, her black dress skipping from side to side. "Restless Movement Yeh, Yeh."

The workers on their coffee breaks stared at us, punctuations of espresso on their bottom lips. "Restless Movement Yeh, Yeh. Restless Movement Yeh. Yeh." "Orc, orc, orc." We danced to the bus stop and she paused and I half expected her to join the queue and the number thirty two on its worming clogged route through Lydon but she smiled and carried on dancing. I was drawn behind her, jutting out my hips to her coco.

We danced along the streets with no more stopping. We swivelled and shuffled out of the docklands and then along the river towards the heart of the city, ever onwards so that time seemed to fade and our movement made the only beat of the passing day. We ignored the stares of the pedestrians and car drivers and snuck into the alleys in the seedier centres of the metropolis, the girl beckoning me onwards in the loop of her music, in the loop of her back switching body. My knees ached, my hips grated, my chest roared but I was reeled inwards, ever inwards.

Dusk came and the streets became hooded and cobblestone lipped. Darkness witched us into the nightlife with its buzzing streetlamps, peepholes and porches huddled under neon brows. And on we danced. The buildings leant, one upon each other, falling into the pit of the city and it was here that we stopped, at a club with the flashing sign 'Below'. Below 'Below' was a single doorway and descending steps. The mouth of the stairwell spat out paroxysms of sound, funky cocky beats, an agitated foundry. The girl gave me a coy look over her shoulder and hopped down into the club. I couldn't help but follow.

It was packed and an odorous sweat arrived like a tide. The crowd waved their arms to a beat from the other side of the cellar. I worked my way across, paddling my hands on the ceiling to the stage where the band was playing. They snarled out their riffs like machine guns. Their shaved heads brushed the low roof as they fretted and pounded their instruments. The dancing French girl removed her headphones and convulsed her body in time to the noises that kicked and exploded around us. I tapped her on the shoulder, I touched her.

"Non," she mouthed, "dance."

It was all I could do in the crowd that carried me in its crush. Someone hit me and then smiled an apology and barged into my shoulder. I struck out and caught him on the chin and he laughed and the thrill of the pain in my fist bit down into the dog bites as the band ratcheted up their guitar and drum beats ricocheted like bullets. The crowd jumped and slid as one, elbowing and febrile in their happy, mutual violence and body was against body and flesh was against flesh and I roared as the singer on the stage roared and I was carried to the front in the dangerous swoon of it all and I saw the singer was spindley thin, turning round his mike stand like a mechanical snake, a prick on a stick, arching up and spraying his saliva fickle flayed.

And my teeth were needles at the back of my mouth, breaking and cracking in the gumline and I ate the flashing darkness of the strobe and a woman and then a man came and kissed me open gobbed and then disappeared and then someone hit me with a flailing leg and I fell to the floor, feet stamping up and down by my hands. A woman tripped up and we stared at each other in the cacophony of limbs. She had crimson lips and I bit at them and she bit mine as leather kicked up around us and we grappled and pulled each other to the side of the floor and tore at our clothes and made to fuck against the wall but she was pushed away and the music carried on regardless; an endless pressure upwards and over and I danced and fought and hit my way to the stairs fighting in the exhilaration, in the thrill of the bang of the music, and I went up the steps and out into the night, bone bright at its trim by the silver moon.

And I danced and I screwed my way across the city; anything and everything as my teeth pointed and pressed in my gums. I saw a plastic litter bin frothing with rubbish and I fucked it in its letter box entry, fucked between the cartons and straws and magazines. I beat myself against the glass of a bus shelter so it shattered and I lifted up the chips like diamonds and threw them into the night. I fucked the drainpipes by the billboards and I fucked the punctuations in the billboards where it told me buy it, to buy them. I danced backwards and on all fours, forward, forward. I moved to the beat of the flashing horning cars, jumping up high to the wire and the railings round a car park. And I fucked between the railings and I fucked the cars in the car park in their exhaust pipes. And I ran on all fours to the patch of grass beside the car park and I rolled in the grass and the condensation of the night and I fucked a plastic bottle and I found a beer can and I drank it spilling it all over my face and I would have fucked it if the hole had been big enough. I got up and I danced, punching the air, running to some streets with couples strolling in arm in arm and I tried to fuck them all, male and female under their long coats and skirts and handbags. And then I fell to the floor and I followed the dash along the centre of the road, followed its serration on all fours, dribbling on it, spewing onto it as the cars swerved and screamed. And my hands bled with the friction and I crawled onto a patch of grass heavenly littered with crisp packets and cigarette polythenes and strips of tabloid sluttings and I gasped. I knelt on all fours in front of a park bench, bleeding from my mouth and the zip of my groin. I howled with the pain and the fury and thrill of the night. I howled at the cavorting lights of the city. And two hair tangled, blue and red faced drunks, sitting on the bench, leant over and rested their lager cans on my back. And then there was a click about my wrists and ankles as policemen put on cuffs and said they were taking me away, taking me away "you fucking nutter." And I tried to move but I couldn't so they had to push and carry me into the car with its blood popped lights. And the drunks laughed and laughed, spilling their sweet alcohol over lethargic hands, their eyes dewy with god knows what tears, god almighty.

Chapter 11

CHOICES

"There's someone here to see you," said the Policeman through the slot of the cell. He narrowed his eyes, rattled the keys and opened up the slammer. I was naked and covered only in a blanket so its bristles scraped against my grazes and cuts.

Mr Cloff walked in. "I hear you've seen the psychiatrists. They say you're sane." I stared at him blankly . "You know the police are going to prosecute you for assault and damage to property? Pet Furnishings will pay bail. But Mr Mantle has some conditions attached."

"Conditions?"

Cloff indicated my gaol. "You want to stay here?"

I cast an eye over the graffitied walls and the dented slop bucket, the creeping darkness. "No."

"Good. I'll get you your clothes. You seem to have shredded them into rags but we'll buy some new stuff at the hypermarket."

I pulled the rough blanket up to my neck and waited for my clothes, shivering.

"I need a dentist," I told Cloff as we made our way to Priscilla in the morning sun. The tumbler of his revolver, resting on the dashboard, reflected the light with angular interruptions.

"There's no time. Mr Mantle wants to see you immediately and since he paid your bail, I'd suggest you do as he says." He looked me up and down. "It makes a change to see someone else with a few grazes. You ought to get some antiseptic on those."

"It's my teeth that hurt," I said and put my hand to my jaw, "I think my wisdoms are coming through."

We turned into a luxury hypermarket and bought an off the peg designer suit, which shrank to fit when you pulled the draw strings in the fabric. We had wild boar soup in the cafe and I was taken, fabric trussed, straight to Priscilla.

*

Security continued to be heavy handed at the wharf; now with a luminous line of security guards outside the reception and a smattering of armed policemen in flack jackets.

"Obviously they're taking the threat very seriously," said Cloff. "The authorities recognise that Pet Furnishings is the prime target for insurrectionist activities. They were going to give you police protection but Mr Mantle wanted me to stay on your case."

After some negotiation with the guards, Cloff and I were taken straight to Mantle's underground office. I sat facing him in a leather chair, rigid with the overwhelming pain in my gums. I prodded at the back of my mouth and it eased a bit; just enough to become fearful of Mantle's tiny eyed wrath.

"Get your fingers out of your mouth Velour. Do you know what you've done?" I picked a piece of boar hide from between my fangs. "Not only do we have to cope with Ibore Davidson's assassination but there are security pictures of you in the papers having, what I can only describe as sex with a drainpipe. If you're not mad, what are you?"

"Restless," I said.

"Look Velour, you're a talented creative, one of our best yet. Only yesterday you came up with a startling innovation but you have to control your energies, your febrile imagination, focus it into the company."

"He's right." I heard the smooth, controlled tones of Ravenski from behind him. She had been sitting on a dog pouffe at the back of the room. The cushion whimpered and wagged its stubby tail

"Ravenski?"

"Ravenski is now staying with us in Priscilla," continued Mantle. "In fact all the executives will be living here, under armed guard. It appears that out there," he indicated the plush leather walls, "is more dangerous than in here," he pointed at the floor and his own paunch. "You too Velour. Not only are you bad publicity but you're a danger to yourself and others." He burped. "I've had problems with creatives like you before but there are ways to solve these strange yearnings. I have plans for you Velour, plans that will make you truly a part of this company and all that it has to offer. But you have to give me control; you have to give me your trust. What do you say?" I looked to Ravenski.

"I suggest we follow Howard's advice," she blinked her brown eyes, "for both our sakes."

I felt the wisdom teeth pointing out from the back of my palate, iceberg pricks against the sides of my tongue. "I.."

"To be blunt," interrupted Mantle, "you don't have a choice. I'm paying the bail and the bribes and if you don't want to end up locked up you'll have to do as I say."

"You know its the right thing," said Ravenski, "the only way."

I let my tongue lie flat in my mouth. The two day old cotton wool felt ugly and sopping. They accepted my silence as an agreement.

"Good. Tomorrow you'll report to Ballistrade's labs. You may go."

Ravenski and I shared a lift to the office. Cloff stood in the corner.

"If you're going to handcuff me," I said to him, "you can lock me to Ravenski."

"There's no need for that," he replied. "You can no longer leave this building without Mr Mantle's express permission."

"Is that lawful?"

"It's bail."

"Better to be here together," I squeezed Ravenski's hand, "than outside alone."

Cloff spent the rest of the journey checking the cartridges in his revolver, a faint blush on his cheeks as Ravenski examined my cuts with careful fingers.

Abel sat outside the office, waiting, arms crossed above his manuscript.

"You deceived me," he said, "You announced that you wanted to read my work but you only desired to spread your spawn across this city." He glared at Ravenski and then returned to glower at me. "The plot is reaching its most fascinating upheaval and yet you do not care, the swallows of beauty fly above you and yet you do not see. The jewels of this crown are within your grasp and yet you do not reach for them. The novel soars in exultation…"

"It's not really a novel, is it?" I said. "It's only two paragraphs."

"Three actually."

"If I really could care," I said, "I would, but I don't." I kissed Ravenski.

"I'm in the peaks of literary ecstasy and you don't care?"

"No. Not really." Ravenski and I went into my office and he pounded from outside.

"Don't care, don't care, don't care…" His voice fell away like an echo and I assumed he had dozed off on his desk.

Eventually Ravenski's bodyguard arrived and escorted her to her own office. I was struck by a brief but fading flash of jealously as they left together.

Abel meanwhile had decided to forgive me. "Just let me read you a bit."

"No."

"I'll shut up."

"No you won't."

"Yes I will."

"…Five minutes. But that's all."

I turned from him and investigated the harbour view as he searched for his single page in the manuscript holder. In a way Abel was right; the sky *was* bluer than I had bothered to notice. The birds dipped and dived between still clouds. Then, as I watched, the sky and the birds and the plaza suddenly disappeared and returned in an instant, as if the whole scene had been spirited away and then retrieved for one brief second. I blinked. "Did you see that? Did you see that?"

Abel ignored me. He had found his bookmark in the grand design.

"You will remember that Roy was on the brink of one of the most important games of his life, only to discover that two players were injured and he had to cover for both of them. We return to the scene in the changing room; "'I'll see what I can do," said Roy, doing up the laces on his golden boots. The roar of the crowd tunnelled towards him. No one had ever played both attack and midfield before but that didn't mean he couldn't be the first. "C'mon lads," he said, "let's show them what we're made of." The team cheered as he mimed a match winning kick into the full length mirror with his Midas boots. Roy admired his own handsome features in the reflection, his beard, his green eyes, his paunchy cheeks, the shaven head.'"

I continued to stare across the plaza, bemused by its momentary disappearance. I could see a lonely jogger padding his way across the forecourt in a luminous top, a brightly coloured fly across the dull pane of my window. "What are we made of Abel?"

"Words mostly. Well my words."

"But out there," I pointed at the window, "do we lead real lives out there?"

"Who cares? What do you think of the latest instalment?"

"Oh yes, very exciting. Do you know a reliable dentist?" I prodded in my mouth.

"Which bits did you like, mostly?"

I felt the iceberg corners of the surfacing enamel at the back of my gums and then came upon a gooey piece of wild boar soup and pulled it out and looked at it. "Um, I liked the golden boots."

"I knew it," said Abel, "did you recognise their cultural resonance?"

"Oh yes." I turned the piece of soggy meat around in the clear light. Now there was a case for flossing if there ever was one.

"Is not Roy a remarkable character; fully rounded, alive, *real*?"

"Oh yes. He's like…well he's like a footballer."

Abel dabbed his fingers in the air. "Ah, with but a few strokes the master paints his picture. The working class hero brought to life, to sing the praises of the humble few."

I turned and nailed my piece of gristle to the blotter with a drawing pin. "Mmm, a working class hero. Do they still exist?"

"Of course, they're the bread and butter, the Irish potato of the new writing."

"Why does Roy have golden boots then, if he's…?"

"It's in the subtext."

"I see," I said, not seeing.

I took my feet off the ground so I could spin around in the chair and the sun winked off my polished shoes. Later I went to get some water from the cooler to find that the water had gone and the fish had died. They lay at the bottom of the plastic tub, spotted black and rotting. I turned the tap and a whiff of rotting fish came to me, a polluted Evian.

The next day I was starved and taken underground. We went straight across the boardroom and continued along the termite corridor that ran from it. But rather than go to Mantle's office at the far end we stopped in front of a steel door marked "Restricted." Cloff pressed a bell and Ballistrade's morose voice came over an intercom.

"Yes?"

"I'm delivering Velour."

"Clearance?"

Cloff looked at his notepad. "Three, two, zero, three, two."

Electronic locks slipped and thunked and Ballistrade swung open the heavy door. It groaned on unoiled hinges. Ballistrade appeared even wearier; his fine blonde hair stuck in places to his forehead. He acknowledged me with a flicker of his eyes behind his smeared glasses.

"Good luck," said Cloff as the door closed and I was left alone with Ballistrade. His lab had the dimensions of a small, low roofed, warehouse. There were four chemistry benches either side of us, leaving a walkway through the middle. On some tabletops lay the carcasses of electronic hardware; on others test tubes and metal vats. Here and there, striplights picked out patches of green, the same linctus that had gathered on Ballistrade's sleeves. Three more doors led off this room; one from the left wall, one from right and another at the far end, opposite the entrance we had come through. There were two technicians working at the benches; they had long lank hair and their white coats were flecked with slime.

The assistants gave a sullen greeting and then resumed their hunched tasks. "This way," said Ballistrade and he led me between the benches to the opposite door and we went into a second space, much smaller than the first and bare apart from an operating table set up in the middle. Its chrome mechanisms reflected the strip light with an icy latticing.

"What's that for?"

He ignored me and led me into another, narrower room where there were steel benches attached to the walls and pegs to hang clothes on. Ballistrade locked the door behind him after we had entered.

"So you haven't been told then?"

"No."

"You better sit down." He removed his spectacles and rubbed them with a whitish square of his coat. For a moment he seemed to have more humanity, his eyes toned compared to the blank walls that shouldered us. "As you are probably aware Mr Mantle has favoured staff, who he brings into the very heart of this company. And so that those staff can be favoured he, err…"

"What?"

"He… he removes one of their testicles and inserts a plastic one impregnated with bromide… 'to dampen down their sexual ardour'."

I didn't reply.

"It's a very simple procedure. I've done quite a few, I'm very fast, and we do it under local." He looked up. "I suppose it's a bit of a shock but it really gets you into the heart of …"

"A BIT OF A SHOCK? You're going to take out one of my testicles."

"Yes it is a little…"

"It's against the laws of human nature…"

"It's not against the laws of this company."

"Have you ever had one of your balls scooped out?"

"No, but then I'm not one of the elite. Look…" he touched the side of my arm where I'd buried my head. "Think of it as not so much losing one ball as…gaining another. Consider what you might lose if you don't get it taken out; your job, your lifestyle, you could even go to prison. I've been told you might lose the woman you're most fond of."

"Ravenski?"

"Miss Goldbird's name has been mentioned. I know it's upsetting for you. Believe me it's not a procedure I like doing, I really don't. The other day I, I…" He wiped his brow with the cuff of his white coat so his fringe became tainted with the slime. He paused and his voice began to break. "The job never started like this. They extended it to… other things. I didn't mind to begin with, I became numbed to the whole thing. It was just a job like any other I told myself. But then things got worse, so slowly I didn't even notice and the further they make you go the harder it is to go back until you're doing things that make you sick while you work, make you wretch while you work and I,…" Now he had his own head in his hands and was whimpering.

Beyond the door I could hear the muffled bell of a telephone.

Ballistrade returned his glasses and tried to wick away some tears with his cuff. "We have to get it done now. Get it over and done with. They're calling for us."

"Isn't there anything else I can do, anything else but this?"

He shook his head and opened the door so the ringing became louder. "Strip down to your underpants," he said. "Hang your clothes on the pegs." He paused. "You don't have to come this way," he nodded at the open door, "but it seems the other way is prison."

There was a mirror in the changing room and I inspected my reflection; the sharp suit, the shiny black shoes, the cropped hair now beginning to grow into a brush, the ungroomed goatee starting to lose its shape and creep up my chin, the cheeks flaccid with their ragged cotton wool but the eyes still a sharp emerald green. I thought of what I had to lose; I thought of Ravenski.

I began to undress and watched the unveiling of my body as if it was another's; the scars, the healing bites on my forearms, the muscles, the prescient outlines. Black spots began to mottle my sight, swelling and joining, patching my body with an inky darkness before slipping away, seeping into the drain by my feet. I stepped out of my socks and walked into the operating suite, clad only in my Pet Furnishing's underpants. The tiles were chill like blocks of ice and here and there I could see drops of blood, leading the way from the changing room door.

Ballistrade was by the operating table, dressed in a blue gown and a face mask. He nodded at the table and I climbed on. There was a window of reflective glass that ran alongside us.

"It's a one way mirror," said Ballistrade, "so others can follow the procedure."

"Who?"

"I'm not sure."

I lay down, and Ballistrade folded green sheets over my chest and legs, leaving my waist exposed. I imagined the faces peering in; the bitter dumpling of Mantle's head, the bruised and knuckle nosed Cloff, Ravenski with her brown eyes. A black line formed at the top of my sight and drifted down, becoming one with the folds of my gown.

A phone next to the mirror rang and Ballistrade answered. "Yes we're ready …Yes…Yes…Of course." He replaced the receiver, pulled on some latex gloves, letting the plastic snap down at the wrist, and wheeled over a trolley. He tugged down my pants and I watched the Pet Furnishings design shrivel into itself. He lifted a syringe, attached a needle, filled it from a vial and squirted some of the liquid back through the point. "Local anaesthetic," he said.

"I used to be afraid of needles," I said, wistfully. "Now I'm quite fond of them."

"All we need," said Ballistrade, "is time. Soon we become anaesthetized even to the application of the anaesthetic." He felt out a crease in my groin, pulled back a tug of skin, inserted the needle and applied the drug. "It deadens the nerve," he explained. He manoeuvred himself so he had his back to the mirror of the audience and wheeled a trolley between us. But instead of unsheathing a scalpel he whispered to me in low, conspiratorial tones.

"I have to take out the testicle and replace it. They," he jerked his head back at the mirror, "have to see that, but it doesn't have to be Mr Mantle's bromide. It could be something else."

"Like?"

"Like this." He whipped back a polythene sheet from a metal tray. The tray contained two objects; one a plastic ball, the bromide imprinted testicle, the other a smaller and fleshier marble. It was webbed with crimson capillaries and lilac veins. "A dog's testicle," he said.

"WHAT?"

"I've found a way of stopping the body's immune rejection of other organs through my work on…other things. But here it is, a dog's testicle, a greyhound's. So now," he glanced from the plastic to the bloody plum, "you have a choice. No one has to know which testicle I insert; they only have to know I take yours out."

"And that's a choice?"

"Two options are always a choice. Now hurry, they'll think something's wrong."

I gazed down. I couldn't see my groin, only my hitched up knee caps, shining like boiled eggs. Yes, I thought, two options are a choice but is that liberty or merely the appearance of liberty? Perhaps, I thought, we have to survive on that, the ghost of freedom.

"Come on" said Ballistrade.

The two balls in the basin gazed at me and above this my reflection in the two way mirror. "Better to be alive with the dog," I thought, "than dead without."

"The dog," I said quietly

"So be it." Ballistrade stood back from the table so the audience had a clearer view of the procedure. He pressed my legs apart and shaved off the pubic hair with a disposable razor. He poured on some antiseptic and cut into the left side of my scrotum. It was a distant sensation; an apparition of pain. Ballistrade articulated his instruments quickly and deftly and removed what looked like a ragged peach stone. He showed it to his audience, and then returned to implant the dog testicle, prodding it in with a pair of tweezers. He winked as he bent across my belly with the sutures.

I didn't follow the rest of the procedure and felt only the knock of Ballistrade's elbows as he poked and sewed the thing in. Eventually the last stitch was done and he rocked back, peeled off the ruby stained gloves, and dropped them into a pedal bin. The phone rang. "All done," he said into it. He turned back to me. "You can pull up your pants. I've put a gauze pad round the ball to stop the ooze. I've got some painkillers for when the injection wears off."

"Can't you do anything for my teeth?"

"Teeth?"

"You see I've got these wisdoms coming through and…"

"I've just taken out one of your testicles and you're worried about your teeth?"

"There's nothing you can do for them then?"

"Like I said, I'll give you some tablets."

"My teeth hurt when I bite on tablets."

"Everything hurts, Mr Velour. We just have to figure out what degree of pain we are prepared to take and for what compensation." He rolled a wheelchair in from the adjacent lab, guided me into it and pushed me into the changing room.

I sat in my office in the wheelchair, facing the window. The mop martial arts dance troupe was doing a lunchtime performance on the plaza. I watched with a listless appreciation. They were like miniature soldiers enacting a battle with their mops. An audience of office workers had gathered to watch. Behind them, police patrolled in pairs, automatic weapons strapped across their chests.

Abel arrived. "So where have you been all this time?"

Cloff followed in his wake, his face billowing with irritation. "I told him you needed a rest."

"It's alright," I said, "he can stay."

Abel removed the second page from the manuscript box he now always carried with him and stood between me and the window.

"We join the action off the pitch; 'Roy turned from the mirror, led his team out of the changing room and down the corridor. The chanting of the crowd was like an echoing canon; "Rovers, Rovers, Rovers." He jogged onto the field and the sound swelled into a roar. "ROVERS." He felt the grass give, fresh and alive. He imagined the vibrations of the cheering reaching up to him, shaking through the ground: "ROVERS, ROVERS"… The referee blew the whistle and its high pitched squeal was drowned in the roar of the crowd. The ball was passed to Roy and he ran it along the wing, dodging one, two, three players. He made a quick pass to the midfielder, Duncan, who knocked it back as Roy strode towards the penalty box. One of the defenders was coming in for the tackle but Roy had sight of goal and went for the strike. He leant onto his left foot with his head over the ball and then…'" Abel paused, holding himself in the guise of his heroic attacker, "'then Duncan stuck out his boot and tripped him up. Roy couldn't believe it. He'd been fouled by one of his own team. The ref. blew for a goal kick. "What's going on?" said Roy as they went back to their own half. Duncan put his hands on Roy's shoulders and then kneed him in the groin. Roy screamed as he fell to the ground but no one could hear him in the crowd.'" Abel let go of the page and it fluttered into his manuscript box. "Makes you breathless doesn't it? The pacing."

"Breathless," I said and then coughed and winced.

"What's with the wheelchair?"

"Recuperation."

"Aha, recuperation before the battle begins, before the first whistle is blown, before the team charge towards their destiny."

"Look Abel, I like your story but I need time to relax. By myself."

"Of course. My solitude is valued above all else. For it is only when I am alone that I can…"

"Thanks Abel."

"Until tomorrow then."

I returned to my anaesthetised gaze over the plaza. The martial arts mop squad were somersaulting over their mops while the office workers nibbled at their sandwich triangles; quiet surrenders in the sun.

That evening, Cloff helped me dress and wash. "Mr Mantle wants you to attend a dinner party". He put a daisy in my buttonhole. "Miss Goldbird's coming."

As he bent down I could smell gin on his breath.

"Were you ever a dog walker?" I asked.

He lifted me into the wheelchair and took off the brake. "Never." He tipped back the chair and pushed me out of the office.

We travelled down to the underground corridor, its strip lights flashing above me like the serrations of an inverted road, and then we stopped in front of one of the stainless steel doors on the right marked 'Restricted.'

"More labs?"

"No," said Cloff, "The Dinner Party." He rapped and the door was opened by a familiar man in a dress suit.

"Names?" he asked.

"Mr Cloff. I've come to deliver Mr Velour."

"Ah yes." He signed a form and took me into the room leaving Cloff in the corridor. The steel doors closed behind us on thick oiled springs.

The dinner party was set in a rectangular red brick room, not much bigger than a normal dining room. Candles on the walls burnt with a low flame so the light was soft and cherry and the surfaces were uncertain with twitching shadows. A banqueting table had been laid out from one end to the other. Mantle was seated at the head. He had a sculpture above him, though its details were difficult to discern in the half light. I was wheeled by the waiter to my setting, second to the left of Mantle. I imagined this conferred some kind of status and I nodded to Mantle as I was eased from the wheelchair and into a tall timbered seat.

I smelt a familiar perfume and found Ravenski had taken the space next to me, closest to Mantle. She was wearing a brown backless evening gown and her black bob had been tidied just behind her ears. She smiled. To my left was Strachen. He nodded formally and his half rim glasses inched down his skeletal nose. He seemed even more pasty, thin and forlorn in the candlelight. I couldn't make out the rest of the crowd and was only just able to define the features of the man sitting opposite, who once again appeared oddly familiar.

Mantle spoke up first. "Welcome friends, to this evening's banquet. Because of our recent security difficulties, we've had to retreat, as it were, into Priscilla. But this is a pleasant retreat I think you'll agree; so much safer and more comfortable than out there…" He curled his thin lips out. "Perhaps I ought to make some introductions. But first we must have light."

The waiter lit the candles that ran along the middle of the table and I was able to see my fellow diners more clearly. Sitting opposite was my Reciprocal, an older and more lined version of myself, who now had some shaven hair growing in patches from his skull.

"Mr Velour this is your camouflage committee member." Mantle nodded in the man's direction. We blinked at each other. "Miss Goldbird and Mr Strachen I believe you already know your counterparts." He pointed at the resemblances of Ravenski and Strachen, facing them on the other side of the table. "Sandra my secretary"; his P.A. was sitting next to Strachen, "and Frances Blencoe"; Frances was beside Sandra and she smiled with her black lipsticked lips. "And on the other side," he indicated the remaining seats, "the reciprocals of Frances and Sandra." It was as if a jaundiced mirror had been set along the centre of the banquet in which our weary reflections had been set to dine with us.

"Now, for sustenance!" He clicked his fat fingers and the waiter, who had his own singular familiarity, went to a serving hatch in the brick wall. He came back with bowls of garnished mushrooms and filled up our jade goblets with red and white wine. As I watched him dip here and there between us I saw the sculpture twitch above Mantle's head. I was about to have a better look when my reciprocal piped up.

"Couldn't you call us by our proper names, Mr Mantle, rather than 'The reciprocals'; we are, after all, on common ground?"

"I don't think that's wise," said Mantle, "in the current situation we should continue with our proper nouns."

The reciprocal snorted but said nothing.

I turned to talk to Ravenski but she had already embarked on a whispered confidence with Mantle. I felt her hand resting on my thigh.

"Not hurtling around so fast now, are we?" said my reciprocal and glanced at the wheelchair by the wall.

"You could never keep up anyway," I said.

"I had to have a break." He dropped his voice. "I gave up chasing you. Do you know how much skill and energy it takes to be an actor?"

"You should try coming up with the ideas," I said, "the concepts that run this company."

He took a gulp of red wine and ran his hand over weedy allotments of hair. "That's where you're wrong," he said, "in fact we", he indicated his fellow reciprocals, "run this company."

"Don't be ridiculous. You just provide the camouflage."

"That's what you'd like to think," he said, "or are told to think. In fact it's us who run the show, from the top floor. We make every decision and direct the company for Mr Mantle. You are made to appear in the driving seat so it takes the attention away from us."

"You're deluding yourself. You're the actors in this company."

"Oh we do our bit of acting but only for 'show'. We're the real deal; we're the ones who turn over the wheels of this organisation. You're the foils, you," he popped a garlic mushroom into his mouth, "are the ones that get assassinated."

"That's a lie," I prodded my fork, "I have to be in the driving seat. I've had one of my testicles removed for Mr Mantle."

"I had mine removed years ago."

"Then how can you be my reciprocal, you can't have been here longer than…"

"Ever heard of plastic surgery Velour? I used to have a face like the poor schmuck before you… until he got demoted."

I sat back, shocked into silence, until Ravenski finished her conversation and turned to me.

"So how was the op?"

"My reciprocal, over there, he says…"

"Must have been painful."

"Of course but…"

"It was the right thing. I've had one of my ovaries done."

"What?"

"We all have to make a sacrifice for the good of the company. I had the thing scooped out. If you want to get anywhere in big business you have to compromise; it's corporate biology and it's great we can make this sacrifice together."

"It's madness."

"It's a leisure, career and lifestyle option."

"So you've still got one left? The ovary I mean."

"Sure, but I'm getting that done as soon as…" She paused in the shadow of my sorrowful face. "Look Telby, we're top of the pile you and me, diamonds in the bosom of plenty, but we have to make a few sacrifices."

"According to him," I hitched a thumb at the reciprocal, "we don't run anything. We just pretend to, for the reciprocals; while they pretend to be us."

"That's bollocks."

"Excuse me." My reciprocal cut in, spluttering his red wine onto his napkin. "That is not bollocks. It is a difficult to swallow fact." Ravenski ignored him and turned to resume her conversation with Mantle.

The reciprocal leant close so I could smell the wine on his breath. "I don't think anyone knows who runs this company. We nick your ideas, you nick ours, everybody steals from each other and the whole big show just rolls on. You want to know what this company is? One, big, happy, thieving family."

I looked across the guests sharing their food and gossip with the brothers and sisters of themselves. "But someone's got to run it," I said, "someone's got to come up with the right formula, the right direction?"

"Maybe. But I don't know who it is and neither does anyone else, including fat chops." He pointed at Mantle. "The one thing you need to know is that I don't chase after you, you chase after me, or perhaps, just perhaps, we chase each others tails." He leant back in his chair and burped.

The waiter removed my plate and replaced it with a saucer of profiteroles. It was then that I recognised him; it was the toilet attendant. He was in a different uniform but he was clearly the same character who'd dispensed towels and cotton wool balls from his booths of convenience, wearing the same black polyester tie. He smiled his knowing smile as I thanked him.

We finished the pudding and the waiter refilled our glasses with champagne. Mantle toasted us. "To one big happy family." We stood, the brothers and sisters of ourselves, and raised our drinks. Even I, with my pain, managed to join the toast. I watched the waiter through the green slur of my glass as he returned our plates to the hatch, his smile still printed on his face like a thin wax seal, his gold chain sparkling on his wrist.

We sat down and finished the rest of the champagne. Irritated by my reciprocal, not wanting to talk to Strachen, and finding Ravenski murmuring with Mantle I took the opportunity to look around the room. The sculpture on the near wall appeared to tremble and squirm in the shadows.

I pulled at the waiter's sleeve. "What's that, over there?"

"A modern sculpture Sir."

"Help me up, so I can see."

He scooped me up, under the arms, and I saw that the piece of art was in fact a dog; a dog nailed to a teak wooden cross. It was a greyhound tacked by its front and back paws in the manner of a crucifixion. It twitched in its pinnings.

"That's enough," I said. The waiter held me where I was. "Put me down," I said. He continued to hold me in the same position. "I SAID PUT ME DOWN." He eased me into my seat as the table went silent.

Mantle burped and lay down his napkin. "Something wrong Velour?"

I shrugged. "Nothing's wrong Mr Mantle."

The waiter served coffee and chocolate mints and I sipped and nibbled as the outline of the soundless dog twitched in my periphery. A black mist drifted across the table, melted into a dark ink on the floor, and then drained into the shadows. I looked around but the others kept on chatting, their lips bruised with chocolate.

Strachen girded himself into conversation. "So how are things in the ideas business?" he asked.

"Fine. And marketing?"

"Fine."

There was a pregnant pause into which our platitudes recharged.

"And your family?"

"Fine."

"How many?"

"Two, a boy and girl."

"Nice."

"Yes."

"Good."

Strachen took another mint and turned to speak to Sandra, Mantle's P.A.

The meal was beginning to repeat up my gullet. I belched, acid ascending to the back of my mouth. From the corner of my eye I saw the dog shake its muzzle. I burped again, put a hand to my belly and pressed a napkin to my lips.

"I think I'm going to have to leave," I murmured to Ravenski, "I'm feeling a bit sick."

"It's the operation," she said, "you always feel sick after the operation."

"What's the matter?" demanded Mantle.

"I'm feeling a bit..."

"Don't you like the food?"

"It's been a long day and…"

"Milk. Bring Velour some milk." The waiter brought over a tureen of full fat milk but it just seemed to make the heartburn worse.

"Helps, doesn't it?" said Mantle.

"Yes," I said and suppressed another belch. The dog continued to twitch above his head.

Mantle saw me glance there. "My own design. Do you like it?" I burped and swallowed and nodded. "Conjures up gothic, renaissance and modern sensibilities…so I've been told. It's conceptual and figurative all at once…so my friends have said."

The swill of wine and profiterole gushed up and spread in a bilious lily across my tongue. "Remarkable," I managed and mopped the acid from my lips with the napkin.

"Which reminds me," said Mantle, "I must show you my latest design. I'm very proud." He leant over and though his reach was limited he still managed to squeeze my shoulder. "I know you're the real ideas man here Velour, it's just nice to get these nails dirty once in a while." He wriggled his fat fingers and pushed himself from the table. "You'll have to give me your opinion." He got out of his seat, wobbled and fell against his placemat before Sandra and her reciprocal helped him to his feet. "O.K.," he said, "everyone follow me."

The dinner party shuffled in line out of the room with Ravenski pushing me in the wheelchair. The toilet attendant watched us leave with the same narrow smile, a tablecloth folded over one arm. The crucified dog hung motionless above him, its jaw slack at a sideways 'V', a drip of saliva falling from its black gums.

"The dog's still." I said to Ravenski as she pushed me out of the room.

"What?"

"The dog on the wall. It used to be moving and now it's just stopped."

"Yes," she said, "it's really very moving…"

"No," I said, "the dog's stopped. It's just stopped."

"We've got to keep on moving," she said, "keep on moving,

don't stop, don't ever look back…" She rocked the wheelchair and tilted it over the brink of the dining room and into the corridor.

"You don't understand it's…"

"Sometimes it's easier not to understand," she said, "because then you can't see and who needs to see as long as you get where you want to go." The door closed behind us on its steel spring and she pushed the wheelchair after Mantle. We came to the third door on the left, Mantle waved a plastic card, the locks shot back and we trundled into the startling glow of the lab where I had been only that morning.

From the wheelchair I had a good view across the benches, green ooze moved uneasily through glass coils to tangled destinations. Some of the coils connected to copper pipes which dipped over the edge of the tabletops and made their way through the walls. Here and there, jars and beakers bubbled with a redder fluid, seething over slow burning flames. There was no sign of Ballistrade and the lab seemed to make guttural warbles in his absence like a pining child.

Mantle waddled to one of the doors midway along the lab, abetted by the Sandras either side of him. He waved his card and it clicked open. The room beyond him was in darkness, but I could see the outline of a ribbed canister held up by a single pillar and topped with a reflective strip. I had a *deja vu*, a quiver of reminiscence.

Mantle peered into the darkness, puzzled, and then quickly closed the door.

"Nope," he said, "wrong room."

"What was in there?" I tried to peer past him from my seat in the wheelchair.

"Nothing of interest," said Mantle as he shuffled past, "I told you it was the wrong room." He led the trail across the lab, unlocked the opposite door and switched on the lights. We went into a chamber that was much the same size as the operating theatre but more chaotic, with the air of a workshop. Engine innards and blades and saws lay in silver trays next to strips of wood, metal pipes and circuit boards. Bits of furniture toppled in various states of deconstruction. "My playground," Mantle told us and we followed him to a podium with a cage on top. Through its metal bars, I could see a bulldog, a very ugly bulldog.

The dog had the sloping face characteristic of the breed but even more pronounced, so the snout, jaw and forehead appeared to have collapsed into the same plane. Its bloodshot eyes were barely visible in a slurry of drooping skin. The canine's nose was like a bubbling ink print on a vellum roll. A plastic straw inserted into a notch in its lip frothed at one end. The pooch's rear legs had been removed and then replaced with a plinth that fitted onto the trunk of the body. At the corners of this plinth were wooden pegs on which it sat on the cage floor. This had the overall effect of turning the dog's rear end into a foot stool.

"My own invention; the bulldog pouffe." Mantle prodded at the cage with a stubby finger. "We managed to breed the bulldog so its face has become wonderfully flat. Of course this caused some breathing problems so we inserted a pipe into its mouth. We intend to solve this eventually with an internal apparatus. The flatness of the face," Mantle began to tilt to one side and his assistants rushed forwards to prop him back, "has meant that the dog is unable to see or smell properly, thus making it easier for the customer to place his or," he smiled at Ravenski, "her derriere."

"You mean people put their backsides on the dog's face?" I said.

"Yes Velour, revolutionary don't you think?"

"Revolutionary," I repeated.

"It's an astounding advance," said Frances Blencoe.

"The avant-garde of furniture merchandising in this country," added Strachen, pushing his glasses up his nose. Everyone in the group added their congratulations.

"Let me show you how the thing works," he said. He opened the cage and, with the help of the two Sandras, heaved his fat backside onto the Bulldog's face. It made a squelching sound and the straw from its mouth wheezed and sprayed.

"How about the bite?" asked Ravenski "Does it have a chip inserted?"

"That's not necessary," said Mantle, "we just pull the teeth out; it prevents the reflex snap." He levered himself further onto the bulldogs face so it creaked back on its pegs. "See how stable it is?" The crowd applauded politely and Mantle slipped off the bulldogs face into the arms of his Sandras.

"O.K. Exhibition over," he said, "I need some sleep. Everybody out." He wobbled into the corridor and the dinner party followed him in a ragged line. The bodyguards arrived to take away their charges and Mantle took our hands one by one. His squeezed my fingers into a stump. "Welcome to the family," he said, "our happy little family."

As Cloff bent down to release the breaks I noticed a silver card lying on the stone floor. It was the same card Mantle had used to open the doors of the underground labs and I slipped it into the folds of the wheelchair.

Cloff wheeled me back to the twelfth floor, helped me into the campbed they had set up in my office, and returned to his own mattress outside.

I tried to sleep but the pain in my groin and the stabbing in my teeth was too much and I twisted in my sheets, trapped in the pool of the moon pouring through the tall office windows. In the end I got out of bed, edged over to the wheelchair and took out the stolen silver card. It had no markings, just a smooth metallic finish.

The silence of Priscilla was interrupted as the lifts growled in their shafts. I found my broken snooker cue staff and used it to prop myself up. I found that if I put a pillow over the end I could use it as a crutch and I limped out to Abel's desk. Cloff was asleep beside it, antiseptic cream smeared over his cheeks. He humbugged into his duvet as I went past.

I took the lift straight down to reception. It was deserted except for a couple of police sharing a cigarette at the front entrance. I bobbed through the shadows to the service lift. One of the guards looked round briefly as it opened and then returned his cigarette to his mouth. The pain in my groin could not exceed my determination as I crooked my way, out of the lift, through the empty boardroom and into the furthest passageway. I stopped outside the third door on the left, waved the silver card so the locks slid back and then entered the lab.

I went straight to the room which Mantle had first shown us; the chamber whose shapes had taunted my imagination with a feverish *deja vu*. Inside I saw the pillar, the ribbed canister and the reflective strip. For a moment I was afraid and took a step away but then, like the explorer driven to taste his own fear, I took a stride ahead. The bruised outline of the shapes expanded. I tried to find a light switch but patted uselessly against the wall. I dropped the staff on the stone floor and the sound echoed along a passageway which seemed to lead from this room into further, darker spaces. The echo faded and was replaced by a clanking sound, the sound of hollow metal tubes being hit. It originated near the abstract shapes before me and was being carried above my head, where it resonated, as if captured, until it too pulsed into the dark corridor beyond.

I stopped, waited for the noises to disappear and tried to find my staff. But the staff had rolled from me and I had to follow the wall hand over hand, carefully approaching the shapes. I found a cavity with a switch and when I flicked it the room was emblazoned with a bright white halogen glow. A sound like a muffled breath, a stifled voice, interrupted the buzz of the strip lighting and I turned to see the shapes that were no longer unclear.

I saw a man's leg, a single leg, its pale wasted muscle the pillar of the form. It held up the trunk of a man's body and was covered with a nappy at the groin. The thing's chest was wasted and its ribs were prominent like a canister. On one side it had an arm outstretched. The arm rested on a pipe that led away from the torso, over to the far wall and through a hole. The thing had no left arm and a glass tube entered into the remnants of its armpit carrying a burbling verdant fluid. I traced the tube back to the wall where it passed through to the lab on the other side and I imagined it conveyed the serums from the bench flasks I had seen there. The kind-of-man's head was shaven and its face difficult to define, obscured as it was by a pair of reflective glasses that covered its eyes and most of its nose. Its lips were thin where they had been sewn together with thread. But through a gap in the side of its mouth another tube entered from the ceiling. This pipe carried some kind of compressed gas that drove the respiration of the kind-of-man's naked chest so that it heaved in and out. Underneath the free hand of this kind-of-man, on a wooden rack that propped up the pipe and the arm, were a pencil and a pad of paper. Incongruously, at the bottom of the single leg that held up its torso, was a shiny black shoe.

I was trapped in the halogen light, too frightened to move or to speak. The limbless apparition puffed its cheeks against its sewn lips, making the stifled sound I had heard earlier. It wrote something on the pad of paper. I steadied myself, shuffled along the wall and then craned my neck to see. In a raggedy hand, almost the scrawl of a child, there was written: "I have no ideas left today." And then: "Please tell me where I am?"

On the floor below the pad was a litter of other notes: "Recycling is the answer", "I need to know where I am," "You will lose secrets as you travel", "If this is purgatory then give me hell." And finally cast to one side; "I dreamt that the sky was the sea and the birds were drowning."

I leant against the wall, panting, unable to escape without my staff. And while I waited the man's, the 'thing's' hand knocked against the pipe so the vibrations echoed and rattled along the plumbing. I saw that the pipe diverged into two before it reached the wall, one connection going into the next room, and the other travelling at right angles into the ceiling. I recognised the rhythms and could not help but translate the pitiful Morse and the replies that chimed in return.

"One of them is here."

"How can you tell?"

"They put the light on and it blinds me."

"How can the light blind you when you wear the glasses?"

"The light seeps in and it devours me."

"Save your poetry, save your thoughts, for reason."

"Reason will not give me liberty."

"Nor will your pretty words."

And then the knocking stopped. This, I knew, was the 'Conversation of Plumbing' and here, in front of me, was the Turner print in all its sunset glory, tubed and pumped and ventilated, conducting its messages through Priscilla's foundations and up to my office. Further along the corridor, I knew I would find the Marilyn Monroe tapping out its plaintive aphorisms. I shuffled back from the thing, the kind-of-man. Green fluid slopped into its armpit. I found my snooker cue staff, replaced it as a crutch, and limped into the dark corridor that led further from this room.

The corridor narrowed down to a horizontal shaft that was musty and still. And then, momentarily, I felt a breeze; a reptilian flicker on my cheek. I wondered if this was what the grave robbers felt as they broke the seals of the pyramids, as they leant upon the thousand year breaths of cursed tombs.

I tapped my staff out in front until I felt another entrance to the right and bent down into this space. I found the switch and when I turned on the lights I saw the amputated form of what I guessed to be the Marilyn Monroe, racked up on a wooden shelf with metal pipes. It had a similar structure to its neighbour with a single leg, a naked trunk in a nappy and reflective shades, but this time it had two arms; one resting on the pipe that communicated with the Turner next door, the other, the right, resting on a pipe that went through the opposing wall. The only difference I could see was in the face, in the cheekbones, what I could make of them behind the glasses. They seemed to rise with more prominence, as if the remains of this kind of man's identity was left solely in his starved inverse, the spectre of his emaciated face, the plundered landscape of his expression. Underneath one hand was a blossom of papers, of scribbled memos. The top one read 'The wise are broken by their knowledge.' and then 'The wayward will lead you from the path of fortune,' and, 'Yes I think recycled toilet paper is a good idea.' As with the Turner print, this source of the Marilyn, this fouled spring of the Monroe started to scrawl for me with its pencil: 'Tell me where I am?' it wrote, 'touch me, please' For a moment I wondered about striking it across the body with my staff, releasing it from its mechanical supports, allowing it to breathe one last quick breath. But I did not want to let go of my own prop, to topple inescapably onto the concrete floor of these cells. I did not follow the connecting corridor that led onwards. I turned my back on them, switching off the bright white bulbs as I went.

Cloff was still snoring in his makeshift bed. In my office I thought I could hear the faint twitches of the dawn but I could see no birds through the windows. I imagined them in their concrete perches, planning their flight paths across the empty plaza and I wrapped myself in my blankets, inconsolably weary.

I didn't wake till midday when Cloff arrived with breakfast.

"Where did you get those?" He pointed at the bites on my forearms as I prodded reluctantly at my food.

"A rabid dog," I said. He raised his eyebrows. "I got bitten by a greyhound," I went on. "It was in quarantine for rabies."

"That's a nasty disease. A cousin of mine got it on a trip to Cairo."

"He should have stayed at home where it was nice and quiet," I said.

"I told him but he wouldn't listen."

I gazed through the windows at the intermittent negotiations of the day. My teeth no longer hurt and my groin throbbed only gently but I was feverish with confusion, with the waking dreams of the night.

"You've been through a lot," said Cloff, "I can understand that. I've been beaten about in my time." I glanced at the fading plumes about his eyes. "So if you want to talk?"

I turned away from him and eventually fell asleep. When I awoke again it was night and the sheets were sticky with sweat. Cloff was snoring outside. I limped across to the window. The city lights diffused into an aura that seeped into the office. I felt out the brush of my scalp and imagined it lit with this radiation, a thin green growth. I conceived what I held in my hands; the skull, the brain, the conscious perception that projected these imaginings that led back to my head in my palms, the closed loop of myself. Which was more important, the thoughts or the touch of the fingertips that surrounded them? How could I know, how could I be assured of anything in the unravelling certainties that confounded the day and stripped the night to its pale bones? Everything I had once known had been torn apart in the cells underneath Priscilla. I gazed at the moon and its singular spotlight. The only solution I could fathom was to share what I had seen with someone else, to see if it unravelled their thoughts as it did mine, and allow them into my confused sight.

I went to the toilet and belched and the belch became a wretch and the wretch became vomit and I was sick and then sick again into the pan until I seemed to be expelling a blackness, an artery of ink onto the ceramic. I closed my eyes and opened them and the blackness had gone but the stink of vomit remained. I felt more certain of my reality in its acid stench, splashed my face with water, and limped out of the office.

Cloff wouldn't wake initially and grumbled and mumbled into his pillow, but then he sat upright allowing a dribble of saliva along his chin.

"Whuh?"

"I don't want to talk," I told him.

"Whuh?"

"I don't want to talk."

"You woke me up to tell me you don't want to talk?"

"I need to show you something, to see what you think."

"Now?"

"Yes. Now."

"It's two in the morning." He yawned and stretched his arms and then quickly lowered them again, over his gun holster.

"Downstairs," I said, "In the labs."

"We have to get clearance for the labs. It's…"

"I've got it." I showed him the silver card.

"Where did you get that?"

"I'm part of the family. Look Cloff, I need to see if the lab makes you sick like it makes me sick."

"Nothing makes me sick."

"And I want to bring Ravenski."

"It's two in the morning. Can't we do this tomorrow; I'll speak to Mantle."

"You said you'd help me." I pleaded from where I had knelt by the snooker cue staff.

"Blessed are the meek," he said, "for they shall be pounded into the earth."

"Does that mean you'll go?"

He took out his revolver from its holster and spun the barrel. Bits of black broke off from its spin, turned across the room like cine reel and then fragmented beneath the glare of the artificial lights. He returned the gun to its holster and dressed.

Even before we reached her room I could hear Ravenski's high pitched laughter and I bent to look through the keyhole. Outlined by its hour glass frame I saw a fingernail tracing its way across a muscular chest. I rammed the door with my shoulder and fell into the office. I saw a flushed Frances Blencoe with her hands on a man's bare chest and Ravenski watching them both from behind her desk.

"What's going on?" I demanded from the carpet.

Ravenski took her hand from her lipsticked lips. "I couldn't sleep, so I got Frances over to discuss some recruitment strategies…"

"And him?" I pointed the snooker cue at the bodyguard.

"Brian…"

"Brian?" I broadened my sloping shoulders.

"Brian was telling us how he worked out at the gym. Frances wanted to see and so…" The colour was beginning to fade from her cheeks. Brian did up his shirt and Frances Blencoe stepped back, disappointed.

"I didn't think you were interested in other men", I said, "I thought that all that mattered was the two of us."

"We were just having a chat," said Ravenski, lifting up her chin and showing her single freckle. "So what do you care? You didn't respond to any of my messages."

"I want you to come with me. I need to show you something."

"It's two a.m."

"I want you to come now."

"But I was having a tête-à-tête, a business ratification. I was *enjoying myself.*"

"Do you want to come or not?" She appraised my stoop, my gaunt face and dark eyes and turned back to Brian.

"Well…"

"It's important."

"We can take Brian…"

"Brian can stay here with Frances."

"Good idea," said Frances.

"I need a bodyguard."

"Cloff will look after us."

The detective looked unhappy. "I'm only meant to…"

"Are you coming or not?"

Ravenski pouted and then walked out of the room ahead of us.

"Don't worry," said Frances, "I'll look after Brian." She blew us a kiss with her waxy black lips and it turned into a charred moth that flew into the light bulb and vanished.

"I want you to see something," I said to Ravenski, as the three of us descended in the lift, "I want you to see what I have seen."

"At two in the morning?"

"Well it's obviously O.K. to inspect Brian's torso at two in the morning."

Cloff checked his revolver in the corner.

I prompted them from the reception into the service lift and thence the underground corridor. By the time we'd arrived at the labs, Ravenski was jittery.

"We shouldn't be down here, not now. This is Mantle's patch…"

"He gave me this," I flashed the silver card at a magnetic block. "We're all part of the family now." The door unhinged and we went in. I paused outside the entrance to the first chamber and Cloff searched out the gun by his armpit, a pincer of sweat advancing along the lines of his jaw.

I dragged the moonlight card through its electronic cradle and led them into the darkness of the first cell. I switched on the halogen lamp and the kind of man beat his hand on the pipe underneath so it clanked. This was quickly followed by a "BANG" and I turned to see Cloff with his gun raised. He'd shot out a piece of concrete on the other side of the room. I turned back to see the kind-of-man blowing out his cheeks as if trying to scream through his sewn up lips. He scribbled frantically on the piece of paper beside him.

"What the hell are you doing?" I pointed a finger gun at Cloff who was still trying to aim his shaking revolver. Intermittently my outstretched fingers aligned with his metal barrel.

"I, I, I, don't know…It's…"

"Put the gun down."

Ravenski had fallen to her knees. She gagged and retched. The kind-of-man went on scrawling on his paper.

Cloff lowered his gun and I let my hands fall by my side. "What is it?" he said.

"I don't know." I limped ahead of them. I could see that the kind of man had written: "Isn't it enough to die once?" And then on another notepad: "Perhaps not, perhaps I need to die again." He hit the pipe under his arm and I was reminded of the amputated Marilyn in the cell beyond.

"We have to go further."

"Where?" said Ravenski, she had buried her head in her hands.

"Into the corridor, into the other cells."

"I don't need to see anymore. I've seen enough."

"Not enough to understand." I tapped my staff out. "Onward". Cloff gazed dumbly at the kind of man. "Onward," I repeated. He shook himself and hauled Ravenski to her feet.

I put the light on in the next chamber to find the subhuman already tapping on its pipes. Cloff and Ravenski stood side by side, their heads lowered; as if they could not entirely accommodate the grotesque pinned out before them. Green fluid sloshed along a glass tube that ran below one of the metal pipes and into the things armpit.

"I can't face anymore," said Ravenski.

The amputated Marilyn knocked on the pipe that led into other, as yet unexplored, tombs. Gas hissed through a hose into the mouth of the aberration and its chest billowed with unsettling smoothness.

"We've come this far," I said. "We have to see what Mantle is making."

"We don't need to know anything," said Ravenski, her voice breaking, "we can blank it out, close it off. I've learnt and you must learn too."

"We can't ignore *this*."

"Why not?"

"We can't turn away from ourselves."

"It's research," said Cloff, "Mr Mantle's project…"

"It's a perversion," I said and turned to Ravenski. She looked at me, her eyes brimming with tears, and I was reminded again of our first meeting on the shop floor. "We need to take one more step, to see ourselves outside ourselves."

"I can't," she said, "leave me behind." She found out the shine of her shoes and I limped to the next room alone.

The passageway was so low it pressed against my head and the walls crowded against my shoulders, holding me up. I threw away my staff and the sound echoed ahead, beckoning. The passageway opened into a wider space and when I found the light switch I screamed.

I saw not a kind-of-man but a kind-of-woman; it was propped up on one leg with the other missing. Both arms were outstretched; the left over a pipe with its attendant glass tube connecting with the last room, the right over a pair of ducts going through the next wall. The hips were covered with a pair of nappies and at the chest was a crepe bandage pressing the breasts flat. The eyes were covered with the same mirrored glasses, the head was shaven and the lips were sewn. But what made me cry out in horror was not this expected grotesque but the remains of a more familiar acquaintance. For what I was seeing was not just a kind-of-woman but someone whom I recognised from the strong thighs, the long nose, the full features and the bronzed skin to be Ibore Davidson.

Facing the remains of Ibore, on a stand, was a pair of lips balanced one side, a spiral of hair above it. I looked from the nappies to the flesh on the stand. Behind me I could hear Mantle's voice, "I've got an idea," and then repeating this, "I've got an idea," again and again in a loop. I turned and saw his image projected on a huge screen on the wall. He was penetrating the organ on the stand, what I could only presume was Ibore's disembodied vagina. The coitus played in a loop in front of Ibore. Each time Mantle reached his shivering climax, he screamed "I've got an idea" and a line of saliva fell from his thin red lips before the act began again, Mantle shunting himself against the excised pubis. I turned back to Ibore and saw the image reflected in the mirrored glasses that covered her eyes, looping its endless desolate horror. I was aware of my breath, in and out, across my teeth, and I forced the air out stronger, harsher, and I howled long and loud and terrified, my voice resonating with Mantle's astonished climax.

Ravenski and Cloff ran into the cell. Cloff once more used his revolver to divine the shadows before pointing it at the apparition of Ibore.

"It's Ibore…" I managed.

The tubes gurgled and the kind of woman began to tap a message into the networking of pipes; an uncertain beat whose code I could not transcribe. It was as if Ibore were searching out a new understanding, an elementary language. Even from where I had fallen I could see she had scribbled endless question marks on the paper squares; defeated hieroglyphics.

Behind us Mantle said over and over, "I've got an idea, I've got an idea, I've got an idea," sputtering, red faced, slow then fast, his belly syncopated with his hips, his hands gripping the metal stand, unashamed in his degradation, riding the automated rodeo of his own fascination, the squalid king of his empire.

The cinematic light fell over all of us, playing off the cheekbones of Ibore, heightening them, transforming her into a sculpted icon, a cameo defamed before her. And Ravenski cried into her hands and Cloff struggled to breathe and Mantle echoed over and over, "I've got an idea, I've got an idea, I've got an idea."

And then this all of this was interrupted. "DON'T MOVE."

I glanced over my shoulder and saw Ravenski with her hands raised above her head and then Cloff, pointing his gun at the ceiling, and behind the both of them, Ballistrade the scientist, aiming a shaking revolver between the three of us.

I ran past him. He fired and the bullet rang off the ceiling and between Ravenski and Cloff. I escaped into the corridor and ran on. I ran past room after shadowed room, empty but for their wooden shelves with tubes and pipes, unconnected, awaiting new kinds-of-men, new kinds-of-women to be plumbed and strapped into their steadying racks. I tripped and fell into an empty chamber, kneeling before the stocks. I held my head in my hands, holding the skull, the china shell that conjured my imagination. And then I heard Ballistrade's voice behind me, penitent and fearful: "We need to talk, in private, in the changing room."

Chapter 12

‹ The Changing Room →

Ballistrade guided us back to the lab. He closed the door on the network of tombs and it seemed for a moment that he was closing the seal on my dreams and I was awakening to an artificial day, strip light bright. We went through the operating suite where only a couple of days before Ballistrade had applied his scalpel, and on into the changing room.

My accomplices were quivering. Cloff walked with one arm wrapped around his chest, as if holding it in, one hand pressed against the gun holster under his armpit. Part of Ravenski's black bob was pressed against the side of her cheek, stuck there with sweat or tears. Ballistrade directed us to a bench that ran on one side of the changing room and took a seat opposite. He had rolled the white sleeves of his lab coat past his elbows and a layer of slime had attached itself to the down on his forearms. His glasses, as ever, were smeared like lab dishes. He removed them and finding that his sleeves were folded back, rubbed the lenses with the crease of his trousers. He looked at me with red eyes. "This is the only place that they can't hear or," he blinked at me, "watch us."

"But only the boardroom and reception have surveillance," said Cloff.

"This whole place has surveillance. Believe me, I installed it."

"Why the gun?"

"I thought you were liberationists, from outside," said Ballistrade, "and I've been working so hard I've not been concentrating…" He removed the revolver from his white coat pocket and fumbled for the safety latch.

Cloff took it from him, flicked open the barrel and slid out the bullets. "You don't know how to use this do you?"

"I'm only a scientist," said Ballistrade. He gazed at the weapon in a daze and then brushed at the dried slime on his sleeves, as if technology was something that just went off in his hand.

"What were those things we saw?" I said, intimating the tombs beyond the changing room.

"We went too far, I know. It's what Mr. Mantle wanted and he's the one who pays the bills; Mantle and the reciprocals."

"The reciprocals aren't the players," said Ravenski, "it's us, we're the…"

"The reciprocals have always been the managers; under Mr Mantle's guidance and so…"

"Baloney," said Ravenski, "the executives run this company…"

"Does it matter?" I said. "Did you see what was going on in those tombs or were you too afraid?" She remained thin lipped. "So?" I said to Ballistrade.

"So I went too far. And once you go that extra mile, you snap the binds that hold you and you keep on drifting. That," he pointed beyond the changing room door, "is Mr Mantle's vision; a stable of creatives perpetuated and designed for the company's profit. Using the latest," he adjusted his rolled up sleeves, "technology."

"So they're connected?"

"They are the first part of a system - cells, in a powerhouse of a brain, linked by the serums, the biochemical elixirs that my lab produces. They sustain each other in an easy to maintain physical grid while the company reaps the harvest of their minds…"

"And they talk with each other?"

"On no," he looked up, "Each is in a separate cell."

"But they *do* communicate," I said, "I've heard them talking through the pipes, in Morse code."

"That's not part of the design, perhaps there's a fault with the connecting…"

"Who are they?"

"I, I'm not sure."

"The last one, the kind-of-woman, it used to be Ibore Davidson didn't it?"

Ballistrade, who had long been blinking back some tears now released the flow and great gobs of pity fell to his lap. "What am I meant to do? They brought her in after the assassination. She was nearly dead. They were asking about the mortuary. So I've been keeping her..," a tear glistened on the ceramic floor, "keeping her alive."

"You call that life?"

"It was all she had left. It was Mantle who did the filming, I couldn't…" He began to break down again.

"What about the other two. Who were they?"

"I don't know. The reciprocals brought them in. They were in a bad way." He sobbed. "They signed contracts to say they agreed, they nodded when I asked them. And then…"

"Then?"

"Mr Mantle was in the theatre." Ballistrade looked at the changing room door. "He forced me to do it. I didn't want to go that far, but he told me to do it and I am his employee, I, I, I…" He began to gasp, breathing too hard to sob.

The three of us watched him silently. I could tell by their eyes that they too had seen what they had always known but never registered; the terror at the edge of their existence, the contortion that they had never dared confront that was now bold before them.

"What were you doing here, so early in the morning?"

"I…I, I was working overtime," said Ballistrade, "to, to, to finish your projects."

"Forget the projects."

Ravenski looked up. "Forget them? But they've got to be ready for Christmas, they're the new merchandising line."

"I think we need to do some thinking," I looked at each of my accomplices in turn, "about our role in the company. And then we can meet back here, tomorrow."

Ballistrade sniffed. Ravenski and Cloff paused and then nodded.

"What do I do," said Ballistrade, "when Mantle finds out we've been down here?"

"Tell him we've been checking up on the new product line, for Christmas." I felt myself imbued with authority. My balls pulsed in their stitched cavities.

When I awoke, later that day, it was with a new sense of purpose. I kicked away the snooker cue staff and got up by myself. Then I swept everything off the desktop; the accumulated bric-a-brac of plastic cups and memos. I folded up my shirt sleeves and noticed the dog bites. They had healed but I was reminded of my greyhound with the silver stripe. I imagined him staring up at me, forlorn, waiting to clasp his incisors deep into my arm from his quarantine. "Bring him here," I thought, "bring him here to snap at my heels..."

I wrote down the address of the kennel and the dog's description and gave the note to Cloff, who, after shrugging his perpetually shrugged shoulders, said he would see what he could do. I was about to start work on a manifesto, an anarchy of the memo, when Abel arrived with his manuscript box.

"I haven't got time," I said, "there are more important things."

"More important than my masterpiece?"

"Than you could ever realise."

"Than I could ever realise?" He asked loudly.

"Shhh."

"Are you insinuating that I have no sensibility, that my perceptive pores are clogged?"

"You don't understand, Abel. There are stranger things afoot than god or beast could imagine."

Abel lay his box on the desk and lowered his voice to a whisper to match mine. "The word is god and this," he rested his hand on the container, "is the completed prophecy."

"But you've only written two pages."

"It's a novella."

I sighed and rolled back from my desk in the swivel chair. "Let's hear it then."

"If you insist." Abel removed his second and third sheets and cleared his throat. "'Roy has just been fouled by one of his own team but no one could hear him in the roar of the crowd...'" Abel raised the paper to eye level: "'He picked himself up and ran, blind to the pain, dribbling and passing and shooting but always attacking. At half time, the team were ready to give up but Roy wouldn't relent. He led his team onto the pitch with a battle cry, punching towards the floodlights. He ignored Duncan and limped as he ran the ball from deep in his own half. The game went into extra time and as Roy watched the last minutes slip away into darkness he wondered if the teams would draw. To Roy this would be worse than defeat; to be delivered into mediocrity. The game wasn't about standing firm; it was about winning against the odds. It was death or glory, black or white. He screamed for his team to push ahead and girded himself for one last charge. The Rover's full back passed it wide to the sweeper who lined it to the winger who volleyed it over the opposition's penalty box. Roy sprinted to the falling target as the goalie raced up. Roy leapt and his golden boot searched for the ball that hung in the air like a floating punctuation.'" Abel stopped and lowered his sheets, breathless with his own oration.

"So," I said, "what happens?"

"You'll have to wait."

"Fair enough."

"Nothing is fair in sex and war."

"Isn't it love and war?"

"You've been reading the wrong books, mate."

Abel left with his box. He seemed for a moment serious in his familiarity, as if finally weary of his pretensions.

I returned to my manifesto but couldn't get beyond the first point, which was 'Out with the old'. I struck it off and wrote 'Out with the new'. And then crossed this through and scribbled; 'Out with whatever has gone before', until deciding on 'Out with what has gone before and will go thereafter'.

I gazed through the office windows at the banalities of the plaza, the strolling couples and the few trees in their concrete beds bowing with the breeze. I meditated on the scene and watched the clouds idle in the swimming pool of the sky. Black patches clogged the cumuli like mud and then vanished.

Cloff put his mouth close to my cheek, so I could feel the damp on his breath. "I found the dog."

"And?"

"It's dead. They told me it had Rabies; it frothed at the mouth, went mad and flung itself at the cage. They had to shoot it." Cloff took my wrist. "These bites, they're from the dog aren't they?"

"Yes."

"So you've got Rabies?"

"Who knows?" I bubbled through the saliva of our intimacy.

Cloff backed away. "You should get a vaccination."

"I've had them…"

"Rabies isn't nice you know. You go mad and froth and fit and…"

"I don't need to be told."

"I think you should lie low. In quarantine."

"There's no time."

"No time for what?"

"To wait."

"To wait for what?"

I wrote in tiny letters on a memo slip and pushed it across the desk.

"Revolution," it said. He wrote underneath: "I'm no revolutionary."

I scrawled in biro: "Not revolution, revulsion." I wrapped one arm around my chest and lifted up the other, in mime of the atrocity below Priscilla. "Are you going to turn your cheek?"

"Who do you think you are, Che Guevara?"

"No," I wrote, "Just another schmuck with, who knows," I lifted my bites, "a couple of weeks to live?"

"So," he blotted the pen into the paper, "you're a schmuck with a death wish."

"A life wish."

"You romantics always die in the end," he wrote, "and die early, there's never been any point in that."

"Better to die in life."

"You," scribbled Cloff and paused, "are beginning to disappear up your own arse."

"No, I'm appearing where you can't be arsed to look." We stopped and stared at each other. "So," I mouthed, "are you with me?"

"Blessed are the meek…"

"…for they will be pounded into the earth."

Cloff pulled at his disjointed nose. I reached over and twisted it in the opposite direction so it fractured with a snap. He screamed and blood poured from his nostrils.

"I think you need to examine your priorities." I led him outside the office and left him alone, praying into the blood of his hands.

*

I was saddened by the death of the greyhound. The dog had been close to my purpose in its savage bites. The scars no longer brought me the same pain and reward but that no longer seemed to matter. For now I had no compulsion, no addiction to the bite. I felt out the points of my molars like the indents of a franking machine. "Bruphalution" I said out loud and then removed my fingers: "Revolution."

My nose was filled with a sudden stink of decay, the same foul stench I had experienced in my first few weeks at Priscilla. I got down onto my knees and sniffed around the office until I came to the wall nearest the Turner Painting. It wasn't hard to pull away the polystyrene tiles to reveal the gap underneath. There amidst the pipes and cables I came across the rotting carcass of a dog. The flesh had wasted so its ribs stuck out like the inverted 'U's of a saucer rack. Its head hung over a loop of electrical cable, its ears like rags, its tail snapped back on itself like a broken aerial. It had no castors but here and there its claws had crooked back where it had been scrambling to free itself.

I prodded the corpse with my snooker cue staff. Then I levered it out from where it had become tangled among the wires and pipes over to a free space in the partition but it slipped off and fell into the floors below. I could hear its bones cracking and breaking as it tumbled into the recesses of Priscilla.

My back ached and I went and lay on the desk and gazed into the coiled moon of the light bulb above. And then I turned to look through the windows. The vista was outshone by the glow of the bulb, which still lingered in the backcloth of my eyes, silhouetting the blood vessels of my vision so they seemed to weave into the plaza like wires. "Revolution," I said. I began to cry and the tears made me blink, shorting and blurring the capillaries of my sight; a breach of grief for the greyhound with the silver striped muzzle and expectant gaze, for the rotting dog in the wall, for the rabid blood that beat through my veins.

Abel was listening at the door. "What did you say?"

I slipped off the desk. "Nothing." The afterglow of the light bulb faded and his outline materialized, holding the manuscript box under his arm.

"What are you doing?" he went on.

"Nothing."

"I don't know what they pay you for."

"They pay me to be a bull in the china shop."

"Are you acquainted with the pastime of bull baiting?"

"No."

"The bulldog is pinned and shaken by the bull but its back remains unbroken because it is bred to have its weight at the head."

"Oh."

"They carry on biting even with their guts hanging out."

"I've no time for history lessons, Abel. Important work to do." I started to push him to the door but he was resolute, juddering back on his heels.

"Even when they're blind and bloody. It's the training."

"Interesting…" I'd managed to force him to the door but couldn't quite push him over the threshold.

"Of course they made a bill to outlaw the whole thing but it was thrown out of parliament. "Any law which interferes with how a man chose to spend his leisure is tyranny." Abel squeezed his shoulders into the gap as I tried to shut the door.

"Profound."

"I'm going to read you the last sentence of my novel."

"It can wait."

"It's the zenith; the denouement."

I managed to push the door past his shoulders but he inserted his head into the space remaining between lock and frame.

"It's not important anymore," I said.

"Nothing is more important than what I have imagined." I closed his shaven skull in the vice of the doorway.

"You'd better go before I crush your head."

"Then do it," he said with a sudden fury. "See how far you're prepared to go." I put my weight against the panel and it seemed to give beneath the spring of his skull. He was silent.

"Abel, Abel?"

"My mind is too powerful for you Velour." I released the door handle, retreated to the window and turned my back on him. "You *really* don't want to listen to my final sentence do you?"

"Give it to me then."

"Why should I give it to you when you don't even have the decency to look me in the eye?"

I turned to face him. "For god's sake Abel, just GIVE IT TO ME."

Abel lifted his chin and the hairs at the exhaust of his nostrils fluttered. He flipped open his manuscript box, pulled out a rivet gun, and let the case fall to the floor.

"Garrick?" I said.

"Yes." He said, with uncharacteristic brevity and a deeper voice.

"The Animal Liberation Liberationist?"

"Yes."

"Please don't…"

But he had already raised his gun, drill like, to the buttress of his shoulder. He positioned himself so he was directly in front of the desk and curled his finger about the trigger.

"PLEASE…"

He fired, aiming just past my head, so the rivets broke the window pane to my right. I closed my eyes and waited for the next round to track across and crucify me. But there were no further shots and I opened one eye and then the other to see Abel, now Garrick the Animal Liberation Liberationist, returning the rivet gun to its manuscript box.

"Move across to the window," he hissed

"What?"

"Through the window."

"So this is it," I said, "I am to fall to my death."

"Hurry."

I walked with my hands above my head in way that I hoped suggested some kind of martyrdom. But there was no cold wind blowing in through the window. In fact the space where the glass had been was now a black cavity. In the adjacent panels, the day continued its parabolic observations. I saw a seagull swoop and a man roll an empty wheelchair across the plaza. It was as if the world had loosened a single tile in its presentation.

"Hurry." Garrick cajoled me into the black space of the broken window. I waited to fall to my death but instead felt the crush of glass beneath my feet. Up close I could see red wires weaving like threadworms into a sheet of circuit board; a model city of microchips. "Right," said Garrick, "behind the screens." He ushered me into the apparent space between the remaining windows and the circuit panels behind.

"Screens?" I asked when we were finally hidden behind the illusory glass.

"Every window is a screen," he said, "and every screen looks at you."

"At me?"

"The screens are electronic magnifying lenses just like every other transparency in this building. We can only talk with confidence in the gap behind them."

"So you're not going to kill me."

"No." Garrick sat on his manuscript box. I looked at him more closely. His eyebrows were heavy over his eyes and the dark shadow beneath now seemed to form a stripe, a mask across his gaze. He fiddled with some of the circuit wires and took out a soldering iron from his jacket. "I have to make them think the screen isn't broken and erase the memory of my rivet gun."

"If you're Garrick," I said, "then who was Abel?"

"Abel was a cover; a thinly painted disguise." He didn't look up from the intricacies of his soldering work.

"So you were never a writer?"

"Abel's pretension allowed me to manoeuvre my way into this organisation. You never even had a secretary."

"But you were on the payroll."

"I have many friends in many places."

"So why didn't you kill me?" I took a step to one side and the glass crunched like gravel.

"I could see that you had had enough of the biology of decadence."

"But you killed McCloy?"

"Yes, I riveted McCloy but he'd defected. He used to be on our side."

"Whose side?"

"McCloy was an Animal Liberation Liberationist, one of our brightest and bravest, until he was…seduced."

"Seduced?"

"He joined Pet Furnishings as a dog walker and accelerated his way up the company ladder, but it soon became clear he had decided to live as a fully paid executive with all its trappings of power and perversion."

"So you killed him?"

"We had no choice. He was about to release vast amounts of information that would have resulted in the downfall of my organisation."

"And what is your organisation?"

"I work alone, among many. I am but one part of the web."

"That sound's very serious."

"It is very serious." He looked at me seriously. I felt Abel had a better sense of irony.

"But did you have to murder McCloy. Couldn't you just silence him?"

"It was better that he was dead."

"Better dead?"

"Better to be dead than remain half alive."

"Like?"

"Like Miss Davidson."

"So you assassinated Ibore as well?"

"We didn't kill Ibore Davidson. It was Howard Mantle."

"Mantle assassinated Ibore?"

"She was a thorn in his side. The reciprocals felt she was far too provocative and, so I'm told, she refused to sleep with Howard Mantle."

"She refused?"

"Like I said, she was a 'thorn'."

"So he had her killed? And then kept alive underground?"

"He imprisoned her body so he could steal her thoughts."

"And the others? The kind-of-men I saw downstairs?"

"They were other executives who had become too wayward with their desires. Mantle kept them alive so he could reap their imagination from the pyre of their bodies. One of them was your predecessor. In fact he used to have this office…until his name was taken from the door."

I tried to swallow. "Are these things, these kind-of-men, are they still alive?"

"In a way." A puff of smoke drifted from where Garrick had attached a severed wire to the circuit board. "They were resurrected from death but not to a new life. They were born into captivity, into the company's violent bridle."

"But why should you care about them? You're an Animal Liberation Liberationist."

"I don't… up to a point. But, as both you and I are discovering, there is a no man's land where the two horrors meet." He stood up and we were silent as the screens hummed.

"I'm sorry I stuck your head in the door."

"I'm a tough nut to crack." He lowered the walnut join of his quiff and for a moment I saw a glimpse of Abel's irreverence.

"So what now?" I asked.

"Revolution. Like you said in your office."

"But I'm not sure what I mean."

"It is not the means. It is the end. We have decided on the outcome and the process will take care of itself." He stroked his quiff, picked up his manuscript box and began to ease himself out from behind the screens.

"Wait." I held onto his case. "Some of us are meeting tonight. You should come."

"Who will be there?"

"Ravenski, Cloff and Ballistrade. They've seen what I've seen. They too have been sickened."

"And you expect me to trust them?"

"I trust them and you trust me."

"Trust is not a transferable commodity."

"If there is going to be some kind of *Revolution*," I lowered my voice, "then there has to be some kind of subversion. And we are all on the inside. If we are going to subvert something, isn't the best way to do so from within? What more valuable revolutionaries could you have than two executives, the top science advisor and a head of security?"

"Every subversive can be seduced. Look at McCloy."

"So what will you do then, sit back and wait for the revolution?"

"Do I look like I sit back?" Garrick raised his manuscript box, a chancellor of the anarchists.

"Then join us."

"Very well but only as Abel. I will show myself only when I am ready." He tipped his hand to his quiff and stepped out of the screen and into the office.

"What about the end of your story?"

"If you can't be bothered to listen to the end of my tale Mr Velour I will find a tale that will listen to my end." His face transformed into the disgruntled snobbery of Abel and he flounced from the office.

I tiptoed out from the electronic gap, disorientated by events that continued to unravel like a ribboning flag.

Later that evening, Cloff returned. He had a large box bandage tied around his nose and strapped behind his head.

"You deserted your post," I said.

"That's because my pode broke my nobe."

"Blessed are the meek," I said.

"But I dobe exped the man I'm meb to be guarbing to beab me ub."

"I wasn't beating you up I was just putting you straight."

"By braykin my nobe?"

"Look just calm down. Follow me."

I led him, carefully, through the broken screen and explained to him what Garrick had explained to me. He didn't appear to be too shocked and was more concerned about his nose.

"Dab dubn't excube you doing dib."

"It's good to see you angry, for a change."

"I'm nob angbee."

"Yes you are."

"Dis ibn't some gaymb, You boke my nobe."

"So where did you run off to?"

"I web to the hobital. Ib wab buddy painfub."

"I bet I straightened your nobe though." I went to press his bandage.

"Geb off. I'm going to garb you outsibe when you can't geb nerb me." He shuffled out from behind the screens and returned to his makeshift bed in the reception.

I lay down on my own campbed and slept, waking punctually for the changing room meeting. The artificial moon waned in its glow, as if the generators that powered its spotlight were finally beginning to fuse.

I had to wake Cloff and he covered his nose with both hands. "I'm not going to pound you," I said, "I promise." Garrick, manifesting as Abel, walked out from the shadows with his manuscript box.

"Where'b he'b cum fromb?" said Cloff.

"He's part of the team."

"I'm writing a political pamphlet."

"We cab trust hib?"

"More than you think."

Reluctantly Cloff followed us and we collected Ravenski from her bodyguard, pretending we had a late night meeting. After one more discussion as to Abel's trustworthiness we took the lifts down to the underground lab where Ballistrade was already waiting.

He gave us cups of mint tea and took us to the changing room.

"Is it really safe in here?" said Abel.

"Safe enough," said Ballistrade.

Abel knocked on the walls and appeared satisfied. "I don't want my readership to know I'm engaged in illegal activities..."

"We hab moreb imporbant fibs to fib abub," said Cloff.

Ravenski swigged her tea. "We're not here to think. We should bite the bullet. We should make a plan."

"Why?"

"So we can flag up all the points that need discussion."

"The labs," said Ballistrade.

"My nobe," said Cloff.

"My book," said Abel.

"The agenda," said Ravenski.

I felt a rage growing inside me, a violent proposition. I leapt to my feet between the two benched ranks and as I stood I felt my blood surge also. I felt it rushing through residual organs and opening closed valves as if to some vestigial pathway, long sealed but now connected between the dog's testicle in my groin, the bladder stone and the cotton wool in my cheeks. I experienced the same aura of giddy elation that used to precede my Brief Periods of Evangelism. It was as if the dormant circuit that had once flickered as religious fits was now complete and flowing.

"LISTEN," I marked the change in myself and in the room, "we will get nowhere by talking." I raised my fists high above my head, the bites a shining weal. "There is no time to discuss this. Death lies like a shadow before us. We must break this company apart and the perversions its stands for. If not at once, then piece by piece."

"Piece by piece?" Ballistrade looked up from under his glasses.

"There are two components to this company. There is what we have seen in the underground labs, the contradictions of a man plumbed into his own purgatory. And then there is everything beyond, outside..." I spread my arms as if to implicate the whole city. "Dogs hammered into furniture, pounded into lounges, a slow embracing, a numbing of disgust."

Abel regarded me with a touch of Garrick's admiration. Ravenski however was not convinced. "Dogs?" she said. "There's nothing wrong with dog furniture; it's been around for years."

"Ballistrade, bring me Mantle's Bulldog."

The scientist left, his white coat crackling with dried blisters of slime, and returned with the Bulldog pouffe. He could only just hold the cage in the reach of his arms and he lowered it awkwardly onto the tiles.

"Ravenski, kneel."

"Don't talk to me like that."

"You have to see." I knelt with her, so we were both on the tiles.

"It's a mutt," she said.

"More closely." I prised apart the dog's skin, pulling back the eyelids, so Ravenski could see the wideness of the pupil; its blank gaze.

"Now what do you see?"

"Zippo, nothing."

"LOOK."

"A bit of crust in the corner of ...'"

"Again."

"I see, I see the reflection of myself," she said "and.....I see some pain. Mine or the dogs. I don't know."

"Both." I let go of the dog and the folds of skin whelped back. "Now the rest of you." I forced each of them to gaze at the bulldog, pulling apart the fat skin around its eyes. Each looked and saw, or said they saw and returned, I imagined, to more humble seats. "We must liberate our understanding, then we can liberate the dogs, then we can liberate ourselves." The words echoed into each other and Ravenski shook her head as if trying to shake off them off. "We need to set up a guerrilla group. I will be captain. Abel will be my second in command."

"Abub?" said Cloff.

"You and Ravenski will be lieutenants. Ballistrade will be scientific advisor."

"You make it sound like a war," said Ravenski.

"The time for indecision is over." I stood between them with my bite scarred arms, hands on hips. "Let us be guerrillas; fusiliers of the first fallen temple. But we need more disciples, and for that we will need more evidence. Ballistrade, you have a camera?"

"Yes…"

"You will take pictures of the executive atrocities and the latest designer dogs. We will use these to recruit in the underground."

"But what if I'm found?"

"Do you wish to return to your experiments?"

He buttoned his white coat. "No."

"Anyone who is not prepared to go into battle should leave now." There was a shifting of backsides but otherwise silence. "This..," I surveyed the bedraggled scientist, the bemused lover, the beaten up detective, the disguised radical, "is where the resistance starts." The bulldog made rasping noises through the straw in its mouth.

"I'm not shub," said Cloff.

I held him by the bandage on his nose.

"Owb," he said as I started to unravel it. "Leave mib alone."

He struggled as I unwound the dressing but Abel held him down. "There," I said and made him put his hand on the swollen nose, "it's straight. Broken back upon itself. Now is the time for vengeance, not for reticence."

I turned to Abel, "We have shown our true colours. How about you?"

"Very well." The liberationist lifted his substantial nose into the air. "I am not Abel. I am Garrick the Animal Liberation Liberationist." He flipped open his manuscript box to reveal his rivet gun.

The other three sucked in bellows of air and felt out their chests, as if fearful the liberationist might rivet them, there and then.

"Garrick is one of us," I said, "There's nothing to worry about."

"And who the hell are we?" said Ravenski.

"Bitten by the dog," I crossed my chest with a scarred forearm.

"What does that mean?"

"We either do or die."

"How can we trust Garrick; the man's an anarchist?"

"Isn't it clear that we cannot trust this company? If we want to do something about this," I lifted my hands back, palm up, as if trying to bear the weight of Priscilla tower, "we have to trust each other. If you cannot trust Garrick then you cannot trust me and you must go." Again there was some general shifting of backsides but no desertion. "Ballistrade," I nodded at the scientist, "you will take the photographs. Cloff will pick them up at first light."

"First light?" said Ballistrade with the weariness of a man who has worked too many dawns.

"Overtime. Payback for the revolution."

"Bullshit," said Cloff.

I rubbed at my goatee and wondered if it might be taking on a weightier curl; the beginnings of an herbaceous growth, a Castro border. "No more bull than that in a china shop. ARE WE TOGETHER," I demanded, "ARE WE?" There was a slow chorus of assent. I punched a bitten arm towards the ceiling. "Let the revolution begin." Black wisps advanced at the margins of my sight, multiplied and spiralled into thin air.

I awoke with the light of the projected sun on my windows but I no longer drifted into the aimless siesta of previous months and met early with Garrick, who I continued to address as Abel. We slid into the space behind the windows as he made the pretence of selling me his latest literary idea: "I want my book to be made into stocking fillers so babies can be inoculated with my genius against the comic book trash of adolescence."

Once behind the screens, we returned to my plans of revolution. "I want to unchain the perversions in the underground labs, liberate those enslaved in the purgatory of pipes and free them from the puppet threads of life."

"And the dogs?"

"When the first manacles on the pipes are broken, we will begin our offensive outside," I pointed through the electronic wall, "liberating the dogs."

"All of them?"

"We will work suburb by suburb, pack by pack, until they too are released." The office door squeaked announcing Cloff's arrival. I ushered him through behind the windows and he shuffled into the narrow mechanical space. He had photos of the kind-of-men in their underground cells together with the latest dog devices sprouting tubes and straws. They were suitably horrific. I divided the pictures between Cloff and Garrick.

"We will use these to recruit to the cause using our underground contacts." I saluted them both with a bitten forearm. "Go. Get."

Chapter 13

Recruitment Consultancy

I invited the Martial Arts Mop Dance troupe to my room. They were a little confused to be invited but arrived nevertheless in their boiler suits carrying their multiracheted mops.

"I have to say," I addressed them, "I was very impressed by your lunchtime display on the plaza."

Their leader, Tony, cast a forlorn glance at the windows and the black space of the broken pane. His straw hair had been startled into a brush as if shocked by some magnetism. "We didn't do a performance," he said, "We didn't get permission; the company said it would be too inflammatory."

"Well, things are never what they seem, from up here. Now, I'd like to discuss your mop techniques and how they might be a valuable asset to the company. If you'd just like to step this way." I led them across and then through the broken window. Eventually the whole troupe, Tony, Jessica, James, Terry and Tricia, had lodged themselves behind the fractured frame with just enough space for each of us to stand side by side.

"Don't be too concerned, it's for our privacy." They moved closer, mops pressed to their shoulders, and I showed them the photos of the atrocities which they passed along the line. I spent another thirty minutes explaining the perversions of Pet Furnishings. Eventually I laid down my proposition: "We are to be the first stone in the avalanche of revolution, will you join our crusade?"

"Well," said Tony, "we come from a workers background and this isn't really a workers issue. It's about animal rights."

"Human rights," I corrected them, nodding at the photos.

"I agree that these are terrible things," said Tony, "but they don't directly affect the cleaners, on the factory floor."

I pressed the pictures to his cheek. "Can't you see? This is your fellow man and woman hammered into perversions of themselves."

"We need to have a meeting."

"This is the meeting. Here, now."

"But it's our jobs," said Jessica quietly, "we need the money. We can't afford a revolution."

"Can't afford this? Can't afford to rage against the destruction of yourselves?"

"We need time to think."

"No, NOW. The meeting is now. If we do not act now, lives will fall away, voices will weaken into hollow mouths." I elbowed the mop head Tony was holding, tilting him and setting a ripple of disturbance down the line. "Look," I gave him a photo of Ibore Davidson tubed and amputated and blinded. "Now imagine yourself here, connected to the chemistry set of their setting sun. IMAGINE. Power up your minds." They passed the photo from one to the other. "So," I repeated, "are you with, or against us?" Tricia, who hadn't said anything, bobbed her mop at the far end of the line and her colleagues followed, turning back a ripple of agreement that reflected onto their leader, Tony. He sighed like an unblocked drain.

"With you," he said, "in fear, but with you." His mop dripped black spots onto his forearm, which dribbled down his elbow, and then disappeared.

"To be afraid is to be alive," I said, "and to be alive, in this company, is revolution." They left quietly, gripping their mops with bright knuckles.

I met up with the Ugly Guitar Band in the underground car park where Cloff had led them. They were carrying their instruments in hard plastic cases and were dressed in jeans and casual shirts. They looked like off-duty mobsters.

"I found them busking," said Cloff, "in the City."

"Is this a safe place to talk?" Even my whisper echoed through the concrete spaces. In the distance I could see a car park attendant lighting up a cigarette in the cup of his hands.

"Behind the skip," said Cloff, "Ballistrade says that's a blind spot for surveillance. We need to hurry; security will miss us from the roll call." Cloff led the group to a dumpster on the lowest floor. Wheelie bins lay tipped over at its mouth like spat teeth.

"This is one weird Gig," piped up a band member with a hairy mole on his cheek as they were ushered into the narrow space behind the skip. It smelt of rotting fruit.

"So what do you want?" said a man with only a few brown teeth.

"I want you to join me in a revolution."

I explained the horrors of Pet Furnishings, passing out the photos of the underground perversions.

"Horrible," agreed bad teeth, "but what can we do, we're just a band?"

"You make the music of revolution."

"We play discordant songs to passers by who toss us a few coins to help us pay the rent."

"I will pay you," I said, "to be part of the revolution. And if you no longer want to be part of it. Then you can leave."

"I don't like the sound of revolution even if *we* are the sound of revolution," said big chin, "it's too dangerous."

"But what if it pays our rent?" said foul teeth.

"How much money?" said big chin.

"Lots of money?" queried poppy out eyes.

"Lots." I imagined the barely plumbed depths of my dog card. There was much scratching of ugly features.

"Perhaps we could get ourselves another shop," said big chin, "put down a deposit."

"Shop? I thought you were musicians," I said.

"We were a cooperative of barbers," he explained, "in the East End. But when it came to renew the lease we were outbid by a glamorous hairdressing group; "Chip Chop: Smart Sculptings for the Smart Generation." The band winced. "The only skill we had left, apart from our scissors, was Barber Shop Singing; we were in a Barber Shop Quintet."

"Except we couldn't sing," said hairy mole.

"Or play our instruments," said bad teeth.

"The only thing we had going for us," added big chin, "is that we were angry."

"Very angry," said poppy out eyes, "and ugly."

"Ten years of fine barbership and we were on the streets with no trade."

"So we formed the Ugly Guitar Band," continued poppy out eyes.

"People pay us to keep quiet." Bad teeth put both fingers in his ears to illustrate.

"We can't help it," hairy mole shrugged his shoulders. "Every time we try and sing our Barbershop Quintet…"

"…with Guitars…"

"…with Guitars. It just comes out as this loud, wailing racket."

"Its good fun though," said poppy out eyes, "cathartic." They all agreed.

I silenced them. "That is the sound," I said, "I want to harness for revolution."

"A dangerous revolution," said bad teeth.

"One that pays well," I said, "with cash."

The group patted out unsyncopated patterns on their cases and formed a huddle.

"I don't know what use they're going to be," Cloff said, "they can't even make it busking."

"They will be part of the consensus of anarchy."

"You're making no sense," said Cloff, "as usual."

"Sense is the enemy of change and nonsense is the powder keg of disorder."

"If you say so."

"I am the Capitan."

The huddle reformed into a line. "O.K. we'll do it," said Bad Teeth, "but we want to see some cash, up front."

"Of course."

The Ugly Guitar Band offered their warty, calloused hands and I shook them one by one. A darkness spread along my fingers and then snapped clear like a camera shutter.

The following night I went with Garrick and Ravenski to "Giuseppe's Cannelloni warehouse". Cloff made a pillow case dummy in the bed in my office and pretended to guard it while Ravenski and I sneaked out through the car park.

Garrick drove us through half remembered streets to the warehouse in whose basement I had once been savaged with petal blossom. The warehouse was an echoing hall with empty shelves racked up to a cathedral high ceiling. We followed the gantries to an open area which had once been the reception. "Goods Out," was written in blistered paint above an exit. Ravenski and I huddled for warmth as we sat on hard chairs behind a trestle table. Garrick sat beside us, his hands resting palm down on the Formica top.

"Do the same," he said, "so they can see we have no weapons." We waited, Tarot like, at the table.

"Are you alone?" I recognised the firm but warm tones of Penelope, the leader of the Gender Go Go Girls.

"Of course."

Penelope emerged from the gloom with two comrades. They were no longer dressed in Hawaiian bikini's but in long purple and velvet dresses with daffodils pinned, broach-like, at their breast. They adjusted their effervescent material and sat facing us.

"I see," said Penelope, looking from me to Ravenski, "that the reprogramming was unsuccessful."

"It might appear so," I said. "But there are more important things to discuss."

"We believe there is nothing more important."

"I assume Garrick has briefed you about this meeting?"

"Garrick has good contacts in the underground. We only agreed to come at his insistence."

"Give them the photos." Garrick handed over the instamatic pictures he had taken.

They looked and listened respectfully until Penelope butted in: "This is not a gender issue. There is no love lost here."

"This is not about man or woman," said Ravenski, "it is about man and woman and dog."

"But sisters," said Penelope, "plainly aren't doing it for themselves." She leant back in the chair and her daffodil perked up, prominent, on her chest.

"We're not trying to say that they are," said Ravenski. "Look, it's not just about man or women is it? It's about the corruption of the body, of the self, of everyone." She pulled her fringe away. "Can't you see that?"

"We operate for the advancement of womankind only," said Penelope, fixing Ravenski with her gaze.

Ravenski picked up the photo of Ibore Davidson, tubed and pumped in her underground cell, and put it on the table with a flick. "And this is not a kind-of-woman?"

"That," agreed Penelope, folding her arms, "is a terrible thing."

"Then for God's sake join with us."

"You want us to put our X's on the line for your Y's," she said, glancing at me and flapping the side of her purple dress.

Ravenski leant over and pulled out her daffodil from where it had been pinned. She tore off the reproductive organs, the stamen and stigma. "The world will be empty of man and woman, empty even of," she plucked away the petals one by one, "...beauty. Is that what you want, a hollow spring?" She flicked the green stem with a finger and it broke. She put it to one side and lay down the final photo, Ibore pinned before her own disembodied vagina, an image reflected in the lenses of her outsized mirrored glasses.

They were silent. "Very well" said Penelope, "but how can we trust Velour, a man with contacts to Ferris Bloom."

Garrick turned on me. "You know Bloom?"

I scoured my memory," uh, the man driving the lorry. He gave me a lift when I crawled out of the basement here. I just dragged myself onto the road and he…"

"Do you know who Ferris Bloom is? Do you know what he produces?"

"He gave me a rose." The Go Go Girls and Garrick took a sharp intake of breath. "He said it was a gift," I added quickly, "I haven't seen him since, it was just a…"

"And what did you do with the rose?"

"I threw it out."

"You didn't unwrap it from its packaging?"

"No."

Penelope regarded me suspiciously. "You know what those flowers are soaked in?"

"Er a special sauce?"

"You know what's in that sauce? Crack cocaine, chicken blood and cyanide. That's how Bloom makes his money. He introduces innocents to his plants. They buy them by the truckload, heat them up, sniff for kicks and are murdered by passion."

"A poisoned rose?"

"Romance Velour, doomed love of the purest packaged kind."

"So I made a mistake with Bloom. But it was just that, a mistake, a chance meeting. I didn't like the rose; I threw it out. Listen; we can make a deal; you help us with the canine liberation, we'll help you shrivel Ferris Bloom."

"How can we trust you?"

"How can you trust yourselves and leave Ibore in the pits of Priscilla."

They left the table and retreated into the racks to talk in private.

Ravenski dropped the broken daffodil stem pointedly, to the floor. "Don't you ever," she said, "bring me pretty flowers."

After ten minutes and some brief chanting, the Gender Go Go Girls returned.

"We," said Penelope, "will support you in the first wave of your 'Revolution' but any sign that it's a product of the phallus and we're outa here." She jerked a thumb over her shoulder, spat on her hand and offered it to Ravenski across the table.

They shook.

"Was that the guy with the cute arse?" I heard one say, and then they were gone, weaving their way into the shelves that smelt of musty pasta. I stood from the table, pushed the chair back, and bits of spaghetti, black and moulding, crunched beneath my feet.

The next day I met an explosives expert, masquerading as a dentist. We had decided to smuggle him into Priscilla under the pretence of sorting out my wisdom teeth.

He had a familiar, Eastern European accent and a thin moustache that stretched below his cheekbones to his sideburns. Garrick stood to one side tapping his foot while Cloff guarded the office door. The dentist bent over as I sat in my padded swivel chair.

"I know you don't I?" I said as he gripped my lower jaw.

"I'm here to examine your teeth, Mr Velour."

"You're Mr Blanoff aren't you?"

He inserted a blunt metal probe into my mouth and prodded the gums. "Possibly." He removed the instrument.

"You were the tailor that made those pectoral basques." I winced at the thought of that snare, tight like a trap across my nipples. "So why are you a specialist," I leant close so only the two of us could hear, "on explosives?"

He took a step back to a silver tray and began to mix some white paste. Then he returned and hovered close to my ear, prodding the goo into a gap between my emergent wisdoms and the rest of the molars. "Yes," he murmured, "I am Mr Blanoff." I winced as he pressed. "And yes I do grow weary of strapping people into basques, pressing them into tighter versions of themselves, so in my spare time I make...," he leant closer and I could feel the flicker of his moustache against my skin, "explosions. Big loud ones."

"Tell me," I said in a whisper to match his, "about your explosions."

"There is not enough time nor enough privacy." He manoeuvred the paste to the back of my gum line. "Everything you need to know is in your mouth." He continued in his softest voice. "A microdot instruction for incendiary manufacture is in the right gum and a concentrated packet of Simtec explosive is in the left."

"Is that safe?"

"As long as you don't crack down on walnuts or pork scratchings." He twisted his moustache and then delved in for a final prod. His probe hooked into a cotton wool ball in my cheek. "Interesting," he said. I glanced nervously at Garrick. Mr Blanoff put his mouth close to mine and smiled so his moustache flexed slowly to his cheekbones. "Don't worry my friend. We are both in the same business; that of making things appear as we intend." He took a step back and wiped the tip of his probe. "My payment?"

I nodded at Garrick who handed over an envelope which Blanoff locked into his briefcase with his instruments. "Remember," he said, "no taking the tops off beer bottles with your teeth." And then he left, leaving black footsteps behind him on the floor that melted one by one.

The following morning, the core insurrectionists met up in the Changing Room. I carefully explained to those present, Garrick, Cloff, Ravenski, and Ballistrade, the progress we had made and who had been recruited, making certain I didn't grind my teeth when Ravenski suggested we draw up a ten point plan.

Then I pointed into my mouth and told them about the Simtec. It was decided that Ballistrade would make trigger explosives from the materials that Blanoff had implanted. He would install the triggers in the underground labs and we would fire them on the first day of the uprising.

"Killing the kind-of-men, the kind-of-women?" said Ravenski.

"Of course. How can we let them live as they are now? The explosives will be attached to the tubes that bind them, destroying their manacles and nourishment."

Ballistrade wiped his glasses. "It is right," he said, "that I destroy what I have created when what I have created is destruction."

"Good, it is decided. We will make an appointment for next Tuesday; the feast day of Saint Frances."

"The patron saint of birds?" said Ravenski.

"Of creation."

"So now you think you're a saint?" said Cloff.

"Of course not," I said and then I made them all kneel and pray, pray to a God that I knew didn't exist. But we offered our hands all the same and the group departed one by one leaving only Ballistrade and I.

I knelt alone before him and he excavated the components of explosion from my mouth; a stolen blessing, restored to him finally; the penitent priest.

Chapter 14

ON THIS DAY

On the day of the explosion, shadows pointed towards the suburbs. I left Priscilla at four in the morning and in the slowly growing dawn the buildings revealed their shade like spreading hands, reaching out towards the residential areas, and Addlebury, my destination.

I walked alone, without my staff. Birds tinkered with the dawn but otherwise the streets were silent. There were some miles to walk but they passed like a sudden scale beneath my stride. I came to Ravenski's flat, in its studio development, perched upon the top of the hill in a moat of grass. A light was on in her room, a warm orange glow in the grey. I took my time as I came towards it, to prolong the pleasure of return.

Ravenski met me at the door and we shared a cup of tea and gazed out across the city from her bedroom windows. I opened one and peered through and felt the cold breeze frisk upon my skin. I closed it again, satisfied. In the distance we could see the docklands and Priscilla tower, still fuming from its pyramid cap, a dampened match. Much closer, dipping away below us, was the battleground, the terraced streets of Addlebury. They were arranged in parallel rows that ran from the brow of the hill, as if toppling, leaning into each other, all of the same 1950's design with small front gardens and sash windows dressed with net. The streets stretched down to a wider concourse, that itself led to a ring road, which wound past the dockland developments and into the heart of the city. To our left, on the brow of the hill, was an old primary school hunkered behind rusting iron railings. To our right was the beginning of a high street. It curved down the hill at right angles to the rows of terraces. There was a garden centre at the near end and, nearer still, the road met a mini roundabout that was directly below us. The mini roundabout led on one side to the terraced streets that dipped down into Addlebury and on the other to the driveway that led to Ravenski's flat.

"On such small stages, great battles are won," I said, sipping my tea in revolutionary fervour.

"When are the others arriving?"

"Twenty minutes."

"So," she touched her lips, "we can visit the White Room." She led me through the gap behind the armchair, and into the pale room.

We stripped to our underwear and I admired Ravenski from the far end of the room. Then we ran into each other like dodgems. I put my thumb into the waistband of her Pet Furnishings knickers and pulled them to her knees and she dragged my boxers to my ankles. No time for foreplay she wrapped herself around my neck, plied her legs around my prick and we collided back and forth across the room. I carried her, joined to my waist, tilting in an hysteria of pushing and shoving like a couple in a rowing boat wrestling for the oars. The transport reached its climax and I fell to the stone floor with Ravenski above me.

"Between you with your one testicle and me with my one ovary we can still make a pretty good go of it."

I wiped the sweat from my forehead. "Two balls actually, one mine, one the dogs." I looked down at where our bodies met. "Perhaps a better go of it."

She held my arms. "These bites, where did you get them?"

"A rabid dog."

"Rabid?"

"An infected greyhound from the dog's home."

"So you could have given me rabies?"

"It's only when you go mad that you're contagious, I…"

"You don't have to explain," said Ravenski, "I knew about the bites. You were followed, even when you first joined the company. We knew you'd been to the dog's home. You were tagged from the beginning."

"But still we kissed and…?"

"Sometimes it's easier to forget, remember?" She leant towards me, both of us still locked in our Tantric bind. "So what if we're doomed? Better to be doomed lovers," she rolled onto her back and I wilted over her like a drooping flower, "than never to have been doomed at all."

"I don't think I'm contagious, I might even be vaccinated, I…" But she kissed me quiet and we rocked backwards and forwards until we were separated. I took her fingers and kissed each one. "We should put the diamonds in," I said, "before the others arrive."

Ravenski went back to the flat and returned with her jewellery box. She opened the lid and a plastic Ballerina popped up. Next to it there were a set of metal prongs that picked out a tune on the Braille of a revolving barrel. The ballerina twisted sadly to its accompaniment;

'Unchained Melody'. Ravenski removed ten tiny diamonds from the box and a tube of superglue and I held each of her fingers and attached the immaculate jewels to her talons. Once so bitten and broken, her nails had returned to their former elegance and she fluttered them with a recovered beauty; a delicacy I remembered from the Pet Furnishing's warehouse so long ago. I thought how far we had come to reach this bond with the stone set ten times, crystal gripped and clawed.

"Ravenski," I said, "there's something I have tell you..." she looked up at me from her glittering fingers, "we've met before."

"This isn't some reincarnation shtick is it?" she said. "Like you were a dachshund and I was a poodle."

"We met at a Pet Furnishings warehouse, years ago. It was your first day..."

She tilted her head back so I could see the freckle under her chin. "The dog comber."

"I was a dog comber then but now I'm Telby. I'm still Telby."

She said nothing.

"I did it all for you. I transformed myself for you." I took her diamond fingertips and trailed them over the awkward allotments on my scalp, the sprouting goatee that had curled into a Cuban beard, the fullness of my cheeks and into my mouth, poking at the wet cotton wool. "All of this for you," I said, chomping on the barrel of her fingers until she removed them. "I sacrificed myself so I could scale the heights so I could ascend the peaks of this company, so I could be by your side. But I couldn't turn my back on the atrocities. So I brought you into the revolution." I prodded out the cotton wool balls from my mouth with her fingers and spat them across the room.

"I knew it was you," she said. "From the first time we met, you twisted me up inside. I tried to forget who you were, where you had come from, what you would bring. I tried to forget the inevitable chaos of desire, the punishing end of love, the fire of the forest. I tried to be strong, I tried to keep my hand at the helm, to be prim, to be businesslike, for the status, the corporate way but I couldn't keep the course. I..."

"Yes," I shouted, "yes." I took her hands and began to waltz her round. "Time," I sang, "goes by, so slowly." I held her pale face, and kissed her as the door bell peeled outside, a wild chorus from afar and

I remembered that first day on the shop floor of Pet Furnishings, a day that time had healed, had knitted to the present.

"Will the dog comber please go to reception for employee training."

Ravenski smiled at me, her face in my hands, her square edged teeth like a carding comb.

We left the White Room and returned to Ravenski's flat. It felt odd as we dressed, as if we were preparing for a housewarming and not the first strike in some guerrilla rebellion. Black patches began to spread from the corners of the room, like accelerating mould on a Petri dish. I rubbed my eyes, pressing flashes of green into the blackness and when I looked again the studio had returned to its plain geometries, its domestic platitudes.

"Where the hell have you been?" said Cloff when I finally answered the door to him, "The truck's out front, by the roundabout. I've radioed to Priscilla for the roll call but it won't be long before they've realised we're not around."

"Through there." I pointed to the hole that led into the White Room and Ravenski pushed him through.

The doorbell continued to ring and the insurrectionists gathered in the White Room, squeezing through the hole. I counted them off one by one; Cloff, Garrick, a shakey Ballistrade, the Gender Go Go Girls, the Mop Squad and eventually the Ugly Guitar Band, trailing their instruments like battered mannequins.

"It's a bit close in here," said Bad Teeth, the band's leader, pulling his guitar to his chest. And I agreed it was claustrophobic; all of us lined upon the square walls gazing at each other, eventually finding a focus in the centre of the room. This was where I took my stand and Garrick handed me the snooker cue staff. I introduced the different factions and then outlined our battle tactics, marking out our positions with the stick.

"Cloff will drive the truck from the roundabout." I made a little circle on the ground. "The Ugly Guitar band will jump from the back of the truck and follow him, playing songs of chaotic uprising and redemption." Bad teeth played a discordant chord.

"Meanwhile the Gender Go Go Girls will hide in the shrubs of the Garden Centre, here." I pointed beside the imaginary roundabout. The gender activists were wearing their purple dresses with a daffodil at the breast. Penelope adjusted hers and started making eyes at the person behind me. I turned to see Bad Teeth of the Ugly Guitar Band reciprocating the woman's gaze.

"Your attention please…" I pounded the stick on the floor. "As the music begins, the Gender Go Go Girls will emerge from their position on the right flank and descend alongside the truck into the streets of Addlebury…" I was distracted by a murmuring and saw that all five of the Gender Go Go Girls were now eyeing up the Ugly Guitar Band who were practicing silent chords along the necks of their instruments, passing their own consuming gazes over the women. I stamped the staff harder on the stone floor and felt a tingling in my hand. It fluttered through my arm and into my armpit. I banged the stick again and this time the sensation shot up into my neck and lingered somewhere about the Adam's apple before fading away. The pink scar of the dog bites seemed to glow. I wondered if the Rabies virus had already embarked on its fatal journey through my nerves, its grand tour of my circuitry, collecting by the sheaths of wires, trembling at junctions, swimming synapses, rooting towards the brain for some final push of madness.

"Ahum," said Cloff. He tapped his wrist watch.

I returned, shaking, to my battle plan and now indicated the imaginary truck descending into Addlebury; "As the Gender Go Go Girls charge towards the lorry, the Mop Squad will join them from the left flank where they will have been waiting in the old school yard." The mop martial artists made snorting sounds and rubbed their stringed poles up and down their sides. They were staring at the Ugly Guitarists who were playing their fingers up and down the frets of their instruments as they in turn ogled the Gender Go Go Girls who nudged and worried one another with their velvet dresses.

I ignored them and carried on. "At the apex of the assault, in front of the truck," I pointed into the midst of the imaginary Addlebury, "will be Garrick, Ravenski and myself. The Go Go Girls and the Mop

Squad will act as support for this glorious spearhead. Does anyone have any questions?" I raised the snooker cue.

But the insurrectionists were clearly uninterested and continued with their frotting, eyeing the opposing groups and generating a perceptible erotic charge.

"What about me?" said Ballistrade. He stood, demure, between Cloff and Garrick against the fourth wall.

"You will stay in the back of the lorry with the equipment. I presume you have the remote triggering?" He nodded and produced a steel container the size of a matchbox with a red button on the front. "Your explosion will mark the beginning of the assault. At that moment we will fire up the truck and roar down into Addlebury." I raised my staff, a broken spear.

The others however didn't appear to be paying too much attention and made sucking sounds with their tongues as they heeded their compadres.

"I made a fat pot of tea," said Ravenksi. She emerged through the hole from her flat carrying a tray laden with cups and a stout teapot. She swayed under the weight before planting it in the middle of the room. I pounded my snooker cue staff, setting up tramlines of rabid tingling.

"What this?" I said

"A nice cup of tea before the final battle." She bent down and poured out a cup. "Who's first?"

Using my snooker cue as a prop I vaulted onto the pile of crockery. "This," I shouted as I stamped up and down, "is not a tea party, it is a revolution." I fell onto the tray, lifted up the teapot and smashed it down so its belly spilled into a growing puddle. I crunched the teacups and then crawled after the ones that had rolled away. The pieces cut into my hands and I bled all over them. I made my fingers into fists and beat at the broken parts while my shoes skidded over the china.

The insurrectionists took this as an excuse to cave into their desires. They charged from either side towards the opposing party, trampling me underfoot. When I got up I could see Bad Teeth was snogging Penelope, pulling at her velvet dress, while she plucked at the strings of his guitar and tried to shove a hand under his jumper. Big chin was stubbling his face into one of the Go Go Girls while she tried to lick inside his ear. The Mop Squad were either tonguing each other or a Go Go Girl or an Ugly guitarist. There were men on top of women, women on top of men, women on top of women and men on top of men. It was difficult to see who was doing what to whom in the mesh of mops, guitars, velvet dresses, bodies and gaping orality. The orgy was about to reach its climax when Garrick, Cloff and I intervened, pulling apart the conjoined mass, levering one, then another out from the scrum until I arrived at Ravenski who was half dressed and had her mouth around the mop pole of Tony, the leader of the mop squad.

"What are you doing?" I said and hauled her to her feet. She returned a bra strap and pulled a bit of mop string from her mouth.

"Well it was obvious you didn't want a cup of tea…"

I retrieved my snooker cue staff and forced everyone to line against the walls. I inspected them as they dressed back.

"We'll have no more of that," I shouted, "the revolution has dawned." I pointed at the skylight that admitted a gold envelope of sun. "Take up your weapons and await the signal." I cued them one by one through the hole. They hunched and left, carrying their mops and guitars and broken daffodils.

Cloff, Garrick, Ravenksi and I remained in the White Room while Ballistrade fumbled in the corner. The scientist had a clean lab coat, but his shirt dangled from his trousers, his tie was askance, and his thin hair had startled into wisps.

"Ah, found them." He put on his steamed up glasses and held the bomb trigger to his navel. "Ready."

"Get into the truck."

"Rightho." He disappeared through the hole.

"You three, with me." I led them, or thought I had led them, outside. But when we arrived at the mini roundabout, I discovered that Cloff was absent.

"Where is he?"

Garrick shrugged. "I thought he was with you."

"He must still be in the White Room. Wait here." Garrick took command and I returned to Ravenski's flat and peered through the hole.

Cloff was kneeling, naked from the waist up, and pulling at a piece of plastic joined by some wires into his armpit.

I wriggled back through the gap; "What the hell are you doing?"

Cloff attempted to press the thing back into his armpit but it popped out, so he pressed the device between torso and upper arm, trying to cover it with the other hand.

I crooked away his fingers one by one. "LET…ME…SEE…"

"It's nothing."

I rapped his knuckles and the device dropped out. It was the Interpit, the communications interface I had seen only once before, plumbed into the chest of Denis McCloy.

Cloff turned from me but I held onto the plastic Interpit. "Who are you?"

"Mr Cloff. Private Detective. Blessed are the meek…"

"Tell me who you are, really." I hauled him over by the sweaty plastic and he tried to wriggle free. "You're McCloy aren't you, Denis McCloy, risen from the dead?" I looked at the man's blue eyes and short teeth, so similar to that of the dandified executive.

"No, I'm Cloff." He managed to retreat a couple of steps.

"You're Denis McCloy, the man with the Interpit that got sweaty at lunchtimes, so sweaty he had to wipe it with a cloth." I pulled him to the opposite wall.

"No, No, No." He staggered back. I pulled him backwards by the Interpit to the middle of the room, where he turned to face me.

"So what if I am? What difference does it make?"

"How can you still be alive when Garrick riveted you to death?"

"That was my reciprocal. He was assassinated by mistake. I was forced to go undercover and have cosmetic surgery; a rush job. Mantle said he wanted me to be your private bodyguard so he could find out what you were up to."

"So, at the last moment, you are to be our traitor. We are to be betrayed by one of our own."

McCloy leant away from me, balanced on a cocked leg by his Interpit. "If that were true, don't you think the police would have found us by now?"

"Garrick told me you were a traitor. He told me you were an Animal Liberation Liberationist but then you sniffed power and then you sniffed the powder and then you turned against the cause."

"Can't you see I've lost everything? I can't even sniff after they snapped my nose. I lost my looks, my drugs, and my position. And then I saw what I might become in the cells in the underground labs."

"So what were you doing," I twisted the Interpit, "if you weren't informing Pet Furnishings of our whereabouts?"

"I was tapping into the network, for the benefit of us all." He glanced nervously at the worming of wires.

"If you were truly on our side, you would cut yourself free."

"I can't live without this," he said, "I wouldn't know how." He pawed at the wires leading into his spinal cord.

"Then live with it, here, half a man. But I couldn't trust you. I would have to let Garrick return with his rivet gun."

"No." He tried to struggle from me but I held him by the pit and we fell together to the floor. I picked up a severed piece of the blood stained crockery and offered it to him. "Take it," I said, "or die."

He looked from my face, to the china, to the cables and then took the piece of porcelain and used its sharp edge to cut through the mealy wires so the thing came away in my hand.

"Now," I said, "are you with or against us?"

"With."

"I shall continue to call you Cloff," I said as I helped him to his feet, "for he seemed a bolder man than you, even in his humility." We left the Interpit behind and its flickering lights continued to play beneath the surface, like the death throes of a stranded jellyfish.

The truck we had chosen was an ex army Bedford and painted in camouflage green. It had a cab at the front and a cargo hold at the rear from which the canvas roof had been stripped, leaving only the metal frame, which made inverted 'U's like a saucer rack. Ballistrade was in the back fiddling with his equipment. The Ugly Guitar Band sat either side. They muttered and nervously tuned their strings.

Garrick was flustered. "Where the hell have you been?"

"Forget it." I turned to Cloff. "Get in the cab and start the engine. As soon as we've triggered the explosion I want you to switch on the noise." I turned to Garrick. "You wait in front of the truck with Ravenski, I'll get Ballistrade to detonate the charge."

I nodded at the scientist. "Up on the roof."

"It's a bit of a climb," he said.

"You heard me."

With the help of the Ugly Guitar Band Ballistrade clambered onto the cab roof. He stood next to the megaphone which was positioned there, pointing over the front of the truck. He wobbled for a bit, steadied himself and held the trigger box with its bright red button close to his waist. In the distance we could see the pyramid capped obelisk of Priscilla; its tip shining like a solitary needle in the sun. Black storm clouds began to reach inwards from the horizon, an encroaching stadium of shadow.

"Press the button," I shouted.

He looked across the terraces of Addlebury, over the urban sprawl to the Dockland developments and the erect Priscilla. "I…I… I'm not sure." The trigger box shook in his hands.

"Press the button."

"How can I destroy…?" The trigger box rattled violently in his hands.

"Give it to me." I climbed up the side of the cab.

"NO." The box jittered out of the scientists hands, rose in an arc from the front of the truck, and then began to tumble like the coffin of a bird, sinking and twisting through the sky. Garrick, I noticed, was already racing towards it; one athletic stride after another. The box fell past the outlines of houses towards a sewer at the side of the road. I imagined it being lost forever but in one final stride Garrick stretched out his foot, arrow straight, a striker, so the point hit the red button and the device was kicked up, floating over the streets of terraced houses.

I gasped and in that breath believed I could hear a cracking; the pipes of torture in Priscilla's basement being snapped from their brackets. I closed my eyes and pictured the kind-of-men, the kind-of-women unbound from their racks and released finally. I saw the green fluids spurting from the glass tubes and then dripping to a lacklustre ooze about them. I saw their blank mirrored lenses fallen from their eyes and I saw them aware, just for a moment, of their own bodies pitched against the backdrop of death; the necessary excavated darkness that would permit them to fall through life, that would allow the sensation of being, the passing of time, the breeze on the face.

I opened my eyes to the revolution. "Now."

Cloff put the truck into gear and it rolled forward, toppling Ballistrade from the roof and into the rear loader. A high pitched squeal screamed from the megaphone on the cab roof. My dog card had been taped to it, and compressed gas was being forced through the small notch in the plastic producing, amongst other sounds, an amplified suprasonic pitch. From the streets below, the dogs howled in reply.

The Ugly Guitar Band jumped from the back end of the truck like an assault squad and began to play their guitars resolutely out of tune. One of them carried a dustbin lid and attached it by a length of wire to the rear axle of the truck. The lid rattled across the tarmac, sending pulses of distortion through the wire and from there into a cable and into speakers that were bolted either side of the dazed Ballistrade. The speakers reverberated like a tin can hail storm.

The lorry rolled into the first terraced street. I ran to the front and joined Garrick and Ravenski, who were scanning for signs of movement behind the net drapes. I saw the first twitch in a pebble dash house on the left. Garrick raced ahead and used one of Ravenski's straightened fingers with its diamond nail to score the outline of a circle into the window.

I pointed to the billowing curtains on the other side of the street and Ravenski and Garrick sprinted over. Behind us the Gender Go Go Girls were leaping from the garden centre, their purple dresses and yellow daffodils bright amidst the placid pot plants. On the left flank, the Mop Squad were vaulting over the iron fence that surrounded the playground, their bleached mops flailing in the sun. Both groups descended in a pincer towards the chaos, around the slowly moving truck.

By now some of the homeowners had emerged, stunned and half dressed in pyjamas and dressing gowns. The mop squad galloped into the melee and using their cleaning implements like chargers pushed through the outlines in the windows that were being etched by Ravenski under Garrick's sure hand. Moons of glass fell into the lounges of the terraced houses making astonished portals. The Gender Go Go Girls leant through these holes, protected by their velvet dresses, and in pairs lifted out the dog furniture, the dog benches, the dog pouffes and the dog seats, all of whom were trying to bark through their safety locked jowls. I helped load the dogs into the back of the truck where Ballistrade put them gently on their sides, one upon the other, with a cushion in between. He removed as many of the wooden runners as he could, pulling out the reinforcing struts that ran over their spine. I saw him mouth "Sorry" to a Chihuahua as he pulled out its teak reinforcement.

By this point, the homeowners had become more active and were brandishing spades and tennis rackets. A few even tried to hold us back as Ravenski and Garrick continued to make incisions into their blank windows. But they were no match for the Mop Squad who elbowed through and fought them off with wooden poles and multiratcheted string attacks. Three of the Mop Squad formed a protective sentry around the truck while the rest continued to push out pools of glass. And just when it seemed a larger posse of owners might overwhelm us; they were thwarted by a fresh and unexpected cavalry. The suprasonic whistle of my credit card had drawn a pack of stray dogs and they funnelled into the street from all directions following the truck and howling in the wake of their liberated kind. They eventually forced the upstart owners to retreat into their porches.

Beyond the inevitable tide of our progress and the retreating owners, there was a single black limousine. And standing on the roof, still in his buttoned janitors coat, was the toilet attendant, shouting and waving his fist in the air, a thin gold chain sliding up and down his arm. And though I couldn't hear what he was shouting I could read his snarling lips. "You bastards, you bitches. How dare you destroy what is mine, mine, mine." So the attendant was to be the final link in the plumbing, planning his dominion in the sink of Priscilla? I watched the stuttering glint of his bracelet. Or was he merely the overseer of the pipes that coursed with cruelty? I looked at the outline of veins on the back of my hand. Perhaps his ideas were just a lancet into our own default blood stream, our civilised evil? I raised my fist to him, the weal of the dog scar bright, and we veered into a side road, rescuing the pets as we went. The attendant jumped off his car and pursued on foot, fighting his way into the pack of stray dogs that pressed around. I watched him stumble and fall and then disappear into the white chop and flash of teeth, invisibly dismembered.

Eventually, at the head of a trail of broken glass, dustbin lid drum and bass, discordant guitar players, dancing mop martial artists, daffodil waving gender activists, Animal Liberation Liberationists and Pet Furnishing's executives the truck came to a halt. Ballistrade hammered on the cab and then climbed onto it. His white coat ballooned about his waist. "We are full," he mouthed, "full."

I took out a distress flare from where I had stored it in my khaki pants and yanked the drawstring. There was a gunpowder scream followed by the rocket trail of an orange firework, a mango fruition that hung iridescent and then floated and fell leaving an arc of smoke as if it weighed down some carbonized stem. I felt the bladder stone rise in its cavity as my belly surged with the thrill of it all. I imagined the stone disintegrating, spreading its rich calcium through my blood and finally releasing its confounding poetry.

At the sign of the flare, the revolutionaries retreated to the truck and climbed aboard, finding what holds they could on the sides of the metal frame and the cab. When I was certain each activist was accounted for, I gave the "O.K." to Cloff, who restarted the engine and the truck advanced onwards through the chaos. The ugly guitar band paddled their instruments in the sea of stray dogs as the Go Go Girls threw their daffodils into the air and the mop squad slung their poles into the gardens. Ballistrade, still on the roof, knelt on one knee and as the truck built up momentum, his white coat flapped behind him, not in surrender but a new flag awaiting some bolder design.

I sprinted behind the truck and Ravenski pulled me onto the rear loader. I sat there with the ranks of liberated dog furniture. Their heartbeats seemed to transmit and fuse into the rabid blaze of my brain. The upright stacks of wooden runners that Ballistrade had pulled from the dogs' spines rested on the bars of the truck and dripped with lines of blood. I leant upon them and cried. The horizon bloomed with darkness, a shadow that accelerated from every direction, rushing inwards to the epicentre of the sky, a black circus top pulled through a napkin ring, till the last of the light remained, a pin hole for an inverted image. And then all was gone.

Chapter 15

LIKE I SAID

Were it true that we escaped in our truck down a little known alley to an underground garage, diverting the police and stray dogs with a trail of false scents. Were it true that we lay low for many weeks and then sent Garrick to find a cave beneath one of the city parks, a cave that Ravenski had always claimed was hidden among the hibiscus. Were it true that we transported the dogs there and, after we'd fed and tended them, carefully dismantled their upholstery and electronic implants.

If only I could say, hand on heart, that Ravenski nursed me through a rabid fever as winter came and the leaves of the park turned over and turned yellow and brown and black upon the cave. If only I could say that I woke from my delirium to see the dogs trotting about with their new prosthetic paws and a canine spark in their eyes. If only I could tell you they were taken to new owners, who shared their lives as a man might with his family, walking them across fields beyond the city, to lakes and hills and unfathomable skies.

If only I could say that we grew as a band of revolutionaries, making tentative links with other groups through our battered technologies, agitating to free the suburbs; unbinding the dogs from the machines of themselves. If I could say this to all of you then how sweet it would be, how bold my hopes.

But I start only with a hard, unknowing seed, pushed deep into the earth, waiting for a light to set it breaking.

Like I said, a funny thing happened on the way to my head. The beginning began but then something happened between the began and the begun, the past and the present, the brain and the tongue, an inhalation of air, a hovering silence. But I can't remember what it was. So with no sure past, I make one up; I tell a tale to give me sense. For truly I do not know who or what I am. Perhaps I was captured, perhaps the company made me. But they have shrouded my eyes so I cannot see, they have made me numb so I cannot feel, they have bored out pipes that run into my body which I can but beat with what I think are my hands, sending out this story, driven by the furies that bleed uselessly to my brain. What else should I do, or did I do, or can I do but pass on the tale buried within me; tell to others that they might hear? When all else is dissolved and I am left alone with these words, with this quick of ideas. When I can see, hear, touch nothing else, what can I do but trill on the pipes, transmit the orisons, tap, tap, tap on the bored out wires?

And now I have reached the end, what is there left to do but play it back again, in reverse. So where shall I begin? With the dog?... Who will hear me? Oh God who made me once in his image, who will hear me? Oh Christ. Oh God almighty.